MERCURY RISES

MERCURY RISES

SCARLETT KOL

The characters in this book are fictitious. Any similarity to real persons, living or dead, places, or events is coincidental and not intended by author.

To those who told me I could,
when I told myself I couldn't.

"We know what we are, but know not what we may be."

- William Shakespeare,
Hamlet

ONE

A half-lit neon sign reflected in the puddles as I lowered my head down and out of the rain as best I could. The Full Moon Hotel and Bar. A place built in a grand vintage style, now so run-down it just looked old. It was a blip. A stopover. The slightest fraction of a map dot that appeared on no one's GPS— ever. But on this dark street, in this backwater town, it was also the only building with any sign of life.

In the window sat a *Help Wanted* sign written in a thick, crooked scrawl. I perked up. Sadly, that dirty piece of cardboard held the most promise I'd seen all day. Overhead, the sky flashed and rumbled as the rain pounded harder on the back of my skull. I took a deep breath and ran for the door.

The thick, earthy smell of the storm disappeared when I walked in, replaced with the stench of stale smoke and fermenting barley, which made my stomach twist. But at least the inside was dry, and not actually the worst place I'd been recently. Most of the tables sat empty, and people at the full ones didn't even look when I walked in, too deep in their own problems to notice mine. In the corner, an ancient jukebox blared a rowdy, country song. Too up-tempo for the clientele, but I had no right to judge anyone. Where people chose to hide was their own business. Besides, I'd only be here a few days at most, so no sense getting attached to the place.

A light over the bar flickered, making the buzz of an angry hornet. Even over the music, I twitched from its irritating drone, but at least following the noise led straight to the bartender.

"Wait, wait." A big bald man behind the counter shook his lumbering arms in front of me. "Before you drip all over my bar, honey, you should know, you're in the wrong place."

I cringed at the pet name, then turned on my best smile. The one I saved for prep school functions and exhausting dinners with my father's important clients.

"Sign says you're hiring." Ignoring his warning, I jumped up on a stool and propped my wet elbows on the bartop. "I need a job."

He leaned against the back counter and chuckled, his big arms crossed over his chest. Blurred colors from faded tattoos peeked through his thick arm hair. "A little thing like you wouldn't last an hour 'round here."

"I can handle myself."

He laughed louder. Hard belly laughs. "What's your name, honey?"

I looked around for inspiration, the bright fiddle music distracting me. "Charlie."

"And whaddya think you can do around here, Charlie?"

I tousled my wet hair and pulled my shoulders back. "I can wait tables, bartend, whatever."

"Uh-huh." A deep wrinkle cut across his forehead. He wasn't convinced. "You know how to mix a drink?"

"Made them for my daddy for years. And trust me—" I let out a pathetic sigh and looked down at my hands. "He drank a lot."

Something crept into the corners of his eyes. Looked like sadness, maybe pity. *Perfect.* Either one would work.

"Most customers don't order anything with more than two ingredients anyway," he said, his voice quieter.

"See? I'm sure I could be just what you need around here."

"I doubt that. Besides, I don't pay much. Don't you got rent to pay?"

I shifted on the barstool, suddenly uncomfortable. "Not quite. That's the problem—"

"So there's the catch. You need a place to stay."

"Only for a little while. Until I get back on my feet."

He grabbed my wrist and stretched my arm across the bar, pulling me off my seat. His thick fingers dug into my skin as he turned it left and right, examining it.

"Hey." I snatched my arm back and rubbed my wrist.

"No tracks. That's good. Whatddya running away from?"

Everything. "Nothing."

"Can't be harboring any runaways around here. Too messy."

"No one's going to come looking for me." *They wouldn't know where to start.* "Even if they did, I'm legal. Nothing they could do about it."

"Sure you are. Got some ID?"

I wrestled a thin wallet out of the back pocket of my soaking wet jeans and slid it across the bar.

He picked it up and held it in his fingertips, far too gently for his stature. His eyes darted from the wallet to me, and back again. In a place like this, he'd probably seen more than one fake ID. I wasn't hoping he wouldn't notice; I was hoping he wouldn't care.

"Okay, Charlie," he said with an edge, knowing full well it wasn't the name on the ID I'd shown him. "One night and we'll see how it goes."

"Yes, sir." I smiled my trained smile again.

"The name's Bill." He reached across the bar with his tree-trunk arm and a hand open to shake. "Big Bill to most everybody."

Of course he was. Small towns and their quaint predictability.

"Pleasure to meet you." I took his hand and squeezed tight. A glimmer of surprise passed through his eyes, likely not expecting a half-decent grip from a drowned-rat girl like me. "When do I start?"

"As soon as you stop dripping all over my floor," he said with a smirk. He grabbed a T-shirt from under the bar and tossed it at me, then slid a small gold key across the bartop. "Clean yourself up and get back down here. You can start by mopping up this mess, then we'll see what you can do."

I grabbed up my backpack from the floor and nodded as I headed toward the lit hallway leading to the hotel.

"And honey," Big Bill said as I walked away. "'Round here, make sure you bolt the door."

AFTER BOLTING the room door as instructed, I locked myself in the closet-sized bathroom and turned on the water. Steam rose from the dingy, ringed tub. The faucet only seemed to have two temperatures, ice-cold or scalding, but I'd rather the latter anyway as the chill from the rain still lingered in my bones.

My wet clothes clung to me as I pulled my shirt over my head. In the dim light, I could see the faint scar on my shoulder, and a blunt ache throbbed in my wrist and elbow where the broken bones had healed. A reminder of who I was. What I was running from.

I slid off my boots and wiggled my toes. My feet tingled and ached, but they were only going to get worse unless I wanted Bill to kick me out into the street. He seemed like a nice guy underneath, or at least he didn't set off my jackass radar. I almost felt bad for deceiving him. Almost.

I reached into the left boot and flipped through the wad of hundreds wedged in the toe. I did the same with the right. Seemed like it was all still there. The hard part was going to be trying to make it last.

Every inch of my flesh burned as I stepped into the shower. It felt good. Clean. As if the hot water were stripping off my last life and letting it ooze down the drain. I closed my eyes. I kind of liked the name Charlie.

TWO

"Disgusting. I need to wash my hands." Big Bill slid the morning newspaper across the bar and headed into the kitchen.

"What's his problem?" One of the day servers, Fiona, snatched up the paper and looked over the front page. "Oh. That's a sweet heap of trouble now, isn't it?"

"What?" I slid to the edge of the barstool and stood on the bottom rung, trying to catch a glimpse of what she was reading.

"Leader of The Five, Vincent Masters, has called a state of emergency over the outbreak of some X9 virus."

"What's that? Some sort of computer thing?" I sat back down and tried to sound disinterested. It was likely a dramatic financial scandal or something else equally boring, but hearing about The Five had me squirming in my seat. It seemed the less I heard about them, the more it threw me off when I did. One more reason to keep running.

"Nope. No computers. It's like a *virus*, virus. A disease, and a nasty one at that."

"Can I see?"

Fiona passed me the paper, and I spread it across the bartop, skimming the article with my finger.

"It says here the X9 virus kills within forty-eight hours. Symptoms start with a cough, then sweats, then emission of blood through the nose and mouth, then hallucinations until eventual death." I swallowed loudly, my imagination forming a gruesome picture of what those symptoms might look like. *Gross.* I shook my head and kept reading. "There have been over a hundred cases already reported in isolated spots down the East Coast."

"Sure hope it stays over there. I'm not too good with blood." Fiona shuddered, the soft patch of skin under her chin shimmying. "Where did you say you were from again? Don't want you infecting us all."

I laughed, a little too hard and high-pitched to be believable, until Fiona gave me a side-eye and I forced myself to stop. Besides, I'd never even heard of this virus until now, and if I actually had it, I'd be long dead. I scanned over the article again, wondering if I knew any of the hundred who had died and hoping with all my strength that I didn't.

Big Bill returned to the bar, the skin on his hands now a raw, glowing red. "Both of you scrub up. There'll be nobody dying around here. Dead bodies are bad for business, and I can't afford to have this place closed."

Fiona shook her head, but marched into the kitchen anyway. I doubted she would actually wash her hands on principle, because Bill had told her to; however, talk of the virus did seem to have her spooked. I gave Bill a nod and slid off the barstool, then headed toward the back.

"You've been doing a good job here," he said once the kitchen door swung closed behind Fiona.

"Thanks. I've been trying my best."

"It shows. But do me a favor; figure out whatever it is that needs figurin' out. You'll waste away here, and I can't have that on me."

Worry fell over his expression. It wriggled in at the edges of his ever-present scowl and put a small dent in his tough-guy mask.

"Don't worry so much. I'll be fine. Besides, I really like it here."

And it was true. The few days' layover had turned into almost three full weeks. The bed was the most uncomfortable I'd ever slept in—a piece of granite covered in sandpaper—but I was so tired at the end of the day, it didn't matter. And I was okay with that. I'd even figured out the whole waitress thing. Remembering the orders was the easy part, and now, if I paced myself, I could go an entire day without dropping things.

Plus, Bill and the staff seemed to like me too. The first few days met with grunts and pointed stares, but now they treated me like one of them. The kitchen staff always seemed to botch an order at meal times, which most often were diverted to me. Not that I really needed charity, but I was grateful. The servers, however, were a tougher group to crack. Middle-aged women with either too much or not enough makeup, who didn't appreciate me cutting into their tips. But after a while, they caved too. I worked hard, and I didn't gossip, which made me okay enough to tolerate. Some of them, like Fiona and one of the weekend girls named Grace, were even downright kind to me, just like Big Bill, although he'd never admit it.

I washed my hands quickly and came back to the bar to prepare for the lunch rush—if anyone could call it a rush. It was the same twenty people every day, coming and going in shifts like they were all on a precisely timed schedule. Once in a while, someone new would come in and they would either join the rotation or disappear, never to be heard from again.

Right now, the 11:36s were arriving and summer sun streamed through the main door as each group made their entrance. In the short moments the door opened, I could see the waves of heat rising off the street. The hot stickiness of the late July air oozed into the bar, even with the air conditioning on full crank. I almost let myself wonder what it would be like to just run through the doors and enjoy the afternoon out in the heat, but I stopped myself. The risk of being recognized was far too high in daylight. Everyone had probably stopped looking for me, but I couldn't take the chance. I still hadn't figured out where I was running to, but the farther away I got, the harder it was to picture going back. Maybe once I decided on my destination, I could stop hiding.

"Is everything all right there, Charlie?" Fiona asked as she laid freshly filled saltshakers on the tables.

"I'm okay. Maybe a little nervous about this virus coming, that's all." If I caught it, I couldn't take care of myself and I couldn't go to a hospital without identifying who I was. Forget X9, catching any virus could be a death sentence.

"Don't worry about it. I'm sure everything will be just fine. Paper said The Five were funding the development of a vaccine already. They'll take care of you. Don't you worry."

So much faith. There were only two types of people in this world: those who believed The Five were the reformation of the country, and those who thought they were the beginning of the end. Fiona was clearly the former, which was definitely the safer opinion to hold. For me, any talk of The Five made my stomach queasy.

"You're right," I replied. "Sorry."

"Nothing to be sorry for. Now, can you grab the cutlery in the kitchen?"

I pushed my way through the kitchen door and hefted the full tray of forks and knives out onto the bar. I laid out a stack of napkins and rolled the pairs of cutlery into tight, orderly bundles. It was a menial task, but the mindlessness settled some of the tension in my shoulders. I brought a few out to my tables, taking their orders and handing the little slips of paper into the kitchen. Customers here didn't need much. Just a cold drink and quick food—at least during the day. They weren't ones for chitchat, and most times if you tried they would ignore you, or worse, make a point of looking annoyed.

I sat behind the bar, still rolling and twisting cutlery, while I waited for my orders. The front door swung open again, and it was hard to see the people just outside from the sun behind their heads, but it was a larger group of about eight.

The door slammed shut behind them, and my heart stopped beating, frozen in place like the rest of me. Eight dark blue coats with red stripes across the left arm. Buzzed heads and thick-soled black boots. A uniform I would recognize anywhere. On the other side of this run-down Midwest bar, in the middle of absolute nowhere, stood a group of officers from The Five's private guard.

I jumped from the stool and snuck off into the corner. The men didn't seem to notice.

"Fiona, I'm swamped. Could you take that table of guys over there?" I hissed as I shrunk down against the wall and pointed to the front door.

Fiona looked around the room and was polite enough not to comment on the lack of customers. "Are you sure, sweetie? Nice-looking young men like that would pay top dollar to see you smile at them for a spell."

"Trust me, I'm sure."

"Well, all right."

I ran into the kitchen. Through the little window in the door, I could see Fiona adjust her apron and rustle her hands through her curly blonde hair before approaching their table. What were they even doing here? They were halfway across the country from where they should be, and I'm sure they were paid well enough that they wouldn't have to eat here.

"Food up," Randy the cook called, banging on the tiny silver service bell.

I ignored it and kept staring out the window. The guards laughed, and Fiona couldn't have batted her eyelashes any harder. The last thing I needed was for them to stick around. *Just take their order and get them out of here already.*

"Whaddya doing? There's food to be run."

I flinched at the voice, knocking the door with my knee and making it swing. Big Bill stood to my left, arms crossed.

"I just need a break. Could you bring it out?"

"I said there's food to be run. Don't forget you work for me, not the other way around." A thick vein in his forehead began to pulse. I'd only seen Bill angry once, when a guy tried to stiff him on a bar tab. An ambulance made sure that guy wasn't coming back anytime soon. The vein had pulsed then too.

"I know, I just ... oh, never mind." I'm sure I could have made something up, but the last thing I needed was a scene. Going unnoticed wasn't going to be easy if Bill reamed me out in front of the whole restaurant. Not that I thought he would, but I had the feeling he wasn't a person who dealt well with liars.

I grabbed Randy's worn baseball cap from its hook on the wall and twisted my dark hair up under it. It barely fit, but it was the best I had. I unrolled the sleeves of my T-shirt to cover the small cloud-shaped birthmark on my upper arm and grabbed the plates. Head down, I marched back to the floor, dropping the food only two seats over from the guards' table.

As I passed, my eyes studied their faces. A few looked familiar, but none of them stuck out in my memory. Hopefully, they didn't remember me either. I tugged the brim of the ball cap lower and headed to the bathroom to hide out until they left. At least Bill wouldn't follow me in there. I glanced back again, making sure they hadn't noticed me. Not one of the men had even looked my direction, or at least I hoped they hadn't. I exhaled, my shoulders falling back from up around my ears. I was safe.

Then *bang*. My head smacked into someone's torso. A navy-blue jacket. I looked up. Tanned skin and familiar hazel eyes stared back down at me. My breath hitched in my throat. This guy wasn't any guard; this one was on my father's personal rotation.

"Sorry, sir," I mumbled, putting my head back down and adjusting the cap.

He placed a hand on his chest. "No, miss, it's my fault. My apologies."

"No harm."

I weaved, he bobbed, and we danced awkwardly in the hallway. Finally, I saw an opening and bolted for the ladies' room. Sitting down on the toilet seat, I pulled off the cap and held my head in my hands. He couldn't have recognized me. Could he? I couldn't remember the officer's name, if I'd ever known it, but I had seen his face enough times around the house. The only thing working in my favor was that as much as I didn't expect him to be here, he would have expected to see me even less.

It took me several minutes to gather my courage to peek out the door. The guards were paying their bills, and from the smirk on Fiona's face, they had tipped well. I waited a few more minutes and crept back into the dining room, just as the front door clicked shut behind the last officer.

"You should've taken that table. So polite, and flush too." She clutched a handful of bills in her deep mauve–polished fingertips, waving them at me.

"My loss, I guess." I grabbed a handful of empty plates from the now-vacant table. "Did they say why they were here?"

"Some training at the military base just outside of town.

Top-secret business. Got a thing for a man in uniform or something?"

"Not exactly. I try to avoid them whenever I can."

THE REST of the day and most of the night flew by as if the universe had sped up to double time. When I wasn't obsessing over every movement I'd made at lunch, I analyzed everyone who walked in the door, waiting for the inevitable to happen. Someone would come for me. But no one did.

"You seemed a bit off tonight. Anything the matter?" Big Bill said as I swept up behind the bar.

"Memories, I guess."

He nodded his smooth, shiny head. I think that's what I liked most about Bill. He didn't push. I had the feeling he had his own secrets to hide, so not prying into others' was his version of self-preservation, or maybe he just really didn't want to know. Either way, it worked for us.

I reached into my apron and pulled out the week's rent. "Thank you for all you've done for me, Bill. I really appreciate you taking me in."

"No sweat. You work hard, and the regulars seem to like a pretty, young face around here. Stay as long as you'd like." He took the wad of bills and slid them in his pocket. "Now get out of here. I'll finish up. You look exhausted."

Walking past, I squeezed his hand and continued on. As I glanced back over my shoulder, he smiled, and for a minute I thought I saw him blush. Bill was the nicest person I had met since I left. I'd miss him.

I ran up the stairs to my room. Time to move on. If there was still a chance of running into my past, I was still too close to the city. Too bad. Part of my heart hurt thinking about how I was going to let Bill down. I stopped at the door and rested my forehead against the rough wood. Maybe if I stayed the night, I could stick around and say goodbye in the morning. Better not. Fewer questions if I left now. Safer for him the less he knew, anyway.

A tight feeling spread across my lungs and up my throat as I slid the gold key in the lock for the last time, but I'd get over it. I had to. I sighed and clicked the door closed. My hand hesitated on the doorknob, the unexpected weight of a stare bearing down on the back of my head. I wasn't alone.

Standing motionless, I scanned the darkness over my shoulder. A voice cut through the black.

"Mercury, I've been waiting for you."

THREE

I knew who it was before I turned on the lights. The smell of expensive hair gel mixed with ambition and a hint of sweat could only be one person—Christophe.

He sat poised on the bed. His left foot was crossed over his right knee and vibrated with either impatience or anxiety from sitting on the cheap hotel sheets. It would've been funny if I didn't want to lunge across the room and strangle him. If I were certain no one would come looking for him, I'd consider it.

Crossing my arms, I leaned against the door. "What do you want?"

Christophe stood and adjusted his French cuffs under his jacket. He used to look like a kid playing dress-up when he wore a suit like this, but right now he finally looked the part. An adult. A man of purpose. It was disgusting.

He cleared his throat. "You know why I'm here."

"Which is exactly why you need to leave." I pointed toward the closed door.

"Why do you need to be so hostile? Your family's been worried about you." He started to walk toward me, an uncertain smile across his lips. "I've been worried about you."

I narrowed my eyes to sharp slits, and he stopped. Smarter than I thought he'd be. I braced myself anyway.

"I don't know why you insist on these games. You've been gone almost three months this time. I think they get the point."

"If they did, you wouldn't be here."

"I know this isn't how you expected things to work out." He ran a hand through his short spiky hair. "I'm not even going to pretend I know what you were trying to do, because the truth is, I don't. I never know what's going on in that head of yours. But I'd like to, if you'd just let me."

"I appreciate the offer, but I don't feel much like talking. So why don't you crawl back to my father and tell him that I'm fine." I moved into the bathroom entrance, allowing him a clear path to the door. "Let him know I said hello."

"I'm not leaving here without you."

"Then I guess I'll have to go without you."

"You'll never make it around the block. He's got security everywhere."

"Fantastic. It was that guard, wasn't it? He recognized me."

He nodded. "There's a helicopter waiting for us not far from here. I'm here to take you home."

Resting my head against the doorframe, I fought back the tears threatening to fall. It was over. All the running. All the hiding. Just over.

He leaned against the wall and tried to look me in the eyes, but I refused to let him. "You didn't think he would let you walk away again, did you?"

"Why not? He can't make me stay."

"Of course he can. You're only seventeen."

Christophe took my arm and pulled me to him. I fell against his chest as his palm rested on my hair, his chin sitting gently on the top of my head. The heat of his skin seeped through his thin dress shirt. It was almost comforting.

"It's going to be okay." His voice rumbled against my cheek.

I closed my eyes and let myself drift deeper into his arms. "You don't know that."

"Once you get home, everything will go back to normal. You'll see."

I cringed. Normal was the last thing I wanted.

"Whatever." I ripped myself away from him, grabbed my backpack from the dresser, and stomped out the door. Once I was in the hall, I wiped my face with my arm and turned back. "Are you coming?"

"MERCURY, YOU'RE HOME," a tiny voice shrieked as I opened the door.

Matty's footsteps echoed through the penthouse foyer as he ran and launched himself at me, his arms squeezing tight around my neck.

"I missed you, buddy." I hugged him back and nuzzled my nose in his curly hair, inhaling his little-boy freshness. No pretension, no perfumes, just Matty.

A second set of steps came into the front hall. Softer, much more cautious.

"Mom, Mercury's home," Matty called to the woman standing in the hallway.

"I can see that," she said as she stared at Christophe and me, keeping her distance. "Now go get ready for bed and tell Henrietta to get you a drink. I'll be up in a bit."

Matty gave me a wide grin. Black empty spaces sat where his front teeth should be. He must've lost a few while I'd been gone. I set him down and he ran back the way he'd come. The sound of him thumping up the stairs bounced off the high-domed ceiling.

Mom walked over and gave me a tentative hug. "Glad to have you back."

"Thanks." There wasn't anything else I could say that felt appropriate. Being polite was all I could manage.

"And thank you, Christophe"—she placed a hand gently on his forearm and gave him the warm smile she refused to give me —"for bringing her back safely."

"My pleasure, Mrs. Masters. Anything to help." He nodded and took his cue to leave, heading deeper into the house.

"Where's Dad?" I asked, not sure I wanted to know the answer.

"He's working in his office and doesn't want to be disturbed. Not that you really care about the people in this house anyway."

Ouch. Maybe I deserved it. Didn't make it sting any less, though.

"That's not fair. If he hadn't—"

"Enough." She raised her hand and turned her face away, the lines around her eyes carving thicker than I'd ever noticed. "I can't deal with this right now. I've heard enough arguing out of you for a lifetime. I'm going to bed."

She didn't bother to look at me again until she'd made her way back across the room. I wanted to say something, but every word on the tip of my tongue would likely come out angrier than I would want. Instead, I hung my head and took her coldness.

"Protests have escalated, so there's a guard at every exit. I don't suggest trying to leave again tonight."

"Yes, Mother."

"And please shower before you touch anything. You smell like a vagrant."

I pulled the collar of my shirt over my nose. It wasn't that bad. Not exactly designer perfume and exotic flowers, but no reason to be so rude.

CLEAN AND DRESSED AGAIN, I lay down on my bed and stared at the ceiling. The room hadn't changed. Same dark oak furniture with burgundy and gold accents. Everything exactly where I had left it, save the pile of clothes I'd scattered on the floor when I'd hastily packed—those were folded in crisp piles on my dresser. It was like living in a storybook castle, lush and virtually frozen in time, as if I'd been gone overnight instead of months.

I doubted anyone believed I would be gone long this time. Or maybe no one cared anymore. I know what they thought: selfish, spoiled Mercury. But it didn't matter what anyone thought. I had an entire future laid out for me. A future I didn't want.

Wrapping myself in the fluffy duvet, I closed my eyes. The clean scent of expensive laundry soap settled in around me as I wriggled beneath the covers. The thread count on these sheets was the highest I'd felt in weeks, soft and silky against my skin. It should be comforting, but it all felt foreign.

I waited, eyes shut tight, but sleep wouldn't come. My head buzzed with too many thoughts, and there was nothing I could do to quiet them. The familiar heavy feeling in my chest had returned, much faster than any of the other times I'd been dragged back home. As soon as I stepped into this house, my breathing had become shallower. The air choked me as I inhaled, my old life reawakening in my blood cells. I'd been stupid to run away. No matter where I went, it wouldn't change who I was.

Tossing the covers aside, I dangled my feet over the edge of the bed and rested my head in my hands. What now? When I was away from here, I had a direction, a reason—I was running. I didn't know my end point, but at least it was forward momentum. Now being back, it was all gone. I had no clarity of purpose. What was it that I was supposed to be doing? What would be expected of me now?

I pushed myself to my feet and stumbled to the mirror, sweeping my long hair up into a ponytail in the lamplight. My face looked tired. Dark circles hung beneath my eyes. I should've crawled back into bed, but there was only one way I knew to quiet the voices. Without that, there would be no chance of sleeping. I changed into sweats and sped out the door.

FOUR

I ran past my father's office, hoping no one would come out and see me in the hall. I would have to face him eventually, but the longer I could avoid it, the better. Everything had gone oh so well with Mom that I could only imagine how awful meeting with him would be. Fortunately, a murmur of deep, heated voices rumbled from inside, so he would likely be busy for hours. At least I'd caught one break.

Two hallways and a set of stairs later, I saw the lights of the gym glowing through the frosted glass doors. I stopped short and considered turning around, but the growing unease in my body forced me to keep going. It seemed too late for the cleaning staff to still be in there, but maybe they were just finishing up, or better yet, had forgotten to shut the lights off. I pushed the door open slowly, so as not to startle anyone still lurking around, and my stomach hollowed when I saw it was only Christophe beating the sense out of a punching bag in the corner.

I tiptoed across the room, hoping not to disturb him, but he was far too into sparring with his imaginary opponent to notice me. From how intense he attacked, he'd either been here awhile already or was going exceptionally hard tonight. His face burned a furious shade of red, and sweat soaked through his tight blue shirt, showing the contours of his athletic body. The benefits of playing varsity rugby last year still hadn't abandoned him, and even though my brain knew I was still mad, my eyes couldn't help watching his taut biceps flex with every punch.

Eventually, I dragged myself away and crept to the far side of the room to my makeshift shooting range. The itchy, unsettled feeling from earlier mixed with a shot of pure excitement and bubbled up underneath my skin. I picked up an arrow and rolled it across my palm. My fingers twitched, aching to draw it back and let it fly. Holding the smooth shaft felt like home.

I opened the storage cabinet, and each bow in its place looked back at me. I ran my hand over every single one, feeling them, remembering them, until I found what I was looking for and pulled it out of the case. It felt like a longbow night, and this one was my favorite. Classic in its design with beautiful polished maple limbs. It'd cost a small fortune, but it felt like an extension of my arm, the woodsy smell taking me to a happier place. I frowned, realizing I should have unstrung it before I left, but it was too late for that; any damage was already done. Besides, it was one less thing for me to do now.

I took my stance and shook out my body, trying to remove the excess stress building in my neck and shoulders. So much tension pulling my muscles tight. Not good.

Arms up. I laced my fingers around the arrow, gripped it to the bowstring, and drew it back. The rough plastic feathers bit into my skin. Slow, still breaths.

Closing one eye, I focused on the target, the arrow spine already lined up perfectly to the bullseye. Funny how some things came back without even thinking about them. To me, this was breathing.

Steady. Steady. And—

"Mercury."

The string slid from my fingers, sending the arrow across the room, not even close to the target.

"Never sneak up on someone with a weapon," I yelled at Christophe, as he lurked behind me.

He shrugged. "Sorry."

"You should be." I pulled another arrow out of the quiver and thumbed the fletching, making a point of standing just far enough away from him that he'd notice. "Why are you still here?"

"My dad's meeting with yours, and then we're supposed to go over some project specs if it's not too late."

I shook my head and rolled my eyes to stare at the ceiling. The bland, white ceiling that I'd much rather talk to than Christophe right now. "Are you enjoying being my father's errand boy?"

"What's that supposed to mean?"

"You know exactly what I'm talking about. You've wanted to be in that boardroom since junior high, and you'll jump at any chance to be included. Hell, you flew halfway across the country to abduct me so you could kiss his ass."

"Actually, I volunteered to go as a favor to you. Your dad would've gone himself until I convinced him that maybe you might be more receptive to me. I guess I was wrong." He rubbed his red knuckles against his forehead, lines from the hand wraps still denting his wrists.

A small twinge of guilt poked at my stomach. Had it been my father in that hotel room instead of Christophe, things would have probably gone worse. Much worse. But I wasn't going to thank him for taking me hostage, even if he did grant me mercy.

"It's not your job to rescue me, Christophe."

"And when did you stop calling me Chris?"

Good question. I couldn't remember when it'd changed, but

from the way his angry glare shifted to the floor, I was sure he knew down to the second. "I thought that was your name now. Goes along with all those fancy suits."

"Wow. You really do have a smart-ass answer for everything, don't you?"

"Have you been comparing notes with my dad again?"

He grabbed the back of his head in both hands and let out an incoherent growl. His jaw clenched tightly as he paced in tiny circles. "Why do you always do this to me? Just shut me out like that? Can't you answer a question without another question?"

"My father trained me well, I guess. One of his many talents."

"Whatever your problem is with him, you need to get over it. Your father is the leader of The Five. He's busy running the entire country. It's kind of an important job."

I looked down and ruffled the plastic arrow feathers. "I know that."

"Do you, though? Do you really understand what that means? What obligations that comes with?"

"Only every day of my life. Why do you think I left? Maybe I don't want to be the good little trophy wife everyone is expecting me to be one day."

Christophe laughed hard. His face strained trying to regain composure, but failed, until he gave up and kept laughing. "You are far too stubborn to be a trophy wife."

"I'll take that as a compliment. Now, if you could run along, I have my own business to attend to."

He opened his mouth like he still had something to say, then slammed it shut without a word. He shook his still perfectly styled head and threw his hands in the air. A deep, throaty scoff followed, telling me what I already knew—he'd had enough.

He wiped his face with the white monogrammed towel

around his neck, dragging out a few more seconds, waiting for the slight chance I might back down, but eventually, knowing better than to expect me to surrender, he walked away.

The salty, sweaty smell of him faded and suddenly my victory didn't feel so victorious anymore. It felt more like when you accidentally bite the inside of your cheek—a little painful, a little bloody, and I already knew it was going to sting a little in the morning.

My weight shifted to my front foot, my heart urging me to go after him, but my head keeping my body in place. I wasn't trying to be so snippy; the words just came out that way when I opened my mouth.

Christophe had been my friend first, then everyone else had to sneak in and steal a piece of him. He was my father's protégé, my mother's favorite, and now The Five's trained pet, and the parts I remembered, the ones I really needed right now, were gone. Sometimes small flickers of the old him would come out and play, but it'd been so long I wondered if they were even still in there, buried beneath all his self-importance and designer labels, or if spending too much time in this house has snuffed them out. How come he couldn't see that I was the only one who never needed him to change?

Drawing the bow again, I aimed and loosed the arrow at the target.

Bullseye.

FIVE

Bodies flew across the screen. A woman rushed at a police officer and he struck her with a baton. Blood sprayed across the pavement. Red splotches on gray dirt.

"Do you need to watch this in front of Mattias?" Mom scolded as she positioned herself between Matty and the gigantic television screen on the wall, her willowy frame doing little to help her cause.

"It's how life works, Giselle. He'll need to learn that one day." My father glowered at Matty, as if his age was somehow his fault. Matty didn't seem to notice.

I considered saying something in Matty's defense, except I was still standing in the hallway, my feet staying stuck to the cool tile floor. Close enough to see without being seen. Bacon grease and freshly ground espresso tried to pull me the last few steps through the doorway, but the need to ease myself back into my *normal* life was stronger. Plus, I'd barely slept, a constant loop of frustrated thoughts spinning through my brain every time I closed my eyes, which made the thought of trying to act okay that much worse.

"He's just a boy, Vincent." Mom put her hands on her hips and did her best to glare at my father.

"For now." He rolled his eyes, more annoyed than intimidated, then flipped off the screen and turned back to his untouched breakfast. "Filthy entitled protesters."

"Well, aren't you pleasant this morning?" Mom sat back down and prepped her coffee. One sugar, two cream, as always.

"Pleasant? Someone hacked into the police mainframe and deleted the records of several high-risk offenders last night. These people will be out on our streets, terrorizing our citizens. Forgive me if I'm less than pleasant."

"I'm sure they can recover the information before there is too much trouble. Have a little faith."

My father made an indecipherable noise under his breath, a grumble mixed with contempt and maybe a swearword or two

Mom sighed. "Do they think it's the same people as the bank fiasco last month?"

He pounded his fist on the table. The cutlery jumped, and the milk in Matty's bowl splashed across his place mat. "Don't you think I'm trying to figure that out?"

Grabbing a stack of papers, he stomped out of the kitchen and past me lurking in the hall.

"Eat your breakfast, then get in my office," he barked, not bothering to make eye contact.

Mom and Matty turned to the doorway.

"Good morning. Sleep well?" Mom said with clipped formality.

I ruffled my fingers through Matty's thick chestnut hair and sat beside him at the table. "Okay, I guess. Still a bit out of sorts."

"You're still here. That's progress," she said.

I forced myself not to answer, even though a response burned on my tongue. Instead, I nudged Matty with my shoulder and watched him teeter in his chair, spilling more milk. He put on a fake pout and jabbed my ribs with his little fist.

"How you doing, buddy?" I asked.

"Good. Me and Henrietta are going to the park today. She told me that we might be able to see some frogs, and I'm going to try and catch one. Wanna come?"

"Sure." I smiled at him, while my mother scowled and shook her head at me. "Or maybe another day."

He scrunched up his nose at my lack of commitment.

"And next week is my piano recital. I'm going to play this song that's super hard, but my teacher says that—"

Mom tapped her hand on the tabletop in front of him. "That's enough, Mattias. Go get dressed and let your sister eat in peace. You can tell her all your stories later."

"Okay." He hung his head and marched slowly out of the dining room like a good little soldier, giving me a quick sideways glance, the sparkle dulled in his big brown eyes.

"You missed your exams," Mom said as soon as Matty was out of range. "We arranged for you to take them over the summer so you don't lose the entire year. Fortunately, your grades were high enough for the school to pass you on that contingent."

So much for peace. I pushed away from the table and grabbed a box of cereal from the credenza, filling a too-small bowl way too full, then returned to my seat, trying to avoid looking at Mom.

"And you missed graduation. There are cards and gifts for you in the study, along with whatever was recovered from your locker."

I took a slow, deliberate spoonful, concentrating unnaturally hard on bringing it to my lips, trying to trick myself into believing I was somewhere else.

"Do you even care?" I heard Mom say, but it seemed far

away and hazy, the checkered pattern of my cereal keeping me too entranced to look up.

I remembered feeling sad the day of graduation. I'd been in a nowhere town with one of those clock towers in the center square. Impeccable neon-green lawns on every street, a function of pride, not price. A corner store with a computerized sign pulsed the date in red lights. I realized then that I'd been gone four and a half weeks, and at that moment I should have been in a stuffy theater clad in my cap and gown. I swallowed hard. The soggy cereal stuck to my throat, struggling to get over the lump building there.

"Why can't you talk to me?" Mom's sharp, angry voice shocked me out of my memories.

Leaning back in my chair, I noticed her eyes. They were blank, a hollowness, ringed in distinct displeasure at my lack of obedience. How could she possibly think I'd get over things as easily as she obviously could? She might have forgotten, but I didn't. "Because I'm not sure you want to hear what I have to say."

"That was rude." She cast her empty eyes away. Her coffee cup hovered in her hand. She hadn't drunk a sip since I'd entered the room; now she just stared at it like a strange piece of art. "Everyone here is trying. It wouldn't hurt you to give a bit of extra effort considering what you've put us all through."

I pushed my bowl to the middle of the table and stood.

"What now?" Mom huffed.

"I'm not as hungry as I thought."

SIX

The office door had been left open a crack. At least my father had granted me the courtesy of not having to fumble with the intricate electronic padlock that stood guard on the hallway wall. Even when you knew the passcode better than your own name, like I did, it was a huge pain to unlock. I tapped my knuckles against the door, knowing no one would likely hear me anyway, but it felt strange walking in here without some sort of announcement.

As expected, the outer office stood empty and eerily still. By 9:00 a.m. this place would be a hub of business and organized chaos that stretched out late into the evening, but it was too early in the day for the constant flow of well-dressed traffic to have started their daily commute.

To the left of the room stretched a dark wooden oval table with plush leather seats lining the sides. To the right sat a cluster of upholstered armchairs and couches. It gave the illusion that anyone who came in here would be comfortable, but I had yet to see anyone leave without a scowl.

Beyond the furniture there were few other decorations, although the grandeur of the windows hid the room's starkness.

Floor-to-ceiling glass walls spanned the far end of the room and overlooked the city. The real world sprawling below was reduced to tiny replicas of buildings and structures you could almost reach out and fit in your hand. From up here, you couldn't even see people, just blurs of traffic and lights that streamed across like colored shooting stars. The office was my father's castle, and all of those things below were his kingdom. His obligation. His power.

Whoever said money couldn't buy everything was grossly mistaken. Money had bought the country out of poverty, it had bought my father his position, and it had bought him the power to do whatever he wanted. The Five were once the five largest corporations in the US, ruling whatever their influence could affect, but bringing them together to bail out years of government misdealing had made them an unstoppable force. The Five replaced the government, entrenched themselves as rulers, and appointed my father their king. All of those specks down there, those dots too small for me to see, lived and died by the decisions made within these walls. My lungs tightened at the thought, but I wasn't sure if it was from envy or pity.

The sound of someone clearing their throat drew my attention from the cityscape. My father stood by a large wooden door that opened to a cluster of smaller rooms off the main one—the inner office. He didn't speak, only pointed inside and walked back through the doorway.

Inhale.

My knees quivered, making my steps clumsy as I walked across the room. The last time I'd been in this office was the night I left. Today's early morning sunlight had diluted my memory of that incident somewhat, but following after my father made it flood back in waves.

The inner office consisted of a series of corridors, all leading to desks, conference rooms, or other places I hadn't been permitted or bothered to explore. Cutting straight through the maze was the hallway to my father's office; the brain that controlled all the lesser nerve endings. Even from down the hall, I could see him sitting at his desk, boxed in by the doorframe. The center of everything.

He didn't look up when I entered, still concentrating on whatever he was writing, his thick fingers gliding across the page on an expensive gold pen. The streaks of silver around the edges of his dark, ivy-league haircut glinted in the desk lamp light. It looked like he'd accumulated a few more recently, several I was sure could be credited directly to me.

Not knowing what else to do, I took a seat in front of the desk. These chairs were stiffer than those out front, and except for my father's desk and a minimalistic set of shelves behind him, there was little for anyone to look at. An entire room designed to encourage people to leave quickly, and it was working.

"You've come back," he said, his deep voice smooth, making it difficult to figure out if he was asking a question or simply making a statement.

"Yeah?"

"May I presume that you have finished with this tantrum of yours? I can't be wasting money and resources chasing after you when you don't feel like being here."

"Then why bother?" I whispered into my lap, loud enough to be heard, quiet enough that he might think I wasn't trying to be.

He ignored my question.

"A lot has happened while you've been wherever it is that you've been. Protests have become violent. There is a domestic terrorist group undermining law enforcement. People are unsettled, and there are allegations of a rebellion brewing in the lower-income classes. Other countries have taken notice."

"And this is somehow my fault?"

He huffed and rolled his eyes up to finally look at me, his stare hard and cutting. "I never said it was. I'm only saying I have much bigger problems to deal with than *you* right now."

That was a relief. A busy father was better than a nosy one.

"Unfortunately, that also means I need to be able to count on you to help out around here."

"What do you need me to do?"

"Be nice and stay out of trouble."

"That's it?" The words came out more flip than they should have.

My father scowled. "Don't be so casual about this. I'm sure this will be a much harder task for you to accomplish than you think, considering your history."

I swallowed hard. Of course he needed to throw that in. As if we both didn't already know that. "It'll be fine."

"It better be." He shifted his wide shoulders back, making himself abnormally large and impossibly rigid, occupying as much space in the room as possible and making me feel about three inches tall. The glower on his face made clear this wasn't just a threat. "Otherwise, you'll be assigned your own guard detail. Morning and night, watching your every move. I doubt you want that."

"No, sir." I sat up straighter in my chair.

"This country is on the verge of a grand-scale war, and I need everyone in my organization to be on point. That means you."

"Okay. Are we done?"

"No." He crossed his hands in front of him, lacing his fingers together. "I'm throwing a gala this weekend for some delegates from the PanAsia Alliance and I expect you to be on your best behavior. We need their support if we are going to show our enemies this country's strength. Use some of those manners I paid so much for you to learn."

"What if I just don't go?"

"I don't recall giving you a choice."

He resumed reading the stack of papers on his desk. *Great.* Barely back home and I already had to face the public. I'd half expected my father to lock me away after what I'd pulled. At least that would've kept me from having to play nice with his socialite friends. The heavy feeling in my chest set in again.

"You may go." He waved his hand, dismissing me, eyes still averted.

I paused for a moment. I felt like there was more to say, but didn't know where to start, or even if it would matter.

"By the way, I've had that despicable place condemned," he added.

I hovered over the chair, my hands still clamped on to the armrests. "What place?"

"The Full Moon or whatever it was that you decided was more important than your responsibilities at home." He stared at his computer screen and clicked away at the keys, like he hadn't stabbed me right in the heart.

"You can't do that."

"Yes, I can. Allowing an underage runaway to rent a hotel room is illegal."

"It's not Bill's fault. I had a fake ID." I dropped back down, my fingers knotted in my lap. By now, Bill would know who I was and the lies I'd told. I blinked back tears, thinking what might happen to him.

"Well then, it is your fault, isn't it? All actions have consequences. You will need to be more conscientious about how your decisions will impact others in the future, won't you?"

"Do any of your actions have consequences, or just mine?" I

bit down on the inside of my cheek. That was not smart. Not smart at all.

He slammed his hands against the desk, pushing himself to his feet. I grabbed the arms of the chair and slid back, knees to my chest. My heart pounded in my head. Why did I say that? He stared at me, his knuckles white and his face the shade of a fresh bruise.

"I'm sorry," I squeaked from my chair, still unable to move. He forced out an exhale with a grunt, the burnt smell of morning coffee still on his breath. Then slowly, the anger drained from his face and melted into something else that I couldn't comprehend. He opened his mouth, but hesitated and sat back down. Something in his eyes sparked. The slick, emotionless business demeanor had cracked a fraction.

Head down in a stack of documents, he refused to look at me. "Get out of here and apologize to your mother. She says you're being a brat."

SEVEN

The dress was simple. Purple with a puffy skirt that hit just below the knee and barely there sleeves that served no function but to irritate the person wearing the hideous thing. I'd bet my mother picked it out. Nothing tight or edgy, or even couture, just the costume of a little princess. I hated everything about it, especially the color. Even the shoes had purple bows on them. Seriously?

The door creaked open behind me, and a head of blonde curls peeked in.

"Kendall," I called, letting her know I'd seen her, a ridiculous grin spreading across my face.

"M," she squealed, then sprinted across the room, arms wide open for a hug. "I missed you."

I hugged her back, trying not to choke on all her coconut-and-hibiscus-scented hair.

She looked fantastic. The dress she wore followed her curves exactly. A black lace overlay showing only a hint of skin. Her dress covered more than mine, but the way her tanned legs and shoulders peeked through the fabric was way sexier than I could pull off, especially in this purple disaster. Twelve years of friendship and I was still insanely jealous of how clothes always looked better on her.

"I'm still pissed you haven't called me," she said, checking herself over in the mirror and running her pinkie along her lips to fix her already perfect cherry-red lipstick.

"Sorry. Everything's been pretty crazy around here. I meant to, I really did."

"I'll forgive you. This time."

She hugged me again, tighter, making it difficult to breathe.

"It won't happen again," I whispered as she let go.

"So where did you go this time?" She spread herself out across my bed, kicking her strappy, high-heeled sandals to the floor, watching me fidget with the stray curl itching the back of my neck.

"A little bit of everywhere."

I cringed, hoping she wouldn't call me out for being vague. For some reason, I didn't want to give her the details of the places I'd been. They were my secret to keep. Besides, Kendall would probably be disgusted with most of them, so no point in sharing.

Fortunately, she didn't seem to care. Instead, she picked at the lint on my duvet and flicked it so it flitted to the floor. "Well, you didn't miss much around here."

"Oh yeah." I guess she and Mom didn't have the same opinion when it came to what was important. For that, I think I liked her more. "How come you're here? I thought your parents hated these types of things."

"My parents felt it was important to show their support for the cause. I'm here to make sure you don't make an idiot of yourself at your dad's big party."

"Thanks." I sat on the bed and leaned over to nudge her with my arm.

"It could be worse."

"Yeah, he could make Christophe babysit me again."

"Ouch. Someone took a bitter pill this morning." She sat up beside me and took my hand. "What's wrong with Christophe? He's even hotter in those suits than he was in his Charlotte Hall uniform. I wouldn't mind a spin if you're not interested."

She raised her eyebrow and gave me a flirty smile that made me squirm. The image of the two of them together flashed uninvited through my mind.

"He's already starting to turn into my father. He's everything I can't stand about my life."

"Stop being so melodramatic. Your life isn't exactly tough. You're practically flipping royalty."

"Is that why I feel like I'm locked up in a tower?"

"Very funny. No one's gonna bother saving you with an attitude like that. You'll probably have to save yourself."

"You'd save me, right?" I laughed as Kendall stretched her feet in the air and stared at her pedicure.

"I'd think about it." She put her feet down and rolled onto her stomach, graceful and a bit seductive, as if she couldn't help being desirable at all times. "By the way, your mom told everyone you've been vacationing on the coast, so I would stick to that story."

I sighed, my whole body deflating into the mattress, making me want to pull up the covers and pretend this night wasn't happening. "They can't even let me be a delinquent properly."

"You know how to be a delinquent as much as I know how to throw a football."

"You're proud of that?"

She shrugged. "You know what I mean. It's just not me."

A soft knock echoed from outside the door. Kendall jumped up, straightening herself and slipping her shoes back on. I rushed over, the layers of my skirt hissing as I moved. I really hated this dress.

Christophe stood in the doorway wearing a perfectly cut tuxedo, the exact right style to make his shoulders look broad and commanding. The girls would love it. I thought he looked like a gorilla.

"Can I come in?" he said.

I rolled my eyes.

"Just for a minute. I promise."

I stepped back and let him enter.

"Why Kendall Drake, you look lovely this evening," he said in a syrupy, smooth voice.

She tittered, her cheeks the color of ripe apples. I made a sour face.

"Would you mind giving me a minute alone with Mercury?"

"Fine." Kendall fake pouted in the cutest way possible, then poked a pale pink manicured finger into his chest right below his bow tie. "But it'll cost you a dance later."

He winked at her and smiled. "How about two? Only if every other guy isn't tripping over themselves to get to you first."

"Deal."

She sashayed out the door, closing it behind her, and the overwhelming feeling of being trapped came back tenfold.

Christophe sighed and looked me over. "You look beautiful."

"Save it. I look like a fancy cupcake."

"Kind of. But if anyone can pull that look off, it's you." He chuckled, and it almost made me laugh too, but I pushed it down.

"Was that supposed to be a compliment? I'm not sure." I flopped back down on the bed, the skirt puffing out around me like a balloon.

"Maybe I can make you feel better," he said as he sat down beside me, the weight of both of us on the mattress almost making me slip on my satin dress. "I wanted you to have this."

He produced a square blue velvet box from his pants pocket and opened it with a squeak. Inside was a black leather cord with a loop on one end, and a delicate diamond-encrusted arrow on the other that acted as both the pendant and the clasp. It was exactly the kind of thing I would've picked out myself. Pretty with a bit of edge, and of course, an arrow. To anyone else, it probably looked plain, but to me, it was breathtaking.

I snapped the box shut. "I can't accept this." Even though I wanted to.

"Why not?"

"You can't just buy me gifts like this. It's not right."

"It's not a gift, it's an apology. I shouldn't have told your parents about finding you without talking to you first."

I slid as far from him as I could get, ramming my hip into the post at the end of my bed. "What are you talking about?"

He ran his hand over his face, clearly realizing he'd spilled information I didn't already know. "I was the one who got the call that you'd been found."

"And then you ratted me out to my parents. Real nice, Christophe."

He hung his head and let out a long breath. "I know that now. I was trying to do the right thing, and I was worried about you."

"Thanks." I crossed my arms. "But I can handle myself."

"I know," he said as he pulled the necklace out of its box. The diamonds glittered under my bedroom lights as it swung in his hand. "I want you to be able to trust me."

"I'd like to, but—"

"We can work on that later. Right now, you need to get down to that party or your head is going to be on a spike in Central Park."

He opened the clasp, and I swept my hair up into my hand. Slowly, cautiously, he attached the cord around my neck, his fingers lingering a little too long at my collarbone. "Perfect."

I looked over in the mirror. It *was* perfect. The right length, the right style. Simple, but pretty.

"Thank you, Christophe. I really like it." My sharp tongue suddenly silenced.

He gave me a sideways smile and offered me his arm. "Shall we?"

"Sure." I stood and took one last glance in the mirror, both of us a bit distorted in the reflection. "Let's get this over with."

EIGHT

The room roared as Christophe opened the door. Voices rumbled and rolled like distant thunder, while delicate music from cellos and violins floated above the noise. Overhead, the ceiling glowed from hundreds of white paper lanterns hanging on invisible threads. Tables draped in deep blue satins seemed to move and flow around the room like water. The smell of lilies —faint, but distinct—filled the air. It was the night sky in the middle of summer. The real ones, outside the city, where the lights of the skyscrapers didn't shine. I didn't think anyone in this room knew what that looked like anymore, but here it was. Every detail exquisite.

"So you like it?" Christophe asked, as we descended the grand staircase into the middle of the room.

"It's amazing," I said, still staring up at the makeshift sky.

He squeezed my arm closer to him. "Good. It's the first time I've seen you look happy since you came back."

I steadied myself on the banister. So many people, so many conversations I didn't want to have. I used to love these types of things, the elegance, the extravagance, but lately they had all blurred together in my memory. One giant loop of pleasantries and handshakes. At least the decor from this party would stand out against the rest. The white lanterns were so hauntingly beautiful, I would do everything I could not to forget them. I should make sure whoever planned this organized all my father's events.

As we reached the bottom of the stairs, it started. The hum of people hovering around us. Glamorous bees in a very upscale hive.

"Think I can leave you alone for a few minutes?" Christophe said, giving me a wink and a smile.

Without waiting for me to respond, he disappeared into the crowd. Probably for the best, as I would've likely said something snarky that I'd have regretted later. Or worse, something I wouldn't regret. I needed to get my mouth under control before I really caused some damage.

I scanned the crowd. Men stood proper and noosed by expensive ties. Ladies dripped with money and jewels that glinted and glittered under the lights. I swallowed hard and my knees shook under my ugly dress. I pushed to my tiptoes and looked around. Where was the bar?

Having a drink in my hands would give me something to do, and an empty glass was always a good enough reason to leave a conversation. However, the only bar in sight was all the way across the room, and getting there would prove to be a challenge.

"Excuse me," I said repeatedly as I maneuvered between guests, the puffiness of my skirt not helping with the tight spaces between the bodies.

Hands extended from nowhere, waiting to be shook. Polite smiles and banter followed me wherever I walked. I didn't really know these people, but they claimed to know me. The little girl they'd seen grow up on the news. I was theirs.

I did my part, responding as they expected. Complimenting

her dress, telling him how much I supported this initiative or the other. Empty words I wouldn't remember by the time I got across the room, provided I could manage to do that.

Almost there. I could see the bartender and his wonderful colored concoctions only a few feet away. I saw an opening and turned abruptly, knocking into another guest.

I glanced up at my suited victim, but instead of a face, all I saw was blue. Deep, dark eyes like the night sky before a storm. Words wouldn't come. He looked about my age, with a hint of something deliciously sinful in his crooked half-smile. Something secret.

I shook my head and looked away. "Sorry."

"It's all right, my fault," he shouted at me over the noise, then continued across the room like nothing happened.

Watching him walk away, something twinged in my memory. I'd seen him somewhere before, or at least that smile. Not close up, but somewhere. I was sure of it. I lunged forward to ask his name, but he disappeared into the thick walls of extravagance and excess.

"There you are."

My father raised his arms and walked toward me, beaming. *So close.* He pulled me into a hug and whispered, "Be nice."

I cringed. He wrapped an arm over my shoulders and ushered me to a group of diplomats and their wives.

The practiced smile spread across my lips by instinct as he maneuvered me into their little group. Most I recognized from buzzing around the office, but there were a few foreign men, clearly here for whatever business my father was planning.

"And this is our lovely daughter, Mercury," my father said as he gazed affectionately at Mom and presented me like a prize show dog to everyone else. His hand rested on the back of my neck, and I fought the urge to shrug him off in front of his important guests. I used to think it was a protective gesture, but now it made me shiver, even in the swelter of the room.

"What an unusual name, Giselle. However did you imagine that?" a woman in an unflattering, ill-fitting silver gown asked my mom.

"The god of business and commerce," my father interjected before Mom was able to respond.

"How charming," the silver train wreck responded.

A salt-and-pepper-haired man I'd never seen before leaned forward to speak. "We heard you just returned from a vacation. How was it?"

Vacation? I wouldn't have considered running away a vacation. I glanced at Mom, her eyes wide as if I'd stepped on her foot. Then I remembered. She'd told everyone I was at the coast. Running away would be a humiliation. A social faux pas. Couldn't have that. Reality was too impolite for this crowd.

"Wonderful," I said. My voice an enthusiastic caricature of a real person. "In fact, I wish I was still there now."

My mother glared at me, but I simply smiled wider. I'd hear about this later, but it was her lie; she should be happy I didn't lay her bare.

"It was a pleasure to meet you, but I really need to make sure I see to all of the guests. Very important to make everyone feel welcome." I shook some hands and gave a polite nod. My father's grip on my neck released. I guess I'd performed to expectations.

"So proper. You must be proud," a voice said behind me as I dashed for a break in the crowd. I didn't wait to hear the answer.

A warm acidic taste built up in the back of my throat and I fought the urge to throw up in my mouth, only I wasn't sure if it was the completely fake conversation I'd just had, or the fact I conducted it flawlessly. And 'god of business and commerce'? What a fantastic lie. I heard I was conceived in the back of some vintage muscle car that gave me my name. Amazing how the story had evolved. A daughter with a serious and inspirational name was more fitting than the truth.

I really needed a drink.

HOURS of pointless and painful conversation later, I found Kendall on the stairs, the center of attention in a group of people our age. There weren't many of us at a party like this, so we kind of gravitated together like well-dressed, well-mannered magnets. Funny I hadn't stumbled upon them before now.

"Staying out of trouble?" she asked as I wedged myself beside her in the circle. "I wouldn't want to get fired from being your handler."

"You haven't seen me all night. You are the worst handler ever."

"Or the best." She draped her arm over my shoulders. "You're still here and I didn't have to hover. Win-win."

"How was the coast?" One of the girls, Davona, asked.

Kendall stifled a giggle.

Great. Not this again. "Good."

"I really wanted to go somewhere this summer, but my parents thought it was too dangerous with all the riots going on. You're so lucky."

"I guess so." I glanced at everyone's faces for inspiration, but came up blank. I'd been away too long to have ammunition for small talk.

"Speaking of riots, has anybody heard about the vigilante group that's been screwing with the computer systems?" Mick, a tall blond, asked, saving me from more questions I couldn't answer.

"I heard they're funding the protests too. Stirring up some kind of uprising," Kendall added.

"My dad actually called them domestic terrorists the other day." I laughed. "Random, huh?"

The entire group looked at me, flat as paper.

"Because they are," Mick said without even a whisper of sarcasm. "They're putting all our lives in danger."

"She laughs when she's nervous," Kendall interjected and jutted her hip into me, but I wasn't sure if she was helping or just setting me up as a crazy person.

"Don't you think that's kind of extreme?" I pushed past Kendall, and she shot me a terrified look before covering her eyes with her hand. "What makes you think anyone would care about coming after you?"

Instead of backing down, Mick stepped closer to me, bordering on socially unacceptable. "Because all of us here are tied to The Five, which makes us all targets. I figured the daughter of the great Vincent Masters would be smart enough to understand how important we are, especially since you're likely number one on their assassination list."

"Assassination list? Seriously?" I jabbed my finger into his chest. "If anyone wanted to kill me, they've had plenty of chances by now."

Mick made a disgusted scoff and flipped his hair off his forehead. "When you end up dead, don't expect me at the funeral."

"Okay, okay, enough, guys. This is supposed to be a party." Kendall squeezed herself between us, locking stares with Mick and gently pushing me away. "Nothing's going to happen. The Five already know about this. They'll keep us all safe."

I backed down, even though it was the last thing I wanted to do, but causing a scene wouldn't be wise either. I crossed my arms. Mick and his smug smirk. I never really liked him anyway.

Kendall ushered Mick back, her hand running playfully up

his arm, then turned to the quiet long-haired guy swishing his drink around in his glass, staying as far out of the conversation as he could get. "Asham, what are your plans for the rest of the summer?"

He looked up, his cheeks flushed. Kendall nodded at him to say something. Anything.

"I don't know." He shrugged. "Nothing?"

Everyone chuckled, even though I was pretty sure he wasn't joking.

The conversation continued, but I stopped paying attention. Had everything changed that much while I was gone so now everyone was completely paranoid? Or was it me who had changed? I knew better than to challenge popular opinion, especially at a function like this one, but my mouth wouldn't stop. The Five would protect us. The Five make us targets. The Five this, The Five that. Being in the world of The Five was exhausting. There were a lot worse things to be scared of than a bunch of hackers who probably never had the guts to leave their hideouts, and there were a lot better things to do than worry about The damn Five.

Eventually I couldn't handle the offside stares and excused myself. I leaned against the banister and looked out over the party. Everything moved around me. People. Sound. Color. It all swirled in my head and made me dizzy. I'd had enough.

Before I could move, Christophe's eyes locked on me from across the room and he beelined through the crowd in my direction. I didn't have the patience to deal with him right now.

Pretending not to see him, I ran down the stairs as fast I could around the other guests and took a sharp left in the opposite direction. I stayed close to the wall, which allowed me to speed up, and I surfaced on the far side of the room by the time Christophe finally made it to the staircase.

That was it. This party was over for me. I'd done my part as

I'd been instructed, but now it was time to get away from this chaos.

"Whoa." A scrawny waiter with a tray full of champagne glasses teetered as he came out a side door. I ran up and helped him steady the tray on his toothpick-thin arms. Even if the tray was stacked properly, he probably couldn't have handled the strain.

Catching the edge of the tray, I managed to save several glasses before they tumbled over onto the floor.

"Distribute the weight evenly and the glasses will be less likely to tip over," I said as I helped him lower the tray to a cocktail table and rearrange the fluted glasses in a more stable formation.

He stared at me like I spoke a foreign language. He either didn't understand my directions or didn't expect them to be coming from me. For all he knew I'd never had to do anything for myself in my entire life.

"Thanks," he said finally, once all the glasses were safe.

The guy seemed nervous. His small, tight face looked a bit like a ferret, and his blatant anxiety narrowed it even more. This might be his first high-end job, but at the very least he should've showered, as he smelled oddly of rotten fish. No wonder his tray was still full. He looked like he wanted to be here as much as I did.

"Remember. Two hands and keep the weight even."

He nodded.

I grabbed a glass of champagne and hid it behind my back. "My consulting fee."

NINE

The champagne was better than I'd imagined. So light there was almost no taste at all, just bubbles. Acidic little balloons that popped in my throat and sent their helium to my head. Must be expensive. I should've grabbed another glass.

I'd wandered the halls of our house looking for a quiet spot to stop. Going back up to my room wasn't an option, because if anyone actually noticed I was missing, it was the first place they'd look. Fortunately, as everyone was at the party, the hallways were completely empty. Except for the throb of noise coming from the other room, it was as close to solitude as I could get.

My ankle jutted out to the left, almost sending me crashing to the floor. These ridiculous heels were so hard to walk in, especially with the beginning of a buzz. I leaned against the wall and pulled them off, holding them by the spikes. My toes unfurled and buried themselves in the thick, silky carpet. An inappropriate moan escaped my throat. Much better.

Tipping my drink upside down, I polished off the last of the champagne, then frowned, realizing I was now stuck with the glass. I could bring it back to the party, but that would mean having to go back to the stupid party. Maybe I'd be better off if I left it in the kitchen.

I walked down the hall, letting my sore feet sink into the carpet, and noticed the door to my father's office open. Odd. This area of the house wasn't accessible to anyone except for staff, our family, or guards. I guess whatever needed to be dealt with couldn't wait.

I pulled the door open wider and peeked in. It seemed empty, save the beams of moonlight cutting across the floor.

"Hello," I called into the dark doorway, but no one answered.

The door to the inner office was closed and it was eerily quiet, the thick walls insulating the room from the party sounds. I shrugged. Must've been an oversight.

I turned to leave, but the serenity tempted me to stay. Instead, I tiptoed in and closed the door. Leaving the lights off and my champagne glass on the meeting table, I stood in front of the wall of windows.

Something about the world beyond the glass called to me. Something bigger, something magical, I felt inside my bones. It gave my soul calm. The city buzzed, electric with a strange beauty that only came out at night. All the lights of the buildings twinkled like stars, and the cars that passed sped in circles like fireflies. I leaned forward on my toes. If I had wings I could simply stretch out and let myself fall.

A distorted image stared back at me. A version of my face reflected in the glass. It didn't smile. It didn't move. It just hovered above the lights. A chill tingled through my palm as I laid it flat against the window, my skin and my apparition connected at the fingertips. Me trapped in here and it slipping away into the shadows of the night.

A streak of color flashed across the window. I spun around. Someone raced from the inner office toward the door.

"Hey," I yelled.

The figure jumped and glanced over at me. He was dressed in a suit and tie, but it was too dark to tell if I recognized him, or what object he had clasped tight in his hand. His twitchy movements made it obvious he wasn't expecting anyone to see him. He ran. I gave chase.

He fumbled with the door, giving me time to close the gap between us, but as soon as he hit the hall, he sped up, too quick to catch. Whoever he was, he didn't want to be caught, which meant he needed to be, if I could only slow him down. I threw one of my shoes at his feet. It hit his leg and bounced onto the floor, sending him teetering to the side. I took advantage of his stumble and willed myself faster until we ran beside each other. Elbow up, I threw my body into his, knocking him against the wall.

I jammed my forearm against his windpipe and pressed, a stiletto in my free hand targeted and ready near his face. I blinked. It was the guy with the stormy eyes I'd almost bulldozed earlier. How did he get up here?

"Impressive. You're a lot stronger than you look." The trespasser smirked at me. The same crooked half-smile he'd charmed me with earlier.

I pushed the heel spike closer to his face. "What were you doing in there?"

"Saving the world."

The whirlwind of the chase catching up to me coupled with his nonsensical words made my head hurt. Or maybe it was the champagne. I squinted. "What?"

"You wouldn't understand."

"Who are you to tell me what I don't understand? You don't know me."

"I know more than you think."

"I thought so. I've seen you somewhere before, haven't I?"

"Yes, you have." He smirked again. "We met at the party, or did you forget already?"

"Not just tonight. Somewhere else. Where are you from? What are you doing here?"

He shrugged, my arm sliding tighter against his neck. "Maybe you have, maybe you haven't. I don't keep track of your social calendar."

I let out an irritated huff. The joy he took from being caught unsettled me. "What did you take?"

"Ratchett," he called over my shoulder, ignoring my question. The short, clumsy cater-waiter raced behind us. The trespasser tossed whatever he had in his hand to the waiter, who caught it and bolted down the hallway.

"What?" I said, more to myself than anyone else.

"Gotta go." In one fluid motion, Stormy Eyes lurched forward, throwing me backward onto the floor. He stopped for a moment, his hand extended, like he might actually help me up, then changed his mind and ran off. "I'm sorry."

I scrambled to my feet and did the one thing left to do. I ran the opposite way down the hall. "Security!"

TEN

Security ran the circumference of the party room, but they couldn't find anyone who matched my description of the ferret-faced waiter and his smart-mouthed accomplice. They probably would've had better luck if they'd actually stopped people and checked them, except the entire operation had to be covert so as not to alert the other guests. An invasion at a party designed to show the country's strength wasn't something anyone wanted to be held responsible for.

I'd been quarantined in the dining room. As much as the thieves were unpredictable, the staff around here knew I was too. The funny part was that I was actually doing the right thing, or at least what my parents would feel was the right thing, for a change.

Someone fetched me a pair of flats and some hot tea. My parents were secretly alerted, and two of the guards checked on Matty to ensure he was still safe in his room.

A new rotation of guards came in and I gave the description of the thieves for the third time. I struggled with why I needed them to be caught. Part of me wanted them found for the obvious reasons, but another part was intrigued. The guy in the suit oozed of a strange something that fascinated me, and if he disappeared, I'd never be able to figure out what it was.

Unfortunately, a search of the entire building came up empty. A tall guard returned to the room carrying the ferret guy's catering uniform he'd found ditched in the trash outside the back entrance used for deliveries. They must've made it out before I had time to get reinforcements. Too late. They'd vanished.

So they set me free. The guards would still be running through the security tapes, but there were no cameras in the office, so they had to rely on the hallway cameras to catch anything. I guess there were some things The Five didn't want caught on film. A blessing and a curse.

As I headed up to my room, I could still hear the boom of voices. I peeked into the main ballroom. The party was still in full swing, like nothing had happened. I rubbed my forehead. Was it all just a dream?

Turning to leave, I caught sight of something at the back of the hall. I looked again. There he was, Stormy Eyes, sneaking out the side entrance. From that direction, the only way out of the building was through the kitchen. I ran to the staff elevator, hoping to get down to the main floor before he made it down the fifty-five flights of stairs. I smashed the lit button on the wall, hoping if I did it more than once the elevator would move faster.

As the doors opened on the kitchen, heat blasted my face, like walking into a sauna. Food and bodies flowed in and out, with hardly anyone casting more than a second's glance at me or simply refusing to meet my eyes, knowing I clearly didn't fit in with the stark-white-uniformed staff.

Carefully, I navigated my way to the rear door. The back entrance had always been the only foolproof exit whenever I ran away, and likely the only way anyone would be able to escape tonight without getting caught.

There was no one outside, at least not yet, so I rushed to the side of the building and hid. A thin sheet of mist hung in the air. The moisture soaked into my skin. It'd probably rain soon.

The sound of cars and footsteps at the end of the alleyway calmed my nerves about standing in the dark by myself. Less than an hour ago, I stood looking over the city like it was a precious jewel; now I was hiding in a corner by a smelly dumpster—one bad enough that there wasn't even one particular smell, just a big cloud of terrible.

Time ticked on, but still no one came out the back. So much for my intuition. He must have escaped another way. Giving up, I started back toward the door, but as I turned the corner, it opened. I ducked back, hopefully unseen.

Stormy. He was alone, or at least I didn't see anyone else. Probably part of the plan. Guards were looking for two people— split up and you look less conspicuous. Smart. Very smart. Besides, this guy could blend in with those hoity-toity types a lot better than his friend. He had an air about him, a polish. The easy way he maneuvered through the crowded party instead of drowning in the sea of arrogance. The too-straight way he stood, his stature screaming with confidence and power. A look I knew all too well. Plus, the suit cut was almost too perfect. Tailored impeccably across his thick shoulders and falling at the right spot on his hips. He wasn't some one-time thief, he was a professional; or, if not, this mission was beyond calculated.

But those eyes. Where had I seen them before? I blinked for a second, scanning my memory for anything that might remind me. Then it hit. I walked out of the shadows as he rushed toward the busy street ahead.

"Corbin?" I called after him. He stopped, then, without turning, kept walking away, but slower this time, the hesitation answering for him.

"I know who you are."

His head fell forward to his chest, but he stopped moving, simply staring at the ground. He didn't turn around, but his voice echoed off the concrete and between the brick buildings. "Are you planning to tell anyone?"

"I haven't decided yet. Are you going to tell me what you were doing?" I took a few steps closer. Thankfully, I wasn't wearing those stupid heels anymore or I would have clicked like thunder through the alley and scared him off. But he didn't run. He either didn't know I was coming closer or didn't care.

"No. It's none of your business."

"You were in my house; it's my business. The best thing you can do is just tell me what's going on."

I heard his deep sigh, even over the sounds of the city surrounding us, then he swiveled his head back, staring me down. "The best thing you can do is forget me."

And then he ran. Fast.

I followed, but he didn't make it easy. His long legs gave him speed I couldn't match, and he was more agile at weaving between the people on the street. At least in the open he couldn't hide.

At the end of the block, the cater-waiter joined him. Corbin nodded and pointed back over his shoulder. Did he still know I was following, or was he just guessing? Didn't matter.

The two bounded through the streets like skateboarders without wheels, up and over things. I tripped a few times, trying to keep my head up without losing sight of them, my puffy dress catching on everything it possibly could.

Around a corner, two others joined the group. They wore hoods over their heads, so I couldn't see their faces, not like I'd actually know them if I did. I pulled back against a nearby building as they stopped to talk for a second. Corbin glanced my direction, and I huddled closer to the bricks. The waiter guy showed the other two what they stole, and the hoods nodded in approval. Then they raced off again.

They zigzagged through the crowd. Not quite running, but definitely a pace to make distance quickly. Down the stairs into the subway. Too many people, but it didn't stop me. I gave them a few second lead, but could still follow through the crowd. Body odor and urine hung in the air. I'd never been so grateful for never having to take a subway in my life. I avoided touching anything, not wanting to risk getting that awful smell on my skin.

They reappeared just ahead of me, across the tracks. As I reached the edge of the platform, a train burst out of the tunnel, blocking my view, then another came from the other direction. When the trains cleared, the thieves were gone.

I stood in the busy station as strangers wandered around me, oblivious that I was even there until they'd bump into me and give a nasty look before ignoring me again. The pathetic-looking girl in the ripped party dress staring out from the platform. They probably thought I might jump.

Then my mind finally caught up with my feet. What was I doing? What was I going to do if I caught up with them anyway? Pin them down and make them talk? Doubtful. I'd tried that once already, and it didn't work out so well. Besides, why did I even care?

I trudged back up the stairs, pushing my way through the people coming down. My chest crushed heavy on my lungs, and I couldn't quite figure out why. I felt completely foolish.

Aboveground, it'd already started to drizzle. I leaned back against the wall of a nearby building and watched people pass. I looked up. A large droplet splattered in the middle of my face, draining into my eyes. *Great.* More drops came, staining my dress with deep plum polka dots. Time to go home.

ELEVEN

Rain dripped from every part of me. My bouncy purple dress had become a drenched rag clinging to my goose-bump-covered legs. My curls fell flat and plastered against my head in a helmet of hair. I needed a towel and a shower and my bed—as soon as possible.

"Where have you been?" my father said, as I walked through the sitting room toward the stairs.

The roar of the party still boomed in the background, but instead of being there, he lurked out here in the low lamplight, all alone. Strange. He still wore his tuxedo, the bow tie loosened and hanging in two strands around his neck. A half-filled glass of caramel-colored liquor hung precariously from his left hand, that was draped over the side of the armchair. He'd either drunk enough to be sedated, or he hadn't figured out what level of furious he was with me yet.

"I saw the guy who broke into your office, and I chased him."

Rain from my dress formed a dark puddle on the carpet, and drops of water ran down the bridge of my nose, tickling my face.

"You chased him? Do you know how foolish that was? What

if he was a terrorist? He could have killed you, or worse." He scowled at me but didn't yell.

I shuddered, trying to imagine what could be worse than being dead in a subway station, and even more disturbing, why my father wasn't screaming at me. I would've preferred yelling.

He took a slow sip from his glass, his eyes never leaving my face. "Why didn't you tell a guard?"

"There wasn't one around. I saw an opportunity, so I took it."

An eyebrow raise. Disbelief or maybe shock. Another calculated sip. "I saw you on the hallway security video. What were you doing in my office anyway?"

I shrugged. "The door was open."

He made a *hmph* noise and stared at the bottom of his glass as he swirled the liquor and ice around. "Someone is already looking into this incident, but I was curious how you happened to be in the right place at the exact right time."

"Luck, I guess. I was trying to do my part. I know how important security is to you." My cheeks burned a telltale crimson. I knew it was a lie, and from the way his lips twisted with amusement, he did too. Fortunately, he decided not to acknowledge it.

"So where did the thief go?"

"I don't know. I lost him about fifteen blocks away."

He bolted upright in his chair, liquor swishing dangerously close to spilling over the sides of his glass. "Fifteen blocks? You ran after someone for fifteen blocks?"

I reflexively took a step back and nodded. Probably farther than that, but I'd lost count.

"Well. Your time away must have toughened you up. At least there's that." He sat back, his posture too rigid to be comfortable, and took another sip, his eyes going glazed and distant. "Go get cleaned up before your mother sees you."

CLIMBING the stairs to my room proved a challenge, but one I was determined to meet. I desperately needed to be out of these clothes—even more than when the night started.

Opening the door, I clicked on the light. A trio of white lanterns hung delicately beside my bed. My shoulders dropped, and I tipped my head toward the ceiling. Christophe. The party wasn't even over and he'd already managed to snag decorations for me. Back when we were together, I would've loved a gesture like this, but now he really needed to stop. Besides, gifts and surprises wouldn't change the fact we'd broken up. Didn't he realize I just wanted the old him back? But I knew the old him was dead, and the second I ran away again was likely the final stab that did him in. Another awful consequence I couldn't fix.

The lanterns were pretty, though. I reached up and twirled one, watching the lights dance along the walls. I made a mental note to thank Christophe anyway. I should at least try to play nice.

I dragged myself into the bathroom and stripped, the nasty dress falling in a wet lump on the floor. My body felt clammy and cold. What the hell was I thinking, chasing a thief through the streets? Or maybe I wasn't thinking at all, and that was the problem.

I stepped into the shower and let the warm water flow over my skin, washing the chill away. I cranked the tap hotter. Once my body thawed, the challenge of standing weighed down on me. So tired. Swaying under the stream of water, eyes half-shut, I didn't want to get out and face the shock of being wet, naked, and cold again. Just a few more minutes.

Leaning my head against the tile wall, I let the water run down my sides and closed my eyes. Through my haze of exhaustion, pieces of scenes flashed in my mind. Bumping into Corbin at the party. Chasing him in the hallway. Confronting him in the alley. His words. Those eyes. So familiar, but from where? Nothing made any sense. My head pounded with so many questions. Who was he? Why was he here? What did he take? And the most deranged question of all—when would I see him again?

TWELVE

Three days. I'd fought the urge to do anything related to Corbin and his gang of thieves for three whole days until it ate away at me. It didn't help that I was bored out of my mind, holed up in a huge house with little to do. What was left of my friends had moved on with their lives while I'd been gone, so that left phone conversations with Kendall and avoiding Christophe as he skittered around our house like a cockroach.

Plus, there were the dreams. I couldn't remember them, but I'd wake up in the middle of the night feeling part confused, part inspired, and part completely lost. Deep down, I think I knew what they were about, but I could never seem to figure it out once the sun came up. Maybe finding Corbin again would make them stop.

I'd skimmed through all the typical socials trying to find a picture of him, even a distant blurry one I could use to figure out where I knew him from, but nothing ever showed up. After about forty-eight hours the world forgot about my father's party and I started to think Corbin never actually existed at all.

Today I'd given up pretending I didn't care and sat cross-legged on my bed, tablet in front of me, ready for research. I pulled up the school's webpage. The thief's first name had come to me, but I still couldn't place from where. Based on his age and the fact the only people I knew came from the same social circle, I deduced I must've seen him at school.

I clicked on every year, searching every face. Nothing. I skimmed through the candid shots. Dances. Fundraisers. Sports teams. A lump built in my throat as I skimmed past the pictures of all of my friends in their caps and gowns. I had missed graduation. The biggest moment of my academic career and I just bailed. I had every reason not to be there, but giving it up now seemed so much worse as I looked over what I was never getting back.

Then I saw him. An old picture of the track team. I enlarged the photo. Corbin Locksley. The hair was longer. Face younger. But it was definitely him. The ridiculously cocky grin across his lips was unmistakable. Even on-screen it looked like trouble. I didn't recognize the last name, but he had to be somebody important if he went to Charlotte Hall. What was he doing in my father's office?

I clicked on the student directory. Since he was junior varsity in the photo, he should've been a senior this year. Libby. Lindstrom. Loxxon. No Locksley. Maybe he failed? I looked at the juniors again. Nothing. He just disappeared. But at least now I had a full name.

I punched it into a search engine, not knowing what to expect. Several pages appeared, but none to do with Corbin. After scrolling down several pages, a headline, "Head of Locksley Chemical Found Murdered," popped out at me.

Eldrin Locksley, owner of biotechnology corporation Locksley Chemical, was found dead in his home last night. Foul play is suspected.

Sad. Maybe that's why Corbin wasn't in the school pictures. Maybe he changed schools after the murder or something. I clicked a few more links, but nothing provided any new information. Over two years had passed and not one more news report mentioned the investigation or whether a killer had been found.

I typed *Locksley Chemical* into the blinking search engine block. A few more articles: "Locksley Chemical Wins Top Prize for Mind-altering Research," "Chemical Company CEO Announces Expansion of Operations Despite Terrible 4th Quarter", "Locksley Chemical Sold to Nott Pharmaceutical Technologies after Death of Founder." I clicked the last article, but there was nothing about Corbin's dad, just share-buyout information. Boring. I clicked on the corporate link. It was still active, but everything off the main page was a bad gateway. The only thing left functioning was a logo and two addresses with some satellite maps: one downtown and one for a warehouse by the old shipyards. I thought back to the waiter, who wasn't really a waiter, who smelled like fish. They must be hiding out at the shipyards.

I searched the information on the warehouse. Last known owner was Locksley. Guess that Nott company had no use for it.

I shut off the tablet. Corbin Locksley. Now that I had his full name and a potential address, what did I want to do with that information?

I CREPT into the dining room to get something to eat, but apparently we had company. The entire room buzzed with suited lackeys, hands full of coffee or buried deep in the pockets of their finely tailored pants. My father's face filled the large television screen along the back wall, and all eyes were glued to his every move.

"Please be assured we will not tolerate this kind of activity and we will find those who look to undermine our country and ensure that justice is proper and swift," the wall-sized head of my father bellowed, splitting the silence in the room. "Thank you."

On the screen, the press flooded toward the stage and started pummeling my father with questions. Every person in the dining room stood still, listening intently, but I seemed to be too late for the party.

I found Christophe in the middle of the room and tugged on his arm. He turned, but without the smile I'd come to expect. Something had happened. Something bad.

"What's going on?" I asked, leaning in close to avoid the icy glares from everyone I'd disturbed while making my way to him.

I followed him as he shuffled out of the crowd and pointed toward the hallway. Once we exited the room, Christophe collapsed against the wall. His skin looked splotchy and puffy, and red lines spidered through the whites of his eyes. I hadn't seen him such a mess since his mother had passed away. He'd spent three days in the hospital holding her hand, and when he came out, he'd looked like this.

"The terrorists struck again," he said, blinking and trying to focus on the floor tiles. "They found some internal memo about how we were planning on cutting an educational support program for inner-city schools and hacked into every network they could find to announce it to the world."

"Looks like he recovered well." I leaned against the opposite wall and tapped Christophe's ankle with my foot.

He looked up, but still no smile. "Should have. We've been up all night trying to spin this in a positive way. He had to promise some crazy new program, that we can't afford, to make up for the one we were cutting."

"Why did this program need to get cut anyway?"

"Too expensive. Needed to divert funds to domestic security endeavors."

I stood up straighter. "Sounds like a real worthwhile cause."

Christophe stared at me through narrowed eyes, sensing not only my sarcasm but my disapproval.

"Things are getting complicated. Maybe you should be happy you're on this side of the fight." He pulled his phone out of his pocket and flitted his finger around the screen, typing with one hand while still trying to keep an eye on me. Maybe he thought I'd leave.

"Yeah. I'm blessed, aren't I?"

He ignored me and kept clicking at his phone.

"Does anyone know who the terrorists are yet?" I asked as I peeked back in at the room of my father's drones, still mesmerized by the sight of their king on TV.

Christophe shook his head and muttered something under his breath. "All I know is if your father ever finds out who's behind this, he'll kill them."

THIRTEEN

Eight days and twenty-two hours. The time I'd spent doing everything but come here. The thought had infected my brain, slowly spreading from the edges of my consciousness until eventually it took over and was all I could think about. Finding Corbin. Getting the answers to my list of questions that doubled every day I stayed away. But standing there in middle of nowhere, the whole idea seemed insane.

Darkness shrouded the shipyard, making me regret waiting until nightfall. Another impulsive decision I'd hate myself for later. I could've come during the day, but the shadiness surrounding my mission made evening the only reasonable time to show up. Besides, if anyone who knew me saw me, I'd have too many things I didn't want to explain.

The sound of every step I took ricocheted off the rows of metal shipping containers and cast-off garbage. The smell of week-old fish mixed with salt prickled my nose. Definitely not the most desirable place for a hideout, but it must keep people from accidentally stumbling across it.

I wandered around for about a half hour and started to think I was walking in circles. The skyline and the shipping containers all looked familiar. The same logos printed across the steel fronts. The same brown rust stains oozing from the seams.

I pulled out my phone and the map from the Locksley Chemical website. Based on the directions, I should've found the warehouse by now. Or maybe I should've taken the first left instead of the second one? I shoved the phone back in my pocket and spun around. No direction looked promising. I let out a heavy sigh. Five more minutes of walking, and then I'd get out of here and come back tomorrow. I continued forward, but something had changed. I heard a new sound. Footsteps. And they weren't mine.

I stopped moving and pushed myself against one of the shipping containers. Covering my mouth with my hand, I listened. Nothing but the night breeze and my pulse in my ears. The dark must've made me paranoid. I started walking again. My steps echoed out of time. I stopped. The other set of steps stopped. Someone out there was watching me. I ran.

Behind me, the footfalls came faster and faster. I glanced back. A hooded figure was chasing me and picking up speed. Pushing harder, I weaved between containers, hoping to lose them in the maze. Metal banged and boomed behind my back. Whoever was following me didn't seem to care about being unnoticed anymore. They were coming, and they wanted me to know it.

Hands clamped down on my shoulders, and my stomach clenched as my feet lost contact with the ground. My elbows rammed into the pavement. Concrete rubbed out the knees of my jeans, taking strips of skin with them. Pain blasted through my head as my chin stopped my fall. I rolled onto my back.

A shock of red hair appeared. Not natural, but glowing neon, the color of a stoplight. She stood over me like a hunter over its kill—satisfied and all too smug. I tried to stand, but she slammed the heel of her boot down on my windpipe. Just enough room to breathe, but not enough to move.

"What're you doing here?" the flaming redhead insisted.

I tried to swallow, but the saliva dammed in my throat. Somehow, I managed a raspy whisper. "Corbin."

"Corbin? Ain't nobody round here named Corbin. Better get your skinny rich ass back to where you came from before I decide not to let you walk outta here." Even with the threat, she didn't raise her foot.

Glaring down with hollow eyes, she made a hacking sound and spit at the ground beside my head. Drops sprayed the side of my face. I forced down the urge to vomit all over her army-surplus-clad foot.

"Red, what have I told you about playing with your food?"

Another voice came toward us. Sounded masculine, but I couldn't tell from my place on the ground. The redheaded beast of a girl snickered, and I relaxed a fraction, knowing at least the other voice was joking. Or was it? I struggled to lift my head and get a better look. Nothing but a tall shadow, a hood over their head shading their face.

"We gots a stray. Looking for some sucker named Corbin. Jus' sending her on her way." She jutted her chin toward me and stepped off. Whoever had come seemed to have a controlling effect on her.

"She's looking for Hawk." The small ferret-looking guy from the party ran into the light and offered me a hand.

I refused, pushing myself up, hand right in the fresh puddle of spit my assailant had left. I cringed and wiped my hand on my pants. *So gross.* "Who's Hawk?"

"You can't bring her with us. You know who she is, don't you?" the tall figure said, as though I wasn't standing in front of him.

"I know," the small guy said, then turned to me. "What do you want with him?"

Standing as straight as possible, I raised my head in the air. I'd seen my father do it a hundred times when he wanted to command attention. "None of your concern."

"What'd I tell ya. This chick is trouble." Red's eyes dropped to slits as she tried to stare the flesh off my face.

"Calm down, Red," Ferret Boy said, stepping between us. Not like he would be much of a challenge for her to rip through, though. "We can bring him a message."

"No, I want to talk to him myself."

He shook his head and huffed. "Fine. Then we'll bring him to you. Wait here."

The trio marched off deeper into the inky blackness of the shipyard.

"You're going to leave me here by myself?"

"We can leave Red with you," the tall one called back.

I cringed so violently, even my liver shook. "No thanks. I'll be fine."

Eventually, their footsteps faded off into the night, abandoning me to an overwhelming stillness that plucked at my wound-tight nerves. For all I knew, those hooded freaks would never tell Corbin I was there, and leave my fate to the mercy of thugs and criminals that would likely drop me dead in a ditch somewhere. But right now, they were the only lead I had at finding Corbin again.

The pale moon disappeared behind a thick patch of slate clouds, shutting out the lights. Shadows crawled out from the spaces between the shipping containers and stretched toward my feet. Somewhere a cat wailed. I shuddered.

FOURTEEN

I'd never been very good at waiting. Probably because I didn't have to do it often. One benefit of being Vincent Masters' daughter meant there was rarely anything I wanted that I couldn't have—immediately. Even the word *patience* made my feet itch to move, and right now they itched so badly I'd considered ripping them off at the ankles.

I'd been sitting here, on the dirty ground, waiting for what felt like hours, but my phone assured me it had only been thirteen minutes. My knees burned as the night breeze blew across my raw, carved-up flesh. My feet tapped, begging me to get up and leave, but maybe it was less my lack of patience and more about being in the middle of a secluded shipyard at night that had me on edge.

Then I heard something. Somewhere in the distance. Not the faraway traffic or cats chasing the shipyard rodents—a new sound. Something was moving, but with a long dragging noise, like a scrape. I scrambled to my feet, and the noise stopped. I squinted and scanned through the blackness. Nothing. At least nothing I could see.

Bang. Bang. Bang.

The shipping containers rumbled. Metal clanging louder and closer. I steadied myself, ready to run if I needed to, but I didn't know which way. The sound seemed to be coming from everywhere all at once. Around me. Above me. Through me.

Thud. A figure jumped from the top of a container and landed right in front of me. I screamed and backed away.

The figure stayed folded in the crouch in which it landed, one sneakered foot behind them, one arm forward to keep them steady, a black, hooded sweatshirt hiding their face. The position looked primitive. Animal. A predator waiting to strike.

"Corbin?" I squeaked. "Corbin Locksley?"

The faceless figure didn't respond; they only stood and swaggered toward me, head still down. I stepped backward, retreating, until my shoulder blades smashed against a shipping container. Trapped.

"Come any closer and I'll make you regret it," I yelled, my arm thrust out toward them, trying to prove that I wasn't afraid, although the shaking of my kneecaps would've given me away.

"Did you drag me out here just to threaten me?" The figure ripped off their hood. Corbin, laughing through his wretched smile that radiated sin and subtext.

I exhaled, waiting for my heart to stop pounding at breakneck speed, then moved to the right, putting myself back into a position where he wasn't hovering over me. Where he wasn't in charge.

I stuck my hands on my hips. "No, but I wasn't expecting you to appear out of nowhere and scare the crap out of me."

He shrugged and leaned forward, still chuckling to himself. "I'm a thief, you know. Stealth is kind of my thing."

I let out an unimpressed scoff, a response feeling like a waste of time, and twisted my hair in my fingers, my hands suddenly feeling restless.

"How'd you find us?" he asked, his eyes tracking my every movement.

"I followed you." I dropped my hair and crossed my arms so he would stop staring. It made my palms sweaty. "When you snuck out of the party, I watched you come down the subway line in this direction."

"Impressive. Who knew someone like you would have such great tracking skills?"

I ignored his assumption and took his words as a compliment. "Then I looked you up online. School yearbook."

"Guess it doesn't matter how you found me. The more important question is why? What are you doing here?"

I swallowed. I'd almost forgotten I'd come here by choice. "What did you mean when you said you were saving the world?"

"You came all the way out here to ask me that?" He raised an eyebrow and looked me over. "You must be crazy."

I shrugged. "There was something about how you said it that just, I don't know, stuck."

"Right. This has nothing to do with me being caught in the office of The Five? Because I'll deny it. You can't prove anything."

I shook my head. "I don't care about that. What were you doing in there anyway?"

"You honestly expect me to answer?" He crossed his arms, and his smile disappeared, replaced by a glare that made him look a little homicidal.

"So?" I asked.

"So what?" His face scrunched up. He didn't appear to have understood my question.

"Saving the world? What were you talking about?"

Corbin thrust his hands in his pockets and paced in tight circles. I wasn't sure if he was choosing his words carefully, or simply deciding whether or not to tell me anything at all. I watched him move, the moonlight making dark shadows across his face, his brow furrowed tight.

"Not everything in this life is fair," he began.

"Tell me about it," I snickered.

His eyes narrowed. He wasn't playing around anymore. I shut up.

"There has always been a division between those people who have and those people who don't. The rich and the poor. Since The Five have come into power, the separation has gotten wider. More people are starving. More people are powerless to make a better life for themselves. While the rich"—he pointed a finger at me—"like you continue your charmed lives at everyone else's expense."

"Sounds terrible, but what does that have to do with you? I know who you are, Corbin. You lived the same charmed life as me. What makes you all righteous?"

He stopped pacing and stared up at the sky. "Things happened, and it changed how I saw the world. I wanted to do something better with my life." His face dropped back down where I could see it, but it was empty now, cold. "I wanted to fix other people's mistakes."

"So you got yourself a gang and became what? A terrorist? A vigilante? Some kid trying to make a mess of things?"

"This isn't some game you play because you're bored," he snapped, his harsh voice bouncing around the yard. "These are people's lives I'm talking about. People who you wouldn't give a damn about if you passed them on the street."

"How do you know what I would or wouldn't do?" I stomped toward him, my finger aimed right at his chest. I glared up at him, the few inches of height he had over me being little deterrent for my anger. How dare he make assumptions about me?

"Because you're right. I *was* like you once, but I gave it all up. My friends, my life, my future, to do something that mattered. But I don't expect you to understand."

He wrapped his hand around mine and pulled it away, his cool fingers melting against my angry, hot flesh.

I wanted to keep arguing. I wanted to tear his head off and tell him he knew nothing about me and what my life was like, but I couldn't. There was something noble about his statement. Whether it was a complete lie, I had no idea, but something about the way he stood and the conviction in his voice made me sure it wasn't. After all, I'd trekked out here, facing potential injury after only talking to him once before. Either he was genuine or he was the world's most accomplished actor.

We stared at each other. Motionless. Soundless. Neither willing to back down, but neither willing to continue. Clouds drifted over the moon again, lengthening the shadows on Corbin's face, thunder rolling in his eyes. He was suddenly much too close.

I snatched my hand from his grip and rubbed my wrist, walking back toward the far end of the space between containers. "How come your friend, the aggressive one, didn't know who you were? It was like I was speaking some dead language or something."

He chuckled at my description of the redheaded girl. "Because she doesn't know me by that name. Around here, they know me as Hawk."

"Hawk?" I burst out laughing. "What's with that?"

"Corbin's a bit pretentious, don't you think? No one was going to take me seriously with a name like that."

"And Hawk is so much better?"

"Said the girl named after a thermometer."

Good point. "At least it's my real name. I didn't make one up to sound cool."

His tone changed again. Serious as a heart attack. "Do you really think these people need someone cool? They need someone to take charge and help them. That's what I do here. I help them."

"Then what were you doing in my dad's office last night?"

He crossed his arms again and steadied himself on his feet. "I told you. I'm not answering that."

"Fine. So how would I get involved in your grand plan of helping the less fortunate?"

"Saying it like that is definitely not going to get you an invitation."

I huffed. "I wasn't trying to be rude. This is all a very new concept to me and for some reason, I feel the need to help. Is that all right with you?"

He shook his head and smirked in amusement. "You wouldn't know the first thing about suffering."

"And I'm sure at some point neither did you. But then something changed for you. Why can't you believe the same thing could happen for me?"

He stood quiet. I hated that. Irritating, uncomfortable silence.

"I can tell you aren't running some amateur operation here. You guys are smart, a little rough, but smart. You've been all over the news with the stuff you've been pulling and no one has any idea who you are."

He lurched forward. "What are you talking about?"

"Don't be dumb. I know you're part of the group screwing with The Five. The hacker stuff, the protests, all of it."

"How do you know?"

"I figured it out. It wasn't that hard."

His mouth dropped open to his chest, and his know-it-all smirk vanished into shock and dread. "You can't tell anyone. If we get caught, all we've done will be for nothing."

"Trust me." I raised my hand, dismissing the idea. "I'm not going to tell anyone about any of this."

"I don't trust people. Trust is something you earn, and from what I can tell, I have absolutely no reason to trust the daughter of a dictator."

Seriously? Hadn't he realized I wasn't the type to be intimidated by catchy mottos and mission statements?

"If you couldn't trust me, you would already be locked up rotting somewhere. I've known where you were hiding for the better part of a week and haven't said a word to anyone. How's that for trust?"

"It's a start." He scratched the back of his head and started pacing again. Quicker. Faster. Furious.

"Does that mean you'll tell me what's going on here? Let me help?"

"No. It just means I'll think about it."

"Then I'll think about not telling the police."

"Fine."

Clearly, he wasn't pleased to be backed into a corner. I had a feeling he didn't like not being in complete control. Sounded like every other guy in my life.

"If you really want to do something meaningful, we have something you can help with going down tomorrow night."

"Really? That fast."

He looked me over carefully. "Unless you'd rather not."

"No. No. I can handle it. Anything. I'll do it."

"All right, then. Until tomorrow." He pulled the hood back over his head and started to jog away. "Why don't you go home and really think about what you might be getting yourself into."

"Wait," I called after him. "How will I be able to get in touch with you?"

"You can't."

I opened my mouth to protest, but it was pointless. Corbin,

or Hawk, or whoever he was, had already disappeared into the shadows.

I MANAGED to sneak into the house without anyone from my family seeing me and the mess I was in. A guard at the door asked if I was all right, then eyed the rips in my clothes suspiciously when I replied that I was fine, but as long as he didn't mention my roughed-up state to anyone, I was safe.

Peeling off my jeans was a painful process. Dirt and gravel had embedded in the flesh of my kneecaps, and my shoulders ached from my arms slamming into the ground. Hopefully, this would be the only sort of initiation I'd have to endure. I trembled. Maybe it wasn't.

Locking myself in the bathroom, I cleaned my wounds and tried not to scream. And for the first time in a long while, I did as I was told. I thought about what I was potentially getting myself into with Corbin and his group of thugs. Did I trust any of them? Probably not. But for some reason, I seemed to trust Corbin. He didn't need to tell me anything, but he did—even if it came off backhanded and rude sometimes. And it sounded like they were doing something of value, something bigger than parties and delegate dinners. Plus, everything they'd done had irritated the hell out of my father, so that was a definite benefit.

I finished bandaging myself up and got ready for bed, both my body and my brain begging for the rest. As I came into my bedroom, something seemed off. The door sat open a crack, but I swore I'd closed it. Guess not. I shut it again and noticed a crème-colored card on my pillow, a pair of widespread wings across the front. I picked it up and admired the black ink–drawn feathers, each one detailed and majestic, like they belonged to a fierce bird or maybe some kind of dark angel. On the back, it read:

1316 *Gate Street. Midnight.*
Wear black. Come alone.
Tell no one.

FIFTEEN

The dull silver numbers blurred under the hazy orangish glow of the main entrance lights, but I wasn't ready to cross the street for a closer look. I pulled the card out of my pocket and read the address again. 1316 Gate St. This was the right place, but nothing about it felt extraordinary—it was just a nondescript office building, wedged in a row of nondescript office buildings. I looked up and down the street, but it was still deserted. During the half hour I'd been skulking here in the shadows, I hadn't seen one person come or go from that building. In fact, no one had even come down the street, except for the occasional car with little respect for the lone stoplight two blocks up that never seemed to turn green.

Maybe I was still too early. Or maybe I'd been played and this was some sort of nasty prank for tracking Corbin down to his secret hideout. *Jerk.* Or maybe.... I exhaled audibly as my body stiffened and twitched while I thought about what horrible trap I'd been set up for.

I could still leave. My brain had gone back and forth between showing up and not showing up so many times that in the end my legs did the deciding for me by walking out the door and bringing me here. But I hadn't committed to anything yet. *I could still leave. I should leave.*

I traced the outline of the black wings with my finger, and my shoulders slumped. I was so stupid. I honestly thought Corbin had taken me seriously, and part of me, a much bigger part than I'd originally thought, was excited. Or hopeful maybe? Whatever the feeling, it was a waste of energy. Him and his band of reckless thugs were probably laughing their asses off somewhere, congratulating each other on making a fool out of a king's daughter. Yep, I should get out of here.

One last look at the empty office buildings, then I dropped the card and watched it flutter to the ground, the soft crème cardstock looking out of place against the cracked dirty concrete. A strange tingle crept up the back of my neck. I jerked my head up and looked back and forth. No one was there, but the feeling of being watched intensified. I tried to turn around, but a hand clamped over my mouth.

"Don't scream," a voice hissed in my ear.

An iron-like arm wrapped around my waist and pulled me off the ground, dragging me into the nearby alleyway. I twisted and fought against the restraint. The grip tightened. I thrust my elbow back into my captor's side, and my raw, scabbed skin made contact with hard ribs. Bright bursts of pain shot across my vision.

"Ow," the voice grumbled.

I pulled my knee forward and kicked back as hard as I could, my heel hitting bone.

The arms released. I whirled around, clutching my elbow.

Corbin leaned against the brick wall, balanced on one foot and rubbing his side.

"What the hell were you doing?" I yelled, pushing at his shoulder, nearly knocking him over.

He wavered and had to hop back a few steps before regaining his balance. "Getting attacked apparently."

"Well you should never sneak up on someone like that. For all I know you were trying to kill me."

"For some reason I think you could probably take care of yourself." He steadied himself on both feet again and held up his hands in surrender. "And I was just playing around, but I swear I'll never try something like that again. Now keep your voice down."

"It's louder than a drunk girl at a boy-band concert. What are you doing, Hawk?" a voice laughed from farther down the alley.

Footsteps echoed louder and louder until the tall guy from yesterday and his fire-engine-tressed sidekick appeared in the dim light from the street. Beneath his black hood, his face dropped and his laughter stopped as he looked at me standing against the wall. Whatever he'd been laughing about was no longer funny with me around.

He tapped Corbin on the shoulder without taking his dark eyes off me. "Can we talk?"

Corbin nodded, and they headed back into the obscurity of the alley.

Muffled angry whispers flooded back with a very clear "What is she doing here?" in the middle, probably with the intent of me hearing it.

The Red girl stared at me as if I carried some kind of disease. Her snarl was more irritated than amused, like the last time we'd met. Being here tonight made me more than a passing annoyance. I inched closer to the wall to create as much space between the two of us as possible. If Corbin didn't come back soon, she looked like she might take a huge amount of pleasure in reaching over and snapping my neck.

The whispers stopped and footsteps crept closer in the darkness. Corbin wore a hard expression, his face unreadable, while the tall guy scowled down at the concrete, refusing to make eye contact with any of us.

Red opened her mouth, but Hawk raised his hand in her direction. "Enough screwing around. We're here for a job. Remember that."

She made a loud huff but didn't argue.

Corbin pulled a phone out of his back pocket and started tapping and swiping at the screen. Corbin's thugs crowded in closer as he held out the device on his palm. I joined the group, making sure to keep Corbin between me and them, and stared down at an intricately detailed grid-like map.

"We'll come in here." He swiped a small X at the corner of the screen, then tapped around the grid. "Security cameras are here, here, and here."

I raised my hand. Somehow, the businesslike inflection in his tone had me thinking I was in some lecture hall instead of a filthy side alley. "How are you going to pull this off with so many cameras watching?"

"Ratchett," Corbin said with a brief sneer, then his face relaxed, possibly realizing how insane this all sounded. "He can override the system and shut down the cameras and locks. Now Tucker—"

"Wouldn't the guard just call the security company when the cameras went out?"

The Red girl growled and began to pace. "You shoulda gave this one lessons in heisting before you dragged her out here in the real world."

Corbin glared at her, but she glared right back.

"Well here's a crash course. Rule number one"—Red counted off with her fingers—"don't ask stupid questions. Rule number two, if you need to know, y'all be told. Rule number three—"

"Enough. She's here because I said she's here. If you don't like it, then leave." Corbin let out an exasperated snort, then turned toward me. Frustration flickered across his face, but he tried to force it back. "Ratchett flashes the cameras for a couple of days before. They go out, then a few minutes later they come back on again. The guards get used to the cameras malfunctioning and don't worry about them for a while, unless the feed doesn't return. Depending on how lazy the guard is, it could be five minutes to a half hour before they bother getting help. Then they need to call the security company, and it's about six minutes before they figure out something's up. Average for the whole process is twenty-nine minutes. We'll be out in twenty-six."

"Tucker," he continued to the lanky guy with the snarky mouth, "you'll need to get through the back-door lock, the office door, and the freezer."

"The freezer?" I spat without thinking. I opened my mouth to ask another question, but pushed it down. They already thought I couldn't cut it; why give them more ammunition?

"And Red, you'll need to run interference if the guards catch on. If things go south, drop everything and run. There's a park four streets that way." Corbin pointed toward the dark end of the alley. "If we get separated, meet in the boarded-up building by the empty pool. You can get in around the back through a loose board spray-painted with *Kill the Rich*."

I swallowed loud enough that everyone turned to look at me. "And what am I supposed to do?"

"Uh." He looked over at the faces of the rest of the crew. They still weren't happy. "You can be the lookout."

"The lookout, are you serious?"

"It's a very important job. If anyone comes around this side of the building, we need to know. Getting in is a lot easier than getting out."

"So I'm just supposed to stand by the door and wait for you. Real nice."

"You can go home," Red said and chuckled to herself.

I scowled at her but didn't bother with a response.

"Are you in or not?" Corbin tapped his foot, his voice harsh.

"Oh, I'm definitely in." I stepped forward and narrowed my eyes at Red.

"Fine. Take this."

He reached into his back pocket and handed me a palm-sized gray device.

"What is it?" I asked, turning it over in my hands.

"A cell phone," Tucker snickered and ripped the electronic block out of my hand. He pried it open, exposing a keypad and a small green screen. "Don't they have cell phones in your world?"

I took the phone back and snapped it closed again. "Yeah. I knew that."

"It's really old," Corbin said, probably sensing my embarrassment. "Harder to trace our communications since no one uses these types of networks anymore."

My cheeks burned bright as a spotlight. Made sense, but how was I supposed to know that?

"One more thing." Corbin reached out his hand, and I handed the archaic hunk of plastic back. He punched in a number and all three of them buzzed simultaneously.

"If you see anything, text the last number on your phone. We'll get it."

"You can actually text on this thing?" I asked, but everyone else was already on the move.

I shoved the cell brick in my front pocket, wrapping my fingers tight around it as I ran behind Red, trying to keep up as they twisted their way through backstreets to come up behind building 1316. Tucker was already in place with his face against the back door, jamming what looked like dentist tools into the deadbolt when I came puffing around the corner.

"Out of shape or scared, rookie?" Red rolled her eyes and turned away before I could retaliate, and from the look she gave me, I doubted she wanted an answer, just to make me feel more like I didn't belong.

"I need something sharper," Tucker said, reaching his hand backward and snapping his fingers.

I patted my pockets for a pin or something, but Red reacted quicker, whipping out a dangerous-looking switchblade from her black boot and laying the bright cherry handle in Tucker's hand.

"Don't break it," she threatened.

A few more seconds and several clicks later, the door opened and Tucker headed inside, waving for everyone else to follow. Red disappeared through the door, and the heavy feeling in my chest that had slowed me down on the run over here crushed against my lungs. Now that the door was actually open, everything seemed to get very real, very fast.

I thrust my hand out, grabbing Corbin by the arm before he could head inside. "Breaking and entering is illegal, you know. Are you sure you want to do this?"

He shrugged and kept walking. "That's why we're here."

I pulled tighter before he could get out of my grip. "How do you know I'm not going to turn you in?"

Finally, he stopped and turned around. "I don't."

He took my hand and pulled it off, letting it drop by my side. His eyes fixed on mine, their color disappearing in the dark. "In a group like this, we can only succeed if we trust each other and take chances. I don't trust you, but I'm willing to take a chance."

"Why?"

"I have no idea." His gaze turned toward the sky. "So please don't mess this up."

He escaped through the door and it clacked shut before I could say the words still stuck in my throat.

Now that they were gone, the night took on an eerie silence. I looked both ways down the alley and shuddered. Probably just the cool breeze on my skin after the run. However, why did every encounter with this group leave me waiting around in the dark by myself?

And the lookout? Really? How dense did they think I was? Must've been a lot, considering I was actually going through with it. I kind of thought we'd be doing something fearless. Leading a rebellion. Freeing political prisoners. Or doing something edgy to get my father's undivided and venomous attention. Nope. We were breaking into an office building that no one cared about past five o'clock. I kicked a rock and listened to the sound echo off the towering offices as it bounced along the pavement.

I paced as my brain ran movie clips of anything they could possibly be doing in a building like this, or even more precisely what they could be doing in a freezer in a building like this. Why did it even have a freezer? I shook off the image of severed hands and internal organs lined up in jars and leaned against a wall facing the doorway. Whatever it was, it better be worth it, and Corbin better plan on telling me what the hell I just got myself into. If I was going to risk getting caught and having my face splashed all over the news, I deserved to know why. Dread crept back into my chest, pressing on my lungs again. Getting caught would be the least of my problems.

Wait. Was that a noise? I lifted my head and scanned through the darkness. Nothing. I probably imagined it as the panic of getting busted had taken over my thoughts. I leaned back again and inhaled as deep as I could, a thick grimy smell attacking my nose, then let the air out in a long, controlled breath. I pulled out the gray block Tucker had called a phone and pulled it open. No touch screen. No apps. Boring. I clicked a few of the buttons, but nothing more interesting than a green screen with a primitive, digital-looking text appeared. I closed the phone, and the time flashed on the front. They'd already been gone ten minutes. Almost—

Another sound. Louder. Closer. A light appeared at the end of the alley. It swept along the walls and crept toward me. With slow, soundless steps, I snuck to the edge of the building and hid around the corner, the cool metal of the walls bleeding through my sweater, likely causing the goose bumps that were spreading across my arms.

The light kept moving forward and a middle-aged balding man in a standard-issue brown uniform appeared from behind the glow. Like an angel walking out of heaven, but wildly less attractive. He looked around, studying the pavement as if I'd left footprints on the black ground. I forced myself to stay still, my knees threatening to give out at any moment. The security guard, seemingly blind to me quivering only a few feet away, walked over to the door and pulled a walkie-talkie to his mouth. "Someone's bust through the lock back here."

A low voice mixed with static came back through the speaker.

"Nope, doesn't look like it," he responded, although I hadn't heard the question. I pulled the cell phone out of my pocket and struggled to type, as each key needed to be hit a series of times before you got the letter you wanted. Who the hell thought this was a better idea than a full keyboard? Finally, I managed to type "guard at the door" or hopefully something that resembled it enough to get the message across, and hit Send.

I peeked around the corner again and watched as the security guard crouched and stared at the lock as if it might speak to him and tell him what was going on.

Get out of the way. If Corbin came out of the door now, he'd probably smash right into the guy. They might be able to get away, but not without being seen, and who knew if they got whatever it was they were trying to get by now. Why wouldn't this guy just move?

I leaned farther out from the corner to see if anyone else was coming. If it was just one security guard, maybe I could convince him I had car trouble or something and lead him away from here. But then where would I go? When I didn't have a car to find, he'd know something was up. *Think Mercury, think.* I leaned a little more.

Clack. Clack. Clack.

The cell phone slid out of my pocket and skipped along the pavement. I pulled back just in time before the guard shined his light my way.

I held my breath and willed myself to blend in with the wall. After a few seconds, the light disappeared again. I dared to look back, and luckily the guard had ignored my clumsiness and resumed his investigation of the door. I reached my arm out to grab the phone. Just a little bit farther. I double-checked that I wasn't being seen, then success—my fingers wrapped around the smooth plastic.

As my fist closed around the phone, it lit up and a shrill sound screamed at me and echoed off the high walls. I'd accidentally turned the ringer on. *Loser.* I fumbled with the buttons on the side and slid it off again. Too late for it to matter.

"Hey," the guard yelled. "Who's there?"

I retreated behind the wall again, but the guard's footsteps pounded my way, the flashlight getting brighter as he got closer. I flipped open the phone and barely read the words *Do something* as I turned and ran.

"Stop!" he yelled as he turned the corner.

His voice lit a fire under my feet. I ran in what felt like circles, but no matter where I turned, the guard stayed close behind. From the muffin top he was sporting, I didn't think he'd be able to keep up, but he was surprisingly fast. I still had a decent distance advantage, but I could only outrun him for so long. My lungs burned. My breaths were coming shallower, and gasping detracted from my speed. Why hadn't he given up yet?

I pushed harder. A second wind took over as my feet moved faster than they ever had before. Corbin's crew should have gotten away by now. If I could just take a few more twists through the alleys, I could likely head for the subway and out of here. If I could figure out where the subway was, considering I had no clue where I was going.

Straight ahead stood another building. I couldn't see the roofs, and running in circles made the walls feel like some sort of sinister maze. I took a left before the wall ahead of me, glancing back to see the guard just appearing around the corner from the prior block. This guy had earned his minimum wage tonight. The alley narrowed, like it was slowly trying to pinch me out. My feet stopped charging, and I almost fell forward with my feet planted and my body still trying to escape. But there was nowhere else to run.

A dead end. Dumpsters and fire escapes and a brick wall. I should've turned right. I looked back and considered running the other way, but the only way out was past the spot where that guard was going to emerge in about five seconds. I had to do something. I jumped at the fire escape ladder. The tips of my fingers brushed the cold metal, but I couldn't quite reach. Footsteps grew louder behind me. I wedged myself between a dumpster and the wall, the putrid smell wafting from inside threatening to end me before the guard could.

I stood in the dark, struggling to hold my breath as my lungs gasped for air. There were only two ways this could go. If he came my way, I was done for, but if he could just run in the other direction, I still had a chance. If he hadn't seen which way I'd turned and I was quiet, maybe, just maybe, he would make the turn I should've made.

The phone in the front pocket of my sweater jabbed into my gut as it sat wedged between the dumpster and me. Stupid phone. If it wasn't for that hunk of junk, I wouldn't have had to run in the first place. But maybe it was my last hope to be saved.

I wrestled it out of my pocket, wound my arm back, and tossed it as far as I could down the alley. It crunched as it hit the ground and skittered across the pavement. Seconds later, the security guard rushed around the corner and followed the noise. His chubby butt sped down the block and disappeared into the darkness. I'd done it. I'd actually done something right.

I stayed perfectly still until I could no longer hear footsteps or the sound of my own blood coursing through my veins and throbbing at my temples. Slowly, I peeled away from the wall and walked back the way I'd come, or at least what I thought was the way back. I'd been so twisted up in these backstreets that in the end I stopped trying to find a way back and started looking for a busy street so I could figure out where the hell I was. Instead, I found myself behind 1316 Gate St. again. The back door swung open in the night breeze. Either everyone had already gone, or they'd been caught. Regardless of the outcome, they'd left me alone again. But after what I'd just survived, I wasn't going to let them see me fail. A noise behind me made me twitch. Coming back to the scene of the crime might've been the worst course of action. Somehow, I channeled the last bit of strength in my calves to keep running back out to the main street and across it, even if it meant risking being seen under the streetlights.

No one was in the alleyway across the street where we'd

first hatched this ridiculous plan, but if I remembered right, Corbin had said to meet at the park. If I could get there, I could show them I wasn't some coward who would run away, and I definitely wasn't some scapegoat that they could put out for slaughter. I kept moving. Four more streets. I could handle four streets.

I gasped for air as my chest burned hot enough that my lungs might combust, but my feet kept propelling me forward, overriding my brain's pleas to stop and give up. Instead, I ran and ran until the buildings fell away and I reached an empty playground. I stopped, scanning the scene for any sign of life. It didn't look like I'd been followed, but it didn't look like anyone from Corbin's crew was here either. I grabbed the tops of my knees and bent over, greedily gulping for oxygen. The only sounds were the frantic banging of my heart against my ribs, and the unsettling squeak of a swing as it moved on its own in the dead-calm night. A shiver rippled across my skin, the stillness suddenly more frightening than the frenzy.

I took one last look back and then headed to a boarded-up building that looked like it might blow over if someone sneezed at it. As promised, neon-green letters glowed in the dark, touting the slogan that always put me a bit on edge. *Kill the Rich.* That was me. That was my family. Little Matty. Everyone I knew. We probably deserved it, but the thickness building in my throat told me just how much the thought terri-fied me.

I'd reached down to move the board out of the way when muffled voices whispered from the other side.

"Seriously, man, she's not coming. Give up on her before she gets us all busted. For all you know she has her daddy's private army camped outside waiting to shoot us down the second we walk out of here."

A guy's voice. Tucker maybe.

"No. She deserves a chance. Or do I need to remind you about how you blew your first shot and you're still here?"

A dissatisfied grunt, then footsteps scuffled along the ground.

"What's with you and this girl? She's a liability, Hawk. A cancer. She's going to destroy us all."

Something inside banged against one of the boarded windows and I jumped.

"Give her five more minutes. After that, take Red and get out of here and I'll meet you at Iggy's."

"And what are you going to do?" Tucker asked.

The voices seemed to fade off, or maybe I just stopped listening. They weren't saying anything I didn't already know, but hearing it out loud hurt. Did no one realize I was risking a hell of a lot more being here than they were? My face splashed all over the tabloids. My father's entire world under scrutiny. I panicked thinking about how pissed my father would be when he found out. *I could just leave. I should leave.* But too late. My hands didn't get the message in time and pried back the loose board, revealing blank, shocked stares from under three matching black hoodies.

I breathed deep and stepped into the hideout, my phony smile pushing its way onto my lips. "So that was fun. What do we do now?"

SIXTEEN

The streets were dark. Few lights worked, and those that did flickered in an ominous rhythm. Buildings looked vacant. As I tiptoed around the garbage built up along the curbs, boarded windows and broken fences decorated with graffiti tags in every shade of angst screamed their silent warnings to turn back. I needed to stay calm, stay alert, but I could barely breathe without gasping in the distinct, unmistakable smell of despair mixed with a hint of terror.

I pulled my hands into my sleeves and balled them into fists as I followed Corbin, Tucker, and Red on their grand tour of hell. It had taken two subway rides and a hike, longer than possibly healthy to get here. Wherever *here* was. If my father knew his only daughter had spent her night trudging through the sketchiest areas of the city, he might actually explode. I shuddered. I needed to do this unnoticed by anyone from my house. However, part of me wouldn't mind knowing that a trained guard, or at least a driver, lurked close by right now.

Finally we came to a stop. Tucker pulled off his backpack and peeked inside, quickly zipping it shut again. I still had no idea of the importance of what we needed to break and enter to get, but from the way Tucker carried the backpack like it was made of glass, I knew at least he felt justified.

After slipping the pack back onto his shoulder, Tucker ran up the stairs of the large plain brown building in front of us. I couldn't see any lights inside, maybe because there were no windows, only mammoth wooden doors and the words *St. Ignatius of the Sacred Heart* etched in the stone above the doorway. Parts of the letters had weathered away, but what remained appeared darker from the layers of dirt caked inside the etched lines. Red made a strange movement between her forehead and her shoulders, then followed after him, Corbin close behind her.

Corbin opened one of the large wooden doors with a creak and everyone else stepped inside.

"Coming?" Corbin said to me.

I stood down in the street, still unsure if I should follow the others. It couldn't be that bad, could it? Taking a deep breath, I forced myself forward.

"Of course."

Each stair seemed one hundred feet high as I headed toward more unknown. Every move I made tonight kept putting me in places where I wasn't sure of myself. I'd seen a lot of different things in my travels away from home, but I'd never felt this uncertain about whether or not I'd make it out alive. I tucked my face into the collar of my sweater, hoping it was only the wind giving me the sudden icy chill up my spine.

Corbin placed his hand on the small of my back and ushered me in, the wooden door slamming shut behind us quicker than I would've liked. Pitch-black veiled the small space behind the grand doors, but a normal-sized doorway across the room pierced the dark with soft voices and light. Tucker headed toward the noise.

"Keep your hood up and your head down," Corbin whispered from behind me, then cut ahead to join Tucker at the front of our line.

I tugged my hood forward and draped my hair loose around the sides of my face. I couldn't risk anyone recognizing me. Not in this place. Not after a night like this. Keeping my eyes firmly planted on the back of Red's unnatural hair, I clenched my fists and followed.

Instead of the meeting place of dangerous and terrifying criminals I had expected to be walking into, it seemed to be a makeshift hospital. Cots with white linens were set up in stations around the room. Old people, young people, even little children occupied almost every bed. I tried not to look at their faces, not let anyone see me, but none of this made sense. Why were they all here?

A girl about my age watched me carefully as I walked by. Her hair framed her face, long and dark like mine, but shiny and not in a good way. She looked paler than a ghost, her lips cracked and devoid of color, blending in with her skin. She sat in the middle of her cot, a pilling fleece blanket wrapped tight around her too-thin frame. Almost like a reflection in a scary carnival mirror. Healthy me on one side and her on the other.

"Watch it," Red hissed as I stepped on the back of her heel.

The sick girl snickered as she watched me get myself back in line. If it were really me, I would've been nicer than to make fun of someone for tripping.

An old lady came around the corner and a broad smile lit up her face as soon as she saw us standing in the middle of the room. Her hair stuck up in all directions, short and graying with a slight curl at the end. Her clothes hung drab and ill-fitted. Cheap polyester navy blue with a white apron over top, and a few splotches of something I hoped was food splashed across the front. Wire-rimmed glasses in desperate need of straightening perched atop her nose.

"Why didn't anyone tell me you were coming?" the woman said in a thick accent I didn't recognize.

"We made all of you a promise that we'd come when you need us, and we always keep our promises," Corbin said matter-of-factly, but with a hint of a smile that said more than his words. He liked this woman. He trusted her.

Tucker put his backpack on a nearby table and produced a foam cooler. He flipped open the top. Vials of blue liquid sat in the box. Probably about fifty. I leaned closer, trying to get a better look, but Red and her big attitude and shoulders kept getting in my way.

"What are they?" I whispered.

Red didn't acknowledge me, but instead cleared her throat in a scoff. I guess that was the closest thing to an answer I'd get from her.

"Ah, Hawk, what would we ever do without cha?" The old lady sandwiched his face with her hands and gave him a big, wet kiss on the lips.

He grinned, red rising up his neck. "Don't worry about it. Just make sure the people who need this stuff are taken care of."

"Of course. We always do. Now come here, you." She turned her attention to Tucker and gave him the same embarrassing smooch. He wrapped his arms around the woman and squeezed hard enough to pull her feet off the floor. She made a whooping sound and slapped him playfully on the shoulder. "Are you all hungry? I can get you something from the kitchen."

"No, we're okay." Tucker took his backpack and swung it over his shoulder again. "Save it for the others."

"My own group of angels. God has special thrones in heaven for all of you."

God wasn't someone anyone talked about anymore. Religion was a history lesson. A legend. Not something I thought anyone still believed.

"How's it been around here, Mrs. O'Connell?" Corbin asked, trying to keep his voice down.

"We've been okay. Less cases this week than last." The old woman beamed, but the corners of her eyes begin to pool. She forced the tears down and adjusted the glasses on her nose. Still crooked.

"That's good. We'll try to get more. It just might take a while. Security's starting to get wise."

"You'll find a way. You always do." She squeezed Corbin's hand. "Now excuse me all, but I have patients to attend to. Stay as long as you like."

Everyone dispersed, leaving me standing by myself, exposed, in the middle of the room. I sped as fast as I could toward the back wall, hoping to hide among a stack of chairs and a dusty old piano that looked like it hadn't been played in decades.

As much as this place creeped me out, for Corbin's gang it seemed like coming home to family. Everyone knew their names and greeted them like long-lost cousins. Even Red dropped her scowl to sit and talk with an old man like he was her grandfather. For all I knew, he was. And right when I'd started to think some evil alien race had abandoned her on earth.

Eventually Corbin saw me lingering in the corner, walked over, and leaned against the wall with his feet crossed in front of him and his hands thrust deep in his pockets. A tired puffiness circled his eyes, but for the first time since we'd met, he seemed almost calm. His shoulders didn't stand at attention, he didn't twitch at every sound, and the sharpness of his stare seemed to fade away, even if only for a few moments.

"Was this what you had in mind when you decided to hunt me down?" he said with a smirk.

"No. Maybe. I don't really know what I was expecting."

"So you didn't think we were kidnapping you and holding you hostage with a bunch of dangerous thugs?"

I straightened myself out. "Of course not. Never even considered it."

He laughed at my awkwardness, my rigid body language probably more revealing than my words.

"That's good, then. We'll go home soon."

Home. My nice warm bed. My nice warm, clean shower. The thoughts felt so good, goose bumps rippled across my skin.

We stood in silence for a few minutes, watching everyone watch us watching them, then when it finally felt that everyone had moved on from the novelty of our visit, I leaned closer to Corbin.

"What was in the cooler?" I whispered.

His eyebrows furrowed, and he peeled himself from the wall to look at me directly. "You really don't know?"

"Of course, not—"

"You're still here." The O'Connell woman appeared in front of us, her soft eyes moving from Corbin to me and back again. "I would have thought you'd be long gone by now."

"You know we always love to visit. Besides, no one can get Tucker to shut up once he gets going."

"I see you brought a new one with you." Mrs. O'Connell stared at me and I cast my eyes to the floor, trying to cover my face as best as I could without being suspicious. The woman stepped toward me and crooked a thin-skinned index finger under my chin, pulling my eyes up to meet hers.

"What's your name, child?"

"I ... I...." Words wouldn't come. I couldn't think of any names other than my own, but I couldn't use it. Far too dangerous.

"No matter." Her warm brown eyes melted like chocolate

fountains. "Sometimes who we're becoming is more important than who we are now."

She gave me a quick wink and her smile crept up enough to tell me that she already knew who I was or maybe, just maybe, it really didn't matter.

"You look run ragged, Hawk. Take this girl home and get yourself some shut-eye. Don't want you showing up at my door as a patient next week."

"Yes, ma'am," he said, giving her a sharp military salute. "Time to go."

THE LONG SUBWAY ride back to my house was quiet. The metal-on-metal shriek of the rails drowned out the sounds of the late-night riders and I snapped myself awake every time my chin fell limp to my chest. Corbin stayed mostly silent, watching, hyperaware of every single movement around us. I couldn't understand how he remained so alert after all that had happened. If I didn't feel gross and horribly unsafe, I probably would've passed out and drooled all over the sticky plastic bench seat.

Red and Tucker took off when we switched trains. I wasn't sure if I should be happy or offended that Corbin had decided to escort me all the way home, but exhaustion dulled my ability to care.

Eventually the train came to a screeching stop, and we filed off, emerging to street level as the orange glow of sun peeked between the buildings, unraveling blankets of night into thin threads of morning.

"Corbin," I started, unsure how to ask my questions, half

expecting to be shut down like I had been earlier. "You never did tell me what was in those stolen vials."

He looked back and forth down the street. Few people had walked by, still too early for that, and those who did had less than zero interest in us.

"You really need to start calling me Hawk."

"Fine. Hawk, what exactly did you steal tonight?"

He stared at me through hooded eyes, then leaned closer and dropped his voice to a barely audible whisper. "It's the cure for X9."

"What?" I blurted, and he hissed for me to hush. "But X9's incurable."

"No, it's not. Ratchett hacked some government sites and found they had a cure, but only enough for select people—government officials, the military, their families. The few clinics that administer it aren't even told what it's for. They just shoot up anyone who comes in with an official prescription from the Department of Defense."

"That's crazy."

"Crazy but true. We only took a few vials the first time, wanted to make sure it worked, and it was like a miracle. Within hours people who should've been dead were back with their families like they hadn't been bleeding out for the last two days."

"So you've been stealing it from the government to give to everyone else?"

"Those people at St. Ignatius won't get access to this medication until it's too late, and by then they will probably infect everyone else around them. It would be a plague in those neighborhoods, while neighborhoods like this"—he rolled his eyes in a tight circle—"will go on not having to worry about dying at random."

"If there's a cure, why isn't it all over the news? Why don't they make more?"

"We don't know. We only know that it exists and we have to do everything we can to make sure those who really need it get it."

I dug my hands in my pockets as I let the concept roll around in my head. A cure for this terrible disease existed, but no one was allowed to have it. That didn't make any sense. Maybe it wasn't really a cure? Maybe it didn't really work at all, but Corbin and all these people believed it did? Maybe it was that placebo effect I'd heard about in science class once? Or maybe he was telling me the truth and someone somewhere was playing a dangerous game with the lives of a lot of people?

As we turned the corner, I realized I had retreated into my own sleep-deprived brain and hadn't spoken a word for blocks. Corbin didn't seem to mind, though. A worried look had set in around his eyes and I imagined he was perfectly fine calculating his next move without me disturbing him.

And then we were home. Or at least behind the building near the back kitchen door. The same place where I'd recognized Corbin for who he was after the gala. The same place he had told me to forget about him. But here we were again. I guess I really wasn't good at following orders.

"How are you going to get back in there without your guards noticing?" Corbin murmured, pulling me out of my head and back into reality.

"I told everyone I was sleeping at Kendall's. I'll tell them we had a fight, and I came home early."

He raised an eyebrow and looked at me with a peculiar smirk. "Must be a girl thing."

"No, it's a me-and-Kendall thing. Besides, the guards are used to me being gone. They'll probably be more shocked that I actually came back."

"What does that mean?"

I sighed. "Never mind. Point is, I'll be fine."

"Good." He nodded sharply and turned on his heel to walk away.

"So now what?" I asked to his back.

He turned around. "What do you mean?"

"With this whole thing. Whatever it is. What am I supposed to do next?"

"Oh." He rubbed his hand over his tired face and scratched the top of his head. "Stop by headquarters tomorrow and we'll go from there. It should be easy to find if you come in the daylight this time, but I can have someone meet you by the shipyard gates. About three o'clock?"

"Okay, maybe." I clenched my hands tight, my fingernails biting into my palms. "But only if you're sure I should come there. I don't think your friends were too impressed with me hanging around tonight."

His eyes narrowed, then snapped open wide once my words finally sank in. "I wouldn't worry about them. Anyone who comes to us has a story to tell, and none of them have happy endings. Until you, of course."

Without thinking, I let out a small muffled laugh that came out more like a snort.

Corbin looked me over with a questioning stare. I bit my lip and straightened my stance.

"Besides," he continued, "whether you believe it or not, you saved our asses tonight. Red and Tucker know that; they just don't know you."

"And you think you do?"

He chuckled. Rows of his white teeth gleamed in the early morning light. "I'm not so sure about that yet, but I have a feeling you like to do things the hard way."

"Might as well focus on what I'm good at."

I chuckled and watched the shadows retreat from the dawn into the corners and crevices of the alley. My chest rose and fell about ten times as we stood in stalemate, Corbin not leaving and me refusing to go inside.

"Maybe you aren't really like them," he said finally as he nodded his chin toward my building.

"Sometimes I think I was adopted or something."

"I doubt that. No matter how many alleys you skulk in, there will always be a part of you that belongs to that world. A part of you that will always be royalty."

I frowned. "What if I don't want to be?"

He stepped closer and pulled my hood off my head, then rested his warm palm against my cheek. My stomach dropped out. I didn't expect him to be so bold and definitely didn't expect myself to like it. "People would follow you with or without the title."

Words caught in a gasp in my throat. I wasn't sure if I should thank him or defend myself, the heat of his skin against mine making things even more cloudy.

"Now, you should get inside before someone catches you hanging out with a wanted criminal."

"Good point."

He dropped his hand and smiled, that one simple gesture making me feel safe and making me want to smile too. Making me think maybe I could be happy.

I turned toward the door and a feeling of dread crept up my back as I thought about having to go in. About having to wait an entire day before escaping again.

"Hey, Hawk." I spun around, but he was already gone.

SEVENTEEN

Three o'clock. Standing by the gates of the shipyards. Waiting. Again. This was getting to be a bad routine. At least this time I'd arrived in daylight, but the way the sun baked down on my dark hair made me wish I hadn't. The heat and the smell of salt and fish, mixed with the dizzy feeling in my stomach from turning around in circles to make sure no one snuck up on me, made me nauseous. Warm acid built up in the back of my throat a few times, but I managed to swallow it back down.

A kid appeared from inside the gate. Short, scrawny, and drowning in an oversized bright blue hoodie and too-large jeans. I watched him approach, grabbing the side of my head to make the world stop spinning for a minute. His hood-covered head was lowered, but I could still see his long dark lashes and wide eyes protruding from his baby face.

He stopped three feet away and scanned me over. A scowl, much older than he looked, curled across his lips. I stared back. Was this kid the one I was supposed to meet? He had the uniform but seemed too young to be involved in something this big. But Hawk said everyone had a story. His was probably one of the worst.

"Are you…? Who sent you?"

The boy didn't answer, only jerked his head back and ran.

I followed behind as quick as I could, but the boy was faster. He jumped on top of old barrels and slid across the tops of shipping containers while I ran below him, trying to make sure I didn't fall behind. He bounced from container to container, like a rubber ball that had been shot out of a cannon. We squeezed down narrow pathways and twisted around so many times I thought he might be leading me back to where we came in.

Then, as we reached what felt like the hundredth turn, the boy disappeared. *Dammit.* Now where was I supposed to go?

I bent over and grabbed my knees, letting my lungs catch up to my heartbeat, then scanned the tops of the containers above me. I turned around and looked back the way we'd come. Nothing. Gone like a ghost.

After taking a few steps to the corner, I looked both ways. Neither seemed to lead anywhere. I wiped the few drops of sweat dripping at my hairline and let out a huge breath. Only three choices. Right, left, and getting the hell out of there.

My feet decided before I did, taking a left turn and continuing forward. Suddenly a dark object landed in front of me. I screamed. It laughed. Light and amused. Almost a giggle. The hooded daycare dropout smiled at me for the first time with a mischievous smirk. Brat.

Without a word, he waved his hand for me to follow, and I fought the urge to yell at him for scaring the crap out of me, especially since I had a good idea who'd shown him that trick. He walked a few more feet, then took a quick glance ahead and behind. Satisfied we weren't tailed, he slid between two containers barely wide enough for him to fit. I squeezed myself into the space, the bolts and jagged metal pulling at my clothes and making me regret following the elf. Just when I thought the container might crush my lungs and leave me trapped forever, I came out the other side. A door, the kid, and Hawk stood waiting for me.

"Good work, Parkie," Hawk said as he ruffled the kid's hair.

The kid looked up at him and nodded, then leaped up on a crate, bounced over to the top of the fence surrounding the building, up onto the roof, and disappeared.

"He's great at getting out of tight situations," Hawk said as he watched him go.

"But he makes a lousy tour guide," I said, straightening my clothes and sliding my sunglasses onto my head to get a better look. "So this is it?"

Metal siding. Flat roof. One uninspiring door. No visible windows.

"Secret hideouts work better when they don't attract attention."

I shrugged. "Guess so."

Hawk grabbed the door handle and pulled it open. I stepped forward to enter, but he quickly slammed it shut again and stepped in front of me.

"Can I talk to you first? Before we go in there, I mean." His face dropped and his eyebrows knit together, irises dark indigo. Serious and all business.

I crossed my arms, took a step back, and nodded.

"How are you?" Hawk asked.

"Fine." I dragged out the word, still waiting for the catch, but he kept unsettlingly silent and unnaturally still. "How are you?"

"Confused."

"Well, it's a door. You pull the handle and it opens."

He rolled his eyes and tried to fight the smirk cutting through his dire demeanor.

"I didn't actually expect you to show up last night, and especially not today."

"Oh." A shadow cast across my skin and gave me a chill. "I'll just go, then."

I turned on my heel and walked away. Hawk caught up and grabbed my arm.

"I didn't say you had to go," he said as he spun me around and let me go. Smart boy. Five more seconds and I might've decked him in his pretty face.

"Then what exactly are you trying to say?"

"I don't know. I figured you would have given up by now."

My fingers curled into fists, my fingernails digging into my palms so hard they might bleed. Given up? Did he seriously think I was some delicate little doll that needed to be handled? I could handle myself. I always had. I always would. And some guy, especially not this one, was going to come into my life and tell me what I could and couldn't do. I already had enough testosterone messing up my world.

I took a step toward him and stood on my tiptoes to gain some of the four to five inches of height he had over me. Hands on my hips. Ready to explode. "Do you seriously think—"

"I'm impressed."

"What?" I shook my head and dropped my heels back to the pavement.

"Don't make me repeat it. Just know that it's not going to get any easier."

"What isn't?"

"What we do here. What we will do." He rubbed a hand over the back of his neck and stepped away from me. "It goes against everything your world stands for. It might get ... bad for you."

"And you're trying to what? Scare me?"

"No. I'm trying to give you an out. If you leave now, there's still a chance none of this will touch you."

"And if I don't?"

"Then I can't control what might happen to you."

"Perfect. I could use less people controlling me." I flipped the sunglasses back down over my eyes to make my point, and hopefully cover the uncertainty that might be bleeding out through my pupils. "Besides, what kind of rebel would I be if I did what people told me to do?"

He pulled his hands together in a giant fist, held it against his mouth, knuckles cracking, and stared at me over the top of his fingers. I planted my feet and straightened my spine, taking his discerning glare and matching it with whatever ounce of confidence I could push back. If he was looking for a sign of me backing down, he was going to have to look pretty damn hard.

Finally he retreated with a heavy sigh. "Fair enough." He yanked on the oversized handle and, with a dramatic sweeping gesture, stepped back to let me pass. "After you."

I took a deep breath and stormed through the doorway with a strut that made me look like I knew exactly what I was doing. Inside, I frowned. All this work for an unimpressive small brown room with peeling wallpaper and a florescent light that hummed above my head.

Hawk closed the door tight with a few loud clicks and the scrape of metal on metal. Without the sun streaming in, the room appeared even more boring, if that was actually possible.

"No receptionist?" I pointed to the dust-covered counter in the corner.

"Funny."

Hawk walked ahead of me and punched a series of numbers in the lock on the door across from the entrance. "Welcome to the Sanctuary."

NOISE. Voices rumbled in the open space, echoing off the high industrial metal rafters and bouncing between the exposed ducts and pipes that hung there. Laughter. Anger. High-pitched gossip. All manner of human sounds to match the groups of people scattered around the large space. Some were sparring in the corner, some playing a game in another, some reading, some talking, and some just hanging out, while others simply stopped and stared at me, their jaws nearly hitting the brushed concrete floor.

Hawk led me right through the center of the room. He walked slowly, giving me time to take everything in. Very little color punctuated the room, just browns and grays like the front office, which probably hadn't changed since it was a warehouse. Wooden tables and plastic chairs stood in long rows like a cafeteria, with the occasional well-worn, mismatched couch thrown in for comfort. A few closed doors led off the main room, one with a glowing Exit sign over the top of the frame, but the others were mysteries.

We stopped near a wall along the back covered in large monitors with lines of numbers and symbols I could only imagine were programming code, and directly in the path of the last two people I wanted to see today. Just seeing that mass of scarlet hair as I approached made me want to vomit in my mouth.

"I didn't realize there were so many of you," I said, trying to see if I could talk without sounding irritated, or worse, afraid.

"There are more of us. They come and go, but not everyone knows everything about what we do. Only a select few." He stopped, and I almost slammed into the back of him as I stared anywhere but forward. "But these are my inner circle. My generals. The people I trust."

For someone who grew up in my world, I would've thought

he'd had better taste in friends. Connections were everything, and these ones would probably get him jailed or killed.

"Over here is Ratchett." He pointed to the guy sitting near the screens with his back to us. He didn't need to turn around for me to recognize the thin greasy hair and sharp features of the guy who had masqueraded as a waiter at the gala. Ratchett raised his arm and made a feeble attempt at waving without prying his eyes away from a computer screen. "If he can't fix it or hack into it, it can't be done."

"And this"—Hawk stabbed a finger in the tall lanky guy's chest with a smile—"is Tuck—"

"I can handle my own introduction. Thank you very much." Tucker stood up straight and pulled the hood off his head, revealing his long straight hair and the geometric pattern that was shaved into the side of his head. "Not just Tucker, *the* Tucker. Specializing in intel, espionage, and all manners of extracting information."

He raised an eyebrow in a frisky kind of way, took my hand, and wrapped it in his palms, more of a fondle than a shake.

"Uh, hi?" I said, staring down Hawk to see if this was normal behavior, but he just laughed. "You're a lot friendlier than when I met you yesterday."

"I make a point of knowing everything that goes on around here, so it stung when I was the last to know about you." He gave Hawk a quick dagger-glare, still refusing to release my hand. "Being the last person at a party is never good form. But I'm sure you know all about those things, right, Queen of the Politikids? I can only imagine what kind of thrashers you throw up in that rock-star-and-a-half penthouse mansion of yours."

"It's okay, I guess."

"I expect you to tell me all about it." He finally let go of my hand, but not without a wink that gave me an awkward, creepy feeling. I'd hoped he didn't hate me anymore, but this wasn't the kind of attention I'd had in mind either.

"Forgot to mention you talk too much too, Tuck," Red snorted from her perch on a table, legs crossed politely, but looking anything like a lady.

"And this would be Red. Weapons expert," Hawk said, stepping away from her so I could see her in all her evil glory.

She scowled at me from hooded eyes. Clearly *she* hadn't changed her mind about me. No matter. I wasn't aching to be her best friend either, but it was always smarter to play nice.

I took a deep breath. "How do you get your hair so red like that?"

"Blood of my victims. Each one dead makes it shine." She snickered and gave a knowing look at Tucker.

Err. She was such a nightmare.

"Great dodge on that security guard, by the way. Hawk told us you pulled some cool-ass ghost move on him. Smart thinking," Tucker said after he stopped laughing.

"Or just stupid. She could've busted us all," Red countered as she flipped open her red pocket knife. The blade looked crude and dirty, and the way she stared at me while she played with it made my stomach churn with a mix of anger and fear. She jammed it tip down into the tabletop. "Didja even clean up the evidence?"

Dammit. The phone.

"Relax." Hawk stepped in front of Red, either sensing the growing disdain between us or just used to having to keep her in check. "I sent Roxy and Raider to look for it."

"And Mercury, is that even your real name or is that something some publicist came up with?"

Wow. Tucker really did talk too much. "Yes. It's my real name. Roman god of business or something like that." I cringed as the words flew out of my mouth uninhibited. I was pathetic. No better than my father.

"And thieves." Tucker rolled his hand regally and made a grand bow.

"Huh?"

"Mercury is also the god of thieves, but commerce and theft are pretty much the same thing, don't you think?"

I opened my mouth, reflexes still programmed to argue, but then thought better of it. "Is Tucker *your* real name?"

"Of course not. Code names only around here. Did you honestly think some meth-head parentals named their baby Ratchett?"

"Hey. I'm right here," Ratchett yelled from the screen wall.

Tucker shouted back, "Your name's weird, man. Own it."

Ratchett spun around on his desk chair, flipped Tucker off, then spun right back to work.

"Does that mean I get a code name too?" I asked.

"How 'bout Princess?" Red laughed so hard she almost fell off the table. Tucker joined in, then, after looking back at me, tried to stifle it.

"It might be early for that," Hawk said with a pathetic smile, likely hoping to hide his own amusement at Red's comment.

"Got any useful skills, Princess? Other than shopping," Red continued, my misery lighting up her face like fireworks.

Besides, someone in my position never went shopping. I had someone who did that for me. Usually my mother's staff and their brutal fashion sense. "I can shoot a bow."

Tucker's head jerked back with an expression of what might be legitimate shock. "A bow? Like with arrows and stuff?"

I nodded.

"Any real weapons?" Red said, now running the tip of her switchblade under the tips of her fingernails as if it was a simple manicure stick.

I cringed. "That is a real weapon."

"If you want a stuffed puppy from the fair," Red snickered.

"Oh yeah?" I said, sick of her trying to make me seem like a pampered, spoiled brat. "Well, if aimed properly, a broadhead arrow at point-blank range can rip through a person and come out the other side. I would say that counts as real."

"Wow." Her lack of enthusiasm coupled with the eye roll made me want to smack her if I didn't think she'd kill me. "And where you gonna hide it? In your purse? We aren't hunting big game here. Key things for an actual weapon are quiet, effective, and concealed. Got it?"

Before I could respond, or retaliate, or figure out what the hell I was going to say next, Red looked past me like I'd disappeared. I turned around.

Two identical white-blonde girls in matching purple hoodies beelined toward us, hair flat-iron perfect with eyes and lips painted peony pink. They marched over to Hawk, and one of the girls tugged on his sleeve while the other dropped a smashed cell phone on the table in front of us.

"See, I told you they'd find it. Good work," Hawk said, giving the girl with his sleeve a pat on the back.

The girl who had the phone made signals with her hands. The other girl made a face and signed back.

"Are those girls deaf?" I leaned over and asked Tucker as quietly as I could.

"No. But their mom is. They cut her supports about six months ago and the twins ended up here. Roxy talks sometimes, but Raider never does."

One of the girls leaned toward Hawk again and cupped her hand over his ear. His lips straightened to a hard line, and he nodded to the entrance room out front. Both girls walked out, with Hawk following close behind.

I stared after them, still slightly shell-shocked from the

mysteriousness of their exchange, then grabbed the cell phone from the table. The casing was completely destroyed, but inside the green screen and its little cursor blinked at me. Incredible. Much sturdier than I would have thought.

"So weapons? Got anything else?" Red didn't miss a moment, especially if it meant she could continue to rate my inferiority against her viciousness.

"How come you need them anyway? Theft is pretty nonviolent."

Tucker patted me on the shoulder. "Don't think because you read the brochure that you're an expert. We've got a fierce little operation going on here. Petty theft is just the appetizer."

I swallowed hard.

"No worries, we aren't going to go looking for trouble; it sometimes just finds us and we need to be prepared."

"But if you ever want to learn how to really cause some damage, let me know. I'd love to teach you a lesson by knocking you on your ass." Red launched off the tabletop and walked past me, not without smashing her shoulder into mine. Pain shot down my arm, but I refused to show any sign of it to her.

Tucker shrugged and followed her, leaving me alone in this room full of people. Now what? I didn't know anyone else here, and Hawk still hadn't returned after taking off with the silent sisters.

I looked around. Ratchett sat hunched, hammering away at a keyboard, his fingers moving faster than I thought the average brain could handle. The numbers on the screens whizzed by in blurs, like they were never meant to be still. I watched for a few minutes, but they quickly made me dizzy.

I leaned against the table where he worked, trying to get his attention while not derailing his train of thought. After several minutes of hovering, he finally got the hint.

"Can I help you?" he said. Not rude, not accommodating, just matter-of-fact.

I leaned down toward him, nervous that someone might hear. "I wanted to thank you for not letting that Red girl rip my face off the other night."

"No problem. And yeah, she probably would have."

I shuddered. Ratchett turned back to his computer.

"I guess she'll get used to me after a while."

He chuckled. "Oh, that'll never happen. Best case, in time, she might be less likely to cause you bodily harm."

"Thanks for the tip."

"No problem," he said, seeming to have missed my sarcasm. "Red is intense, but she's loyal to a fault. Taken a lot of bad stuff for us."

"But what's her deal? Why is she even here? All that anger and stuff doesn't seem to fit."

He finally gave up trying to type, pushed back on his wheeled chair, and turned to face me. Must not be used to talkers.

"Hawk did her a favor a while back, and then she just appeared and hasn't left since."

"What kind of favor?"

"He wouldn't say. Not his style. Must've been big, though."

"And him?" I pointed to Tucker talking on a cell phone in the corner. "What's his story?"

"Parents moved from PanAsia for a better life. They never found it, so Tucker came to us."

"And you?"

"I have my reasons."

"Oh."

He took advantage of my brief second of quiet and went back to whatever he was doing. I looked around again. I probably should've left him alone. It was likely what he wanted, but standing beside him at least made it look like I had someone to talk to and wasn't completely abandoned. I'd been trained in all manners of etiquette. I could schmooze the most powerful men and women in the world and have them eating out of the palm of my hand. It was my gift. It was who I was, but in here, all of that felt stripped away. I doubted any of my regular tricks would work with this crowd. I was an outsider.

"You've got to be shitting me!"

I jumped as Ratchett yelled and flew backward in his rolling chair, throwing a pair of headphones across the room, barely missing the skull of some dark, floppy-haired boy.

"A complete waste!" Ratchett dropped his head in his hands and rubbed them over his increasingly red face.

Hawk appeared in the doorway and crossed the room in five long rigid strides. "What's going on, Ratch?"

"The info on the key is gone."

"What do you mean gone?" Hawk grabbed the edge of the desk, his eyes flitting left to right as he looked over the screens. "Can you retrieve it?"

"No, gone as in, no longer there. Destroyed. Vanished." He made a frustrated groan. "There was time-triggered security embedded in the files. Once they're away from their host network too long, they shred themselves."

Hawk hung his head, the same irritated red bleeding across his skin.

"What's going on?" I asked.

This didn't seem like the right time for a question, but trying to follow tech speak with no idea of the bigger problem was too difficult. Or maybe Ratchett always had a short fuse?

"Remember when you asked what I took the night of the party?" Hawk sighed and pressed his fingers against his temples. "Well, it was information. A backup of all the network files on your dad's computer."

"You hacked The Five's network?"

This whole time I'd thought he took something physical, tangible, but it was a lot more valuable than I'd ever imagined. Hawk and his operation weren't just poking at The Five. They were going to tear its insides out. *Awesome.*

Hawk linked his fingers behind his neck and stared at the ceiling. "Yeah. Not like it matters now. We can't use anything we don't have anymore. All that work for nothing."

"What I need is direct access," Ratchett mumbled toward the floor. "Something permanent. Something where I can monitor the information coming in and out without actually extracting it." He turned and looked at Hawk. "Any chance you're willing to go back in there?"

"No way. That last job took almost a month of planning and we were almost caught." His eyes darted to me, but this time, they weren't friendly. "They aren't just going to open their doors to strangers again."

Ratchett finally sat up and pointed at me. "She's not a stranger. She can do it."

"Oh no." I put up my hands and tried to back away, but rammed the back of my thighs against the tabletop, making the lower screens shimmy. "I don't know how to hack stuff. Besides, the office is under lockdown after you broke in last time. I'm not allowed in there."

Hawk's face flipped from despair to hope. "But you could get in if you needed to, right?"

"Maybe. But I really shouldn't. Isn't there another way?"

Ratchett shook his head. "Nope. Any backdoor-entry attempts will be too easily detected. I need to get to the source from a valid access point. Am I the only one around here with even *basic* computer knowledge?"

"I'll go." Tucker jumped in the middle of the conversation.

"I've been dying to see that place, and I wasn't invited to the fancy-ass party you two went to. It's my turn."

"Like they'd let a skid like you in there," Red scoffed, joining our circle around Ratchett.

Great. More opinions I didn't want.

"What's that supposed to mean? Do you think you're a better choice?" Tucker popped his neck at Red and threw his hands at her.

"Hell no. Don't want to be anywhere near them rich snobs."

Ratchett stood and jumped in between them. "You're not going anywhere near this, Tucker. Remember Concord?"

"Still bringing that up. So I screwed up. Once."

Red snorted, rude and loud.

"Okay. Maybe a couple of times, but I won't do that again. I promise." Tucker turned to me with a pleading smile, like it was my decision to make. "You could get me in, right?"

"Well, I...." What was I doing? There was no way I could consider this. Too many chances to get caught. Too many things at risk if I did. My stomach churned just thinking about it. Disobeying my father in his own house was not worth the price. "No. I can't do it."

"Scared you'll get grounded, Princess?" Red mocked in a high-pitched sugary voice, with a hint of drawl. Way too sweet to be coming from her mouth.

Yes. "No. It's just too risky. There are guards all over the place. And what if someone recognized you? There would be no escape. You'd be done for."

"Yep, scared. You had no problem breaking and entering yesterday. This is your own damn house; it's not even a crime."

"I'm not scared," I shouted, a little too sharp and a little too loud, so that everyone in close proximity stopped to stare. Even Red's too-big mouth shut for a second. "I'm just.... No. I'm not doing it."

Hawk looked from Tucker to Red to Ratchett, hoping for some help that none of them seemed willing to give. Instead, they gave him the same look, the one that said, *No, you fix this.* He stepped closer to me and dropped his voice to keep the onlookers out.

"Hey. It's not a big deal. We'd be quick. In and out and you'd never even know we were there. You can even choose which one of us should do the job. It would be a huge help." He locked his eyes on mine and stared. The type of stare that made people all gooey inside. The one that made you feel included and respected and important. The one that made you feel seen. Too bad for him, I was way better at it than he was.

"Do you honestly think that's going to work on me? I learned to manipulate people before I could walk."

He deflated, the stare dropping away as he realized my immunity to his negotiation superpowers. "Then what'll it take?"

"A lot more than you have to offer." I put my hands on my hips and glared at him, but he stepped closer and glared right back, neither of us backing down. The small space between us charged with pride, power, and fire. "Fine. I'll think about it. But I'm not promising anything."

EIGHTEEN

Family dinner. Mom had been harping on all of us to have one since Christophe dragged me home. No one really wanted to be in the same room with each other, but for some reason, faking to care was still acceptable. Already borderline late, I'd spent the rest of the afternoon wandering around the shipyard, trying to find my way out and refusing to go back and ask for help. The extra-long shower to scrub off the fish smell didn't help my timing either. The skin on my arms still burned pink and raw, but at least my mother wouldn't wrinkle up her nose the second I walked into the room. I'd even put on one of the hideous dresses she'd picked out for me once upon a time that had been wasting away in the closet with the tags on. One of those lace-and-floral things that was less my style, more expensive table-cloth, or maybe Victorian doily. And it itched. Bad.

Rich smells of butter, rosemary, and cream drifted out into the hallway on the notes of a string concerto piped in through the formal dining-room speakers. My mouth watered so hard I almost forgot I was walking into what would probably be the most awkward meal I'd had in months. What most people would deem as normalcy was completely foreign to the inhabitants of this house.

As expected, I arrived last. All eyes turned to me, but everyone still tried to be pleasant, which meant I couldn't be that late.

My father sat at the head of the table, flanked by Christophe and Bernard. I hadn't expected the Royces to be invited, but I shouldn't have been surprised. Mom had always considered them family. Maybe more than I ever was. Matty sat between Bernard and Mom, fidgeting in his seat and making shapes out of the deep purple napkin on his lap. He looked up at me and grinned, which made me a feel a little better.

"We were starting to think you'd made better plans," Mom said as I circled around and headed to the one empty seat beside Christophe.

Everyone chuckled. Christophe stood and pulled out my chair.

"You look pretty," he whispered in my ear as he helped push it back in.

I hoped with every ounce of my being that he was lying, because if he actually liked this look, then no wonder he wasn't dating other people and kept lurking around my house. Not a single girl in this end of the city would be caught in public in this dress.

"We were just discussing the day your mother had with the Women's Alliance for Safer Communities," my father said, bringing the conversation back from my disruption.

"As I was saying," Mom continued with a smile, "the Alliance has come up with some fabulous ideas to help deter youth from getting involved in antigovernment rallies and protests. I think this could be a real advantage for us."

"And what are they planning to do?" Bernard asked, thankfully asking my question for me and without the snark that I would've added had it crossed my lips.

"Well, right now, plans are still preliminary. In the meantime, they are planning a luncheon to raise awareness for the issue."

I coughed, trying hard not to have my first bite of dinner fly out across the tablecloth. My father gave me a stern look.

"Sorry," I mumbled, wiping my face with a napkin. "Food is still a little hot."

My father raised an eyebrow as he cut another piece of his own, perfectly edible entrée. "Then maybe you should let it cool and tell us all about what you've been up to today, Mercury."

Of course. The one question I couldn't answer. "Well, I spent the morning with Matty, and then I met up with a few friends and we just kind of hung out, I guess."

"It's delightful to know that you're doing something constructive with your time." He put a forkful of food in his mouth, his flat expression unimpressed but at least not questioning my story. My shoulders dropped as I let out a sharp breath and sunk deeper into the plush cushion of the dining chair. *Planning your downfall with a bunch of thieves and delinquents* wasn't the answer anyone would want to hear, even if part of me wanted to know what he'd say if I had said that.

"Speaking of constructive," Bernard said, "I received the plans for the military facility we were contemplating near the Canadian border, should the need arise."

"Excellent. We need to be prepared should we receive any more information regarding...."

My father rambled on about his project as I poked my fork at my fancy chicken and let it slide around the plate. It looked delicious. Juicy and flavorful, the mark of an extremely talented kitchen staff, but for as much as my empty stomach rumbled when I walked in the room, the return of the nagging thoughts in my head about what Hawk had asked me to do had suddenly killed my appetite.

What Hawk was trying to do was important. I got that. It's just that too many things could go wrong. Too many things no one would understand. Hawk had tried to warn me that choosing this path would get tougher, but instead of listening, I acted like a total snot. What was I even trying to prove? Why did I even care? *Argh.* Did I hate them or myself for getting into this predicament?

Christophe pulled out his cell phone and held it just under the table, quickly sliding his fingers over the screen. I leaned over and tried to see what he was looking at, any distraction from my own life welcome, but he swiped around so fast I couldn't get a good look.

Mom cleared her throat. "Chris, dear, could you please put that away? Whatever it is can wait."

He stared at the screen, clearly not agreeing with my mother's opinion on priorities, but eventually nodded and slid the phone into his pocket as slow as possible to get the last few seconds of screen time he could.

"Leave him alone, Giselle. There's nothing wrong with dedication." My father gave Christophe an adoring look and patted him on the shoulder. Unfortunately, looking at Christophe made it too easy to see me. "It would be nice if more young people had the same ambition."

"Besides, he's been very busy. He's joined the task team searching for the vigilantes. What a menace," Bernard said, his eyes full of pride for his son.

Christophe's cheeks flamed at the attention. Seemed odd, considering he'd been craving this kind of recognition. Maybe it felt like too much now that he actually got it.

"Yes," Christophe said. "They struck again last night. Stole a bunch of narcotics from a downtown lab."

I coughed on my chicken. "Narcotics. They don't sound like the type of organization that would bother with stealing drugs. How do you know it's them?"

Christophe looked at my father, then his father, before answering. Was there some secret government bro-code hierarchy he needed to fall in line with for now? "Funding maybe. To attract followers. The drug trade has deeper ties in organized crime than you could possibly imagine."

I made a quick snort, then tried to cover it with my napkin. Organized crime? Hawk and his misfits? Not quite.

"The security guard from the lab chased one of them, but they managed to get away."

I swallowed, my hand starting to twitch a little in my lap. "Really? Did they get a description?"

"Not exactly. Some tall, muscular guy."

A guy. Honestly? I wasn't sure if I should be grateful or offended. "So what does that mean for your investigation? Does the security guard know anything? Was there any other evidence?"

Christophe laughed and put his hand on my shoulder. "Easy, Mercury. I know everyone is concerned about these criminals still free on the streets, but—"

"But we'll take care of it. If they want to push us, we'll push right back," my father finished with a pleased smirk, then took a deep gulp from his wineglass.

"What does that mean exactly?" I asked.

"It doesn't concern you."

"And why not?"

"Can we please keep business for after dinner," Mom interjected. "This is supposed to be a relaxed family meal."

"Sorry, Mrs. Masters," Christophe said, while everyone else retreated into their plates.

But I couldn't give it up. They knew about the robbery last

night, but at least it didn't seem like anyone knew about my involvement. Or was Christophe covering for me? I tried to look him over in my peripheral vision, but he didn't seem to have the odd peaked left eyebrow that he did when he lied. Maybe he really didn't know.

"And thank you for the invitation to the Breaker Gala tonight," Christophe continued, still kissing up to my mother.

"What's that?" I whispered to him, trying not to call attention to myself.

"It's a charity event," Mom, who clearly had the hearing of a predatory bird, said. "Very good cause. Very well attended."

Well attended. I knew what that meant. A bunch of stodgy politico types parading around trying to outdo each other by how charitable they could be, when most of them didn't even know what the event was for.

"There will actually be quite a few young people; you should join us," she added.

I tried my hardest not to eye-roll. "Right."

My father pointed his glass at me. "It's about time you started making appearances at society events. It's important for your future."

"What, so you can find me a rich husband to take me away and make some sort of strategic alliance?"

Forks clanged against plates as the conversation halted. It had rolled off my tongue as a joke, but came out with a bite everyone at the table clearly felt.

"At least that would make you a contributing member of this family, instead of just a scandal waiting to happen." My father tried to curl a smile and brush it off, but his building anger got in his way as he stared right through me.

"A scandal?" *Shut up. Shut up. Shut up.* "Like anything I do could be worse than how you've screwed up an entire country."

My hand shot over my mouth, but there were no more

words to hold back. Every muscle in my body clenched as I sunk back in my chair, wishing I could fall right through the floor and out of this room.

"How dare you speak to me like that. You ungrateful little brat." He jumped to his feet, his wineglass falling to the floor with a smash, red splattering across the slate tile floor.

"Vincent," Mom said, trying to hush him.

"Uh-oh." Matty's tiny voice came from the corner as my father stared me down. "Mercury's in trouble."

"Mattias. Out." Mom snapped her fingers and pointed to the hallway.

"But—"

"Mattias."

He grumbled and scrambled out the door. Taking his cue, Bernard nodded at Christophe and they both stood as if in a choreographed dance they had practiced. Christophe brushed his hand across my shoulder as he left, his eyes never leaving me until he disappeared around the corner.

"After all your mother and I have put up with from you, you should be grateful we are even willing to let you out of this house." The fire in his blood bubbled, bled up his cheeks and across the scowl lines gouged across his forehead. "You have no idea what is going on outside these walls. No idea what it's like out there in the real world. I've protected you from that. I've kept you safe and comfortable. For what? To have you lunge out at me anytime it suits you because you're bored and selfish."

"Protected me from the real world or tried to cover it up from the press?"

He lurched forward, but Mom held his arm and stared up at him while he ignored her, his glare locked only on me. "Vincent. Let it go. She's just testing you."

He shirked out of her grip, her graceful body jerking from the sudden movement. "Go get ready. We're leaving soon."

She shook her head at me, but scurried out of the room. Ever the obedient wife.

"Do you set out to disappoint me or does it simply come instinctively to you now?" he said, his tone morphing to a weird state of calm. Emotionless. Flat. Scary.

I didn't answer, not knowing if he really wanted a response. If only I'd learned to keep my mouth shut about five minutes before.

"When you were a little girl, you had so much potential. You were charming, sweet, and you did what you were told."

He circled the table and walked toward me. Every single footfall against the tile vibrated through my body. I couldn't move. Even if I could, my wobbly legs would've given out if I tried to run, and as big as this house was, I had nowhere to hide.

"Now look at you. You're a disaster. You scream about things you know nothing about. You can't be relied upon to present yourself appropriately in public. You're rude, ignorant, and ungrateful. You might be my biggest failure."

Gutted. His words pierced through my skin and jabbed at my organs. I swallowed down my protests and focused on the vase of hydrangeas on the credenza, an itchy feeling creeping under my eyelids. A feeling I refused to let win.

His suited arm lunged in front of me. All my muscles tensed. He grabbed the plate from under my nose and I held my breath.

"You need to remember your place around here," he said, the fierce growl returning to his voice. "You are never to speak to me like that again."

I flinched as the plate shattered on the floor behind me, but I didn't turn around. With one last huff that made the small hairs on my neck stand on end, he stormed out, staring at the overhead camera on the way, leaving me alone in the oversized dining room. I sat there staring at nothing, one fist tight on my fork, the other twisted in the silky tablecloth at my lap, forcing myself to breathe. The violins cried through the speakers, but I just sighed and wished I'd kept my mouth shut.

Eventually, the tension drained out of my muscles and I could move again. I picked up the broken china pieces and stacked them on the table, each one dirty with the dinner I never finished eating. A small sliver of porcelain stuck in my index finger and blood pooled at the spot when I pulled it out.

"What happened in here?"

Christophe leaned against the doorway, probably still unsure I'd welcome him or if he should keep his distance. Caution was a skill easily learned growing up in this house.

"It fell."

I grabbed a napkin with my wounded hand and hid my bloody finger behind my back as he walked across the room.

He leaned over and flipped another piece of plate onto the table. "Missed one."

"Thanks."

"Fighting with him only proves him right, you know. If you really want to make him listen, you need to show him that you're not just some whiny kid. That you're capable of making your own decisions."

"Doubt it."

"Maybe not, but what you're doing definitely isn't working. It wouldn't hurt to try a new strategy."

"I'll think about it."

"Hey." He put his hand under my chin and turned my head up to face him. "You really should come tonight. It could be fun. I'll help you fight off all those potential husbands."

He chuckled and the sound made the queasiness in my stomach settle for a second. Underneath all his new self-impor-tant style, I could still see the warmth he'd always kept just for me. I only wished things were simpler between us again. Like it used to be.

"Thanks, but I have work to do." I shook my head gently so he'd move his hand and stop staring at me with those wide hopeful eyes. "Going to get some college applications together so I can get out of this place."

"Sure."

He lowered his head to stare at his feet, then dug his hands in his pockets and backed toward the doorway, looking up at me when he hit the entrance. "If you change your mind, I can have them send a car for you."

"I'll think about it."

He nodded, his smile disappearing and leaving his lips in a hard line as he headed off down the hallway.

I watched the empty doorway with a heavy feeling pressing against my lungs. Once I knew Christophe wasn't coming back, I chucked the bloodstained napkin on the table and wriggled my cell phone out of my bra. My fingers hesitated over the screen, but eventually I texted the random number Hawk had given me.

It has to be tonight.

NINETEEN

The taillights of the car carrying my father and his entourage had barely turned the corner when Hawk bounded down the sidewalk. His timing was risky, but at least it didn't leave me much opportunity to second-guess my decision to call him.

"I thought I told you to dress nice," I said, looking him over. Worn-out sneakers and ill-fitting cargo pants. More donation-bin chic than designer.

He shrugged. "What?"

"Have you really been out of this world that long that you don't know how to put together an outfit? At least lose the hoodie."

"Sorry, I must have forgotten my argyle sweater vests when I moved out of my penthouse."

"Very funny. Do you honestly expect that people aren't going to ask questions if I walk around with some guy that looks like a street kid?"

He slipped the sweater over his head, static catching the navy T-shirt underneath. A flat stomach and toned abs appeared above his belt, taking me by surprise. *Nice. Very nice.* I looked away quickly before he could realize that his flash of skin and the red splotches spreading up my neck might be connected.

"Am I presentable now?"

I turned back and gave him a last once-over, rushing over his torso so I wouldn't think about the rest of the body he had hidden under there, but the way the sleeves clung tight to his biceps didn't help.

"Better." I shook my head and started up the stairs to the door. "Now. Don't talk to anyone. Don't touch anything. We get in. We get out. And you get the heck out of here. Got it?"

"Sure." He followed close behind me up the stairs and through the main hall. He didn't gawk or stare like most guests on their first visit to the house, but I had to keep reminding myself it wasn't the first time he'd been here, and I didn't bother asking how many times he'd been here with no one knowing, because I wasn't sure I wanted to know the answer.

"Am I allowed to ask what convinced you to go along with this?"

I marched forward, hoping he didn't notice the slight hesitation in my step. "No."

"Whatever it was..." His voice dropped to a whisper that fluttered the small strands of hair at my temple as he leaned close. "Thanks."

I smiled, but pushed it down as we rounded the final corner into the long corridor outside the office.

"Remember to make this quick," I said as I pulled back the decorative cover of the keypad.

"No one is to enter the office without express permission from The Five," a voice boomed behind us.

A guard ran toward us, all clang and clatter and conviction. As he came closer, I recognized him immediately. Hazel eyes and a too-blunt haircut. The guard who'd found me at the Full

Moon. The only things missing were the stench of stale beer and a sticky, broken tile floor.

I straightened myself as tall as I could and stood in his way.

"You can't tell me what to do. Do you know who I am?"

He nodded sharply and stood rigid with his arms crossed behind his back. "Yes, ma'am, but I am on specific orders. No one is to enter the office without permission, especially no outsiders."

He jutted his chin at Hawk.

"This is the super genius hired to help me write my college entrance essays, but I forgot my drafts on my dad's desk and I need to go get them. You wouldn't want to waste my family's money, would you?"

"You'll need to wait until he returns, ma'am."

Seriously? I looked him over for a minute. Lips in a tight line. No eye contact. No emotion at all. Another brainwashed errand boy. My father must order them in bulk and store them in the bottom drawer of his desk for emergencies. I stepped closer to him and lowered my voice, his pupils following my every move as he remained stone-still.

"Okay. I know you were the one who told my dad where I was hiding out."

The guard still wouldn't look at me, but blood began rising along his jaw. *Good.* Guilt was a great emotion to exploit.

"So basically you owe me. Now all I am asking is for you to look the other way while I go into the office and get my stupid essays. I'm the one entering the code. I'm the one in the office. The only thing you need to do is not stop me."

"I'm not going to be responsible for this, ma'am."

"I promise. If anything goes wrong, this is on me. You did your job, I just didn't listen. Trust me. That's more believable than the idea that you actually let me in. Besides..." I hated myself as the words crawled up my throat. "You wouldn't want me telling Daddy you knew I was staying at a shady bar in the middle of nowhere for weeks before you reported it?"

He hesitated. The clenched jaw and shifty eyes told me he was weighing his options. A lie from me, even a lousy one, could have him reassigned to crossing guard duty in half the time it would take me to tell it—if he was reassigned at all.

His shoulders fell as he sidestepped out of my way.

"No one is to enter the office without permission," he repeated through gritted teeth. "Have a nice evening."

With a swift nod and a sympathetic *good luck, buddy* eye roll at Hawk, he marched back down the hall like a good soldier. Smart guy. Walk away and don't get blamed.

I tapped in the passcode, as natural as breathing, and did a quick last-minute check down the hall as the keypad made its familiar double beep and the door clicked open. No other witnesses to worry about. Even though I'd threatened him, I didn't need that guard suffering the same fate as Bill because he was good enough to help me. No more casualties from my mistakes.

Inside, the room was dark. The regular city lights shone, but the overcast sky shut out the moon. An eerie glow about the place radiated in a strange way I'd never noticed before. Maybe it had something to do with the possibility of getting caught. Or maybe the moon didn't want to see what we were up to tonight. Either way, it gave me a creepy feeling in my bones that I couldn't will away.

I pushed open the door to the inner office, peeking down the hallway to make sure no one had stayed late. Seeing and hearing no one, I waved Hawk to follow. "I think we're good."

He bounded across the floor in three wide steps and carefully, quietly shut the door behind us.

"What were you whispering to the guard to make him take off like that?"

"I just reminded him he owed me a favor."

"For what?"

"Don't worry about it. Maybe you're not the only one with a secret life."

He didn't say a word, just nodded with a satisfied smile. He didn't pry. I liked that.

I headed down the hall and pushed on my father's office door as I turned the handle. My shoulder slammed into the door with a *bang*. I turned the handle again, but it didn't budge. Weird. The inner offices were never locked.

"My turn," Hawk said as he pulled some sharp-looking tools from a case in his back pocket.

I guess that was a benefit to being a thief: locked doors meant nothing. He kneeled and started to work as I watched back down the hall.

"Could you stop that? You're making me nervous," Hawk said as he kept his head level with the lock, his hands working quick and precise like a surgeon's.

"What?" I responded as my tapping foot echoed through the hall. I stopped and tucked it around my other heel.

The door clicked and creaked as it opened to the dark office. I flipped on the lights, half expecting my father to be sitting there, even though I knew he was across town and at least six scotches in.

"Score." Hawk tucked away the lock-pick kit and rushed around the far side of the desk. He tapped the keyboard, and the monitor lit up on the password screen.

"Dammit," I said, looking around my father's desk for inspiration, even though it was hard to find with the noticeable lack of pictures or anything remotely personal in sight. "I didn't even think about a password."

"Already covered." Hawk's long fingers clicked across the keys and the lock screen disappeared. "*MissMurky1201star*, or did you forget I've already hacked into this system before? No idea what it means, but it must be something important since no one bothered to change it after last time."

"It's me," I said, the thought stabbing me in the heart.

"Huh?"

"My little brother couldn't say my name right, so he always called me Murky. My father added the Miss. The numbers are my birthday."

Hawk shrugged, and I turned to stare at the shelves of plaques and awards, all the words swirling together in an unreadable mess. Why did he have to use my name for a password? It was a simple thing, something that shouldn't make the tops of my cheeks flame, but it did. It made me angry. And sad. And then angry again. He hadn't even called me that in forever. Long before we were both on opposite sides. Long before the first time—

"Okay, Ratch, we're in. What now?" Hawk said into one of those ancient bricks pretending to be a phone.

He flipped a small, black thumb drive out of his pocket and jammed it in the side of the computer. Honestly, how big were those pockets? He must have at least half a criminal toolbox in there.

"Uh-huh. Uh-huh. Okay." Hawk nodded along as files and folders flipped across the screen in flashes.

I leaned over his shoulder and tried to follow the pathways, but nothing he clicked or typed made sense to me. "What are you doing exactly?"

"I have to bury the watcher file deep enough no one will find it, but someplace no one will think to look, either. At least not right away."

"And how did you learn how to do all this stuff?"

"If you want something bad enough, you figure it out."

"Hey," a voice yelled from Hawk's phone, loud enough to make him pull it away from his ear.

"All right. Ratchett taught me everything I know. He is a technology god and I would be nothing without his help."

A deep laugh came from the phone.

"And done." Hawk pounded the Enter key and the bright blue password screen appeared again. He clicked off the cell phone and grabbed the thumb drive, shoving both in his bottomless pocket. "Let's go."

I ran after him, locked the door behind me, and kept an eye on every door until we emerged in the outer office. The dark clouds had vanished and the entire room now lit up in a whitish-blue moonglow.

Without thinking, I stopped and stood in front of the windows. The night pulled me toward it. A magnet. Or a mirror I couldn't help getting lost in. A fascination. An obsession. Maybe all of the above.

"What are you doing?" Hawk called from the doorway.

"Sometimes I used to stand here and wish I could jump from this window and fly over the city and then somewhere, anywhere, that wasn't here."

"Is that what you were doing the night of the party? Thinking about flying?"

My father's party seemed long ago and far away now.

"Yeah ... I think I was."

He walked over and stood beside me, both of our blurry bodies reflected in the glass. Two watery apparitions. But Hawk's image wasn't staring out—it was looking right at me.

"I remember you standing here. The way the light came through the windows and across your face. You looked upset. A strange kind of beautiful sadness." He inhaled deep, then rubbed his hand against the back of his neck. "I wondered what you were thinking about."

Something changed in his face when he looked up again. The steady sureness I always saw had drifted off somewhere among the stars, and left something behind that gave the moon competition for my full attention.

"Then you chucked a shoe at me and body-checked me into a wall."

I laughed. Maybe a little too much. Then shoved my hands deep in my pockets. "You deserved it."

He stepped closer. Not too close, but enough to make me very conscious about the haggardness of my breath and if I'd remembered to brush my teeth after dinner. He pulled his arms tight to his sides, his muscles flexing against his sleeves and clouding my thoughts. I wondered what it would be like to be in those arms. What Hawk might do if I was.

"Who let you in here?" a low voice snapped. My head whipped toward the door to see my father standing there, red-faced and large.

I backed up a step. "Sorry, I was just showing a friend around. I didn't think you'd mind."

"Well, I do mind. This is a place of business, not a museum."

"Yes, sir."

I nodded at Hawk and started for the door. Before we had a chance to pass, my father tapped him on the shoulder. "And who might you be?"

"Uh... This is Kendall's cousin. He's visiting from down South," I said. I really should've planned a better excuse.

"South?" My father's brows knit together. "I thought all the Drakes came from the Northeast."

"Distant cousin. Twice removed," Hawk added, extending his hand. "Max."

He eyed Hawk over, but took his hand and shook it roughly. "Pleasure to meet you, but if you don't mind, I have something to discuss with my daughter. Would you mind showing yourself out?"

Hawk looked at me with curious eyes, but did as he was told and headed for the door. Probably realizing how lucky he was to be walking out of here instead of being dragged in handcuffs.

"Send my regards to your aunt and uncle," my father called after Hawk as he watched him walk away, scrutinizing every step.

The party shouldn't be over already, but the undone bowtie draped around my father's neck and the open top button of his perfectly pressed white shirt meant he was definitely home for the night. I snuck a glance at my phone. Only nine thirty. Something serious had brought him back here. Something bad. A tremble started in the backs of my knees and ricocheted up my spine. Whatever he wanted to discuss couldn't be good. The list of all the things I'd done in the last few days that he would disapprove of looped in my brain and my head spun. Or maybe the air around me had gained a hundred pounds and had made it hard to breathe.

Five seconds. That's how many I counted from the time Hawk slipped out the doorway until my father went nuclear.

He sternly waved a stack of papers in my face. "Who do you think you are, sending money to that criminal?"

"Excuse me?"

"Don't pull that with me. William Mackenzie from that sickening backwoods Full Moon establishment. You sent him $200,000 two weeks ago."

"He lost everything. You took away all he had."

"No, you made that decision, then you used my money to buy your way out of it. I can't be tied to funds sent to unsavory characters. What you did was irresponsible, criminal, and extremely immature." Spit flew out of his mouth. His head erupted in flames. My entire body tensed. "I will *not* let you ruin my reputation because of your ignorance."

I didn't have a chance to move. His hand came down flat against my cheek, pushing my face to the side. The pain exploded behind my left eye and the sour taste of blood flooded my mouth. An all too familiar feeling, and likely just the beginning.

His hand lifted again, and I clenched my fists, hoping it would hurt less the second time, and knowing it wouldn't, but when the hate flashed in his eyes, his hand didn't fall. He turned sharply, with Hawk's hand tight around his wrist, twisting his arm behind his head.

"I don't think that's a good idea," Hawk said, staring my father down. Both stood in a deadlock. Hawk refusing to let go. My father refusing to back down.

"This is none of your business," my father snarled.

"It is when I see someone hit their own daughter."

"You didn't see anything." He jerked his arm out of Hawk's grip. "I recommend you leave before I have someone escort you out."

Hawk stood there staring back at him, as if his words had come out silent.

"Guard!"

Hawk gave me a sorry glance and bolted for the door. His loud footsteps disappeared down the hall as another set came pounding into the room.

"Yes, sir," the hazel-eyed guard said as he tried his hardest not to look at me and think about what I could've done to destroy him.

My father's voice hissed low and venomous. "Get out of my sight."

I ran. Tears welled up behind my eyes, but I wouldn't let them fall. Instead, I held my cheek, the skin beneath my fingertips feeling like it might explode and leave a trail of skin and blood on the expensive carpet. One more thing in this house I'd be responsible for messing up.

Two flights of stairs and three hallways until I surfaced safe in my room again. I closed the door and leaned my forehead against the sleek lacquer finish. I flexed my jaw. Pain shot up through my temple and pulsed in my brain. It hurt, but no permanent damage. It could've been worse. So much worse.

"Are you okay?"

My body jumped. I turned around to see Hawk sitting near my window.

"You're still here?"

"Yeah. I couldn't leave. Not after that." He stood and walked toward me. I couldn't move, my limbs standing firm. If I didn't waver, it meant I wasn't weak. "I needed to make sure he didn't try anything again."

"It's not as bad as it looks."

He stopped in front of me and stared at my cheek. Fifteen minutes ago being this close would've made my stomach flip; now I just wanted him to go. "This isn't the first time, is it?"

I shook my head, regretting it immediately as pain-induced vomit rose in my throat.

"Come here." Hawk took my hand and marched me into the bathroom. I think I felt him squeeze my fingers once, but I wasn't sure if it was in support or urgency. "Up you go."

He grabbed my waist and tossed me on the counter like a kid with a skinned knee. Funny, that's exactly how I felt. Like a stupid, scared kid. Hurt and humiliated.

"It's really not that bad. I'll be fine."

He ignored me and ran the faucet. A blanket of goose bumps formed on my arms from the chill coming off the cold water as it splashed in the sink.

"If you're fine, your face must be made of lead." He gave me a half-hearted smile and tried to laugh, but it came out forced and unnatural.

He wrung out the cloth while I watched his knuckles turn white against his cold red skin. Watching him move hurt less than watching him look at me. The sick feeling building in my stomach stung much worse than the pain in my face.

The ice-cold cloth gave a frosty jolt that rushed through my jaw as he pressed it against my cheek. I hissed as I sucked air through my clenched teeth. "Hopefully it won't bruise too much."

Hawk brushed a strand of hair behind my ear, his fingers grazing slowly against my temple. "Is this why you didn't want to help get me into the office? What might happen if you got caught?"

I didn't answer, but from the way his eyes narrowed and his lips twitched as if he fought saying something he might regret, I knew it didn't matter. He'd already figured it out.

"Thanks, but I can take care of it." I clamped my hand over his on the cloth. He held steady for a moment, his icy fingers warming under my fiery palm. I relaxed my grip, and he got the hint, finally sliding his hand out from under mine.

He let out a long, defeated sigh. "How long has this been going on?"

"I don't remember."

"How often does it happen?"

"I don't keep track."

"Have you told anyone?"

"No."

"How bad has he hurt you?"

Too many questions. "I think you need to go. I kind of feel like being by myself right now."

His head ticked back, confused. If he expected to give me a hug and a pep talk and have me unload all my screwed up stories on him, I wasn't that girl. I was too messed up to be that girl, and it stung knowing he knew that about me now.

"If that's what you want."

I nodded.

He lifted his arm and made an awkward fist pump like he might've considered touching me but didn't want to cross some imaginary line, then started to step away. He hesitated for a second. "But if you don't think you're safe."

"It's over. Please go."

He backed out the door, not taking his gaze off me until he turned at the threshold. I had never seen that look before. What was it? Concern? Maybe pity? I hated pity. The thought of it crept up the back of my throat and sat behind my tonsils, heavy like a bag of marbles. I leaned my head against the wall, my hand still holding the cloth tight against my cheek. The cold and the pain made me numb. My face, my hands, my soul. For some reason, keeping the fights with my father a secret kept them from being real. The bruises and the broken bones were just thoughts, and if I didn't think about them, they didn't exist. My own private nightmare. Mine alone. But now someone knew.

Running away always managed to dam everything up until I had time to forget again, but having someone know made all that pain flood over me again. The world hazed as teardrops fell into my lap. I only cried the first time he'd hit me. I swore I'd never do it again. Something inside must've broken this time. *Hawk, what have you done?*

TWENTY

Twenty-six minutes. The amount of time I'd stood outside the Sanctuary, the door handle in my sweaty hand. The amount of time I'd tried to tell myself that if I could just pull it open and get this over with, things would be okay. The amount of time the door had remained shut.

Last night I'd cried—deep, dark, ugly crying from a place beaten down and dead a long time ago. This morning, that place went numb again. Numb and embarrassed. Hawk knew my secret now and suddenly had power over me. He knew the one thing I'd never told anyone. He had the power to destroy me, but I wasn't going to let that happen.

One last deep breath from the bottom of my gut and I yanked the door open, running as quick as I could through the security door before I changed my mind.

"Look, it's Hackerette," Tucker announced as I burst into the room. "Back for another fix of badass. It's addicting, isn't it?"

"Morning, Tucker," I said as I calmed myself down and walked over to where he and Red were sorting through a pile of wallets. "Do I want to know what you're doing?"

"Probably not." He laughed and looked at me, his smile

falling into his lap. "Question is, what have you been doing? I didn't think purple was your color."

I'd spent an hour with the most expensive concealer I could get, and I thought I'd done a pretty good job, but clearly not. Now that my face burned five shades of flaming, I probably needed three bottles of it to try to look normal.

"It's nothing ... it's...."

"It's my fault," Hawk said from behind me. I'd been relieved I hadn't seen him when I walked in, but now hearing his voice pushed my shoulders up to my ears.

"She was leaned over watching me pick a lock. I turned too fast and hit her with my elbow. A simple accident."

"That is the dumbest thing I've ever heard." Tucker said, eyeing me up and down. I didn't blame him. His excuse was weaker than saying I ran into a door. If Hawk hadn't cut me off, I could've done so much better.

"Then you know it's true. If I was going to lie, I would've come up with something else."

Tucker nodded, seemingly satisfied, or just knowing better than to push the issue.

"I didn't know you were coming," Hawk said, his breath moving the hair on the back of my head.

I turned around and watched him try to cover up his reaction from seeing my clearly-not-disguised bruise spread out across my cheek.

"Why wouldn't I be here?" I asked, making my voice as calm as I could with my knees still shaking.

His lips kept quiet, but his stare screamed in indigo. I looked away. Holding on to silent shame cut deeper than anything else, but fortunately was much easier to ignore.

"Okay, then." He dragged the words out like a knife across my skin. "Since you're here, did you want to see what we found from the mission last night?"

"Sure."

He stepped aside to let me pass, then ushered me to the oddly empty chair where Ratchett always sat. With or without him, the screens wrapped data like a marquee. I blinked, still not having learned my lesson not to stare directly into the ever-moving glow.

"So what did you find?" I said, skimming over the desktop, half expecting some sort of important document to come jumping out at me. Whatever it was. Whatever the mission involved now, I was in. I needed the distraction.

"It looks better than I thought it would. Does it still hurt?" Hawk said. His hand reached up and stopped near my collarbone, clenched into a fist, and dropped again.

"Nope. Like I told you yesterday, I'm fine."

"It's okay if it does."

He put his hand on my shoulder, strong but gentle, his warm skin so close I could tilt my head and rest my cheek on his knuckles.

Instead, I shrugged it off and turned around. "And it's even better if it doesn't."

I couldn't stand to look at him. His big sympathetic eyes mixed with a tragic knowing smile. The one I never wanted to see. Why couldn't he leave it alone? I wasn't going to be the type to sit around and cry about it, at least not today, so why should he?

"And I don't need you to defend me, all right? I can handle myself in front of other people, you know," I said, my back still to him.

"I wasn't saying you couldn't. I was just trying to make things easier for you."

"Well, stop. If I wanted a publicist, I'd hire one."

"Fine." He tossed up his hands and backed away a few

inches, the breeze from his sharp movements cold against the skin on the backs of my arms. "Sorry I asked."

I almost felt bad, then decided against it. He had no right interfering in my business. He already knew far too much.

"I just thought ... never mind, I've got somewhere to be." He shook his head and started toward the door.

Dammit. He couldn't just leave after that. "Wait. Where are you going?"

"If you're here when I get back, I'll fill you in."

"And what am I supposed to do until then?"

He didn't turn around. "You seem like you can handle yourself. Figure it out. Make friends or something."

The door clicked closed, and I scanned the sets of eyes around the room that had watched my outburst. Make friends? He had a funny sense of humor.

I flipped through the papers sitting on Ratchett's desk, but they didn't really mean anything to me. Everything in unreadable scribbles with numbers and codes that didn't make sense out of context. Maybe I should just go home. Or maybe.... I looked around. Since when was I ever not the most popular girl in the room? I'd trained for years to be charming and interesting. Be exactly what everyone wanted me to be.

In the far corner, people played some kind of card game. I was good at cards. I always beat the nannies when we played poker, and I took the boys at Charlotte Hall for their trust-fund dividends all the time. I walked over and sat on a nearby table-top. Immediately, the laughter stopped. A girl with chunky turquoise streaks tried to hide that she was staring at me from behind her hand. Everyone else just dropped their eyes and kept their mouths shut.

"Mind if I play?" I asked, plastering on my practiced smile. "I can promise to go all-in for the first three hands."

"Can't have more than six," one of the older boys grunted

from his spot on the floor, as he held his hand close to his chest, like I might try to read his cards.

"But there's only five of you."

"Someone else is coming and they've already got dibs."

"Well, maybe until they get here, I could—"

"No, we're good." The boy scanned the other faces. Everyone shook their heads so slightly, probably hoping I wouldn't notice.

"Right." I jumped up and watched them dart their eyes to each other in some secret silent language I was clearly not welcome to learn. "Maybe next time."

Well that failed miserably. I walked around slowly, trying to ease myself into any conversation that would have me, but instead I managed to snuff out all interactions like the pathetic weird freshman who tried to sit at your cafeteria table on their first day. But now I was the weird kid. Seriously? I was never the weird kid.

I wandered back to Tucker and Red.

"Got a problem, Princess?"

I cringed. Red talking to me actually made me sort of happy. So pathetic.

"No. Just bored."

"Uh-huh," she muttered and chuckled at Tucker.

He kicked her underneath the table and she laughed harder.

"Don't think your prep-school pedigree's gonna help you much with this crowd. Maybe you need to try a different strategy," Tucker said.

"Yeah, maybe."

I looked around the room again. Everyone had gone back to forgetting I existed. At least they didn't stare.

"Hey," Tucker said, brushing his hand over the tips of my fingers to get my attention. "Number one rule around here is trust, and until they all know they can trust you, it'll be rough."

"Right. Trust is something you earn or something like that." I fluttered my hand in the air, dismissing Hawk and his ridiculous rules.

"Someone's been studying their rookie handbook. That's a good place to start." Tucker grinned a little too hard, feeding my self-pity. If he didn't believe it, how was I supposed to?

"Besides, they know you ain't really one of us."

"Red," Tucker scolded.

She shrugged and flipped her hair in one harsh fluid motion, adding even more attitude to the nasty look she threw me.

"Ya know it's true. You're up here"—she held her hand above her head and flicked it in the air for effect—"we're all down here." She dropped her hand under the table as far as she could reach. "Ain't nobody gonna buy what you're selling until they know you're all-in."

"I am all-in. Don't you know what I'm risking to be here?"

Red stood and walked right up in my face. "Being watchdog and breaking into your own place isn't real convincing." She jerked her head to the side, and I felt her neck crack down in my knees, then she cackled and stormed off.

"Don't listen to her. Sometimes people need time to accept change. Just chill," Tucker said, watching Red strut her way across the room.

Chill? I definitely wasn't capable of chilling. That familiar itch had been growing in my palms since the second I woke up this morning. The one that tempted me to pack a bag and get as far away from the city as I could. No one would care if I left anyway.

I clenched my hands into fists and dug my nails into my skin so hard I might bleed all over my freshly manicured fingertips.

"Hey, Red," I called after her. "Still interested in teaching me how to fight?"

Her face twisted into a smirk of delight, the closest thing to a genuine smile I'd seen since I met her. Even from across the room, I could feel her vibrating with excitement. I'd probably painfully regret challenging her, but I didn't want to feel weak, even if it meant going toe-to-toe with a hellbeast like Red. I needed something to make my head stop thinking.

Tucker jumped in front of me. "What are you doing? She's like a pitbull; she'll bite and not let go until she tears off an arm."

"Don't think I can take her?"

He scoffed. "Uh, no."

"Well, everyone around here"—I raised my voice—"seems to think I can't cut it, so either I prove you all right and walk away like a spoiled coward, or I step up and take her on."

Tucker chuckled and looked me over. "Hopefully you're a lot faster than you look, because you're going to need all the help you can get."

A CROWD of hoods appeared around us. On top of the shipping containers, creeping in from the dark corners of the yard, all gathering to watch me get my butt handed to me. I'd hoped this might get me some attention, and it had definitely worked, but I'd likely regret this wish coming true.

Red stood across the empty space, a sneer on her lips and a stare that reminded me how risky this idea really was. What the hell was I thinking? She'd probably kill me, but somehow it'd probably hurt less than I already did. Sore. Raw. Broken. Hopefully whatever she did to me would knock something back into place.

Tucker leaned in to whisper, although no one stood close enough to hear anyway. He probably saw it in some old movie or the sports channel or something cliché like that. Next thing I knew he'd be standing here spraying water in my face and trying to towel me off.

"Remember, you don't want to hurt her, you just want to immobilize her."

"Are you sure about that? Hurting her might be the best fun I have all day."

"Not funny, plus not freakin' likely either." His face dropped and his giddy smile disappeared. "The best self-defense is to avoid a fight in the first place. We don't fight for fun around here; we fight to survive, and only when we need to. Besides, if you think for one second you're actually going to get the upper hand on that girl, you won't, and there will be a world of hurt that's going to be more painful than being wrong."

"Okay. Okay. What do I need to know?"

"First"—he held up his fingers in the air as he went, as if I wasn't hanging on his every word—"keep moving, it'll make it harder to hit you. Second, keep your arms up and elbows out; they are more damaging than your hands. Third, kicking is never useful unless you're close enough and you'll probably fall on your ass. And last and most important, do not show fear."

"She's not a dog, Tucker."

"No, she's worse. Don't get me wrong, I love her nasty, but I know not to get on the bad side of it."

Tucker sighed and put his hands on my shoulders as if he'd never see me again, his floppy dark hair falling in front of his eyes, so I couldn't tell if he meant it. "All right. Remember what I told you. Try not to die."

He yanked me forward into a most awkward hug, his chin digging into the top of my head as his lanky arms wrapped all the way around me and then some.

"I'll try," I said, my words muffled from my face squeezed against his sweater.

He let me go, his scent of smoldering fire and cinnamon still clinging to my skin. I took a deep breath. *Go time.*

Red stood in the middle of the yard, picking at something under her fingernails. Her calmness putting every one of my reflexes on edge.

"Are you ready yet?" she called.

I stepped forward and tried to remember what Tucker said. *Arms up. Keep moving. Confidence.* All the sets of eyes, that I'd forgotten were watching, bore down on my back.

Red readied herself as she saw me advance. Feet planted. Knees bent. Arms out. "Try something."

"What?"

"Whatever you got."

Shifting my weight from side to side, I looked her over, trying to find the best place to strike. I'd never been in a real fight before, at least not one with fists. I'd always been on the receiving side, never daring to hit back, hoping that letting it happen would make it end quicker so I could start forgetting. But right now I remembered. I pulled my arm back and swung.

Red's fingers clamped around my wrist. The crowd cheered. She whipped me around and pressed up behind me with my arm sandwiched between us and my fingertips high enough to grab the back of my skull. The bones in my elbow felt like they might snap if she even exhaled the wrong way. I grunted to myself, but refused to give in. I squirmed under her grip until she let me go with a push, almost sending me facedown into the concrete.

"Never let your opponent get a hand on ya. If they do, you're good as dead. Got it?"

I nodded and shook out my arm, my nerves crackling under my skin.

She waved me forward. "Again."

I circled her, looking for an opening, but she turned with me, anticipating, knowing my every move before I made it.

"C'mon. Do something," she coaxed.

I hesitated. She swung. I jumped back, feeling the air rush past my stomach where her hand should've connected.

"So ya are paying attention."

I lunged. Knuckles bounced off her rock-hard shoulder. She twisted back. I swung again. A slam against my left leg. The sharp jolt up my spine as I slammed into the ground. The sour taste of blood as I bit my tongue. The rough roar of the crowd cheering again.

"Never get too close." She hoofed my shoe, intensifying the growing ache.

I retreated to Tucker, who was already waiting for me.

"Okay, so that sucked."

"Really?" I said as I rubbed my calf where Red's steel-like toes had made contact. "I thought you said kicking was bad?"

"I said only kick if close enough. You got too close, so she kicked, but you're the one who still ended up on their ass." He chuckled at his own joke. "Ready to give up yet?"

"No. I can't walk away now. Not with everyone watching me."

"Who cares about everyone else? You're gonna get hurt. Just wait for Hawk and—"

"No way," I snapped, almost too quickly. "I started this and I'll finish it. Any more advice?"

He shook his head. "You're not using your speed to your advantage. She's big and tough, but you're quick. That might give you a head start. And look for weaknesses. Anything that can give you an advantage."

"Great. What are her weaknesses?"

"I don't think she has any, but typicals are nose, throat, jaw, groin, thumbs, ears, and knees."

"Got it."

I shook my body out. Tension rose in my shoulders from my fall, but I wouldn't know the full extent of that pain until morning, and right now it didn't matter. Hawk already thought I was weak. I knew it from how he'd looked at me today. I was damaged. Breakable.

"You're tougher or dumber than I think, aren't ya?" Red said as I came back to face her again.

I didn't respond. Instead, I took my stance, one foot in front of the other. Arms up and ready. This was just like the archery range. Red was another target. I never quit until I hit my target.

I swung. Missed. She swung. I backed up. She tried again. I pivoted less than inches to safety.

"There ya go." Red's lips bent in a smirk.

Finally. Getting somewhere. Then, *smack.*

Her hand landed right in the middle of my fresh bruise. Pain blasted through my cheek and seared behind my eyes. Something in my brain clicked. The sensation replaying every time I'd been hit before. Every. Single. Time. Replaying in a vicious loop. A blur of red, purple, and pain.

I pulled back and let loose with everything I had. Red's fingers clenched my arm. With a grunt, I pulled down hard and broke free of her grip, twisting sharply to replace her hold on me with my own on her. She tried to retract, but I moved faster, grabbing her wrist and reefing her arm behind her back. She growled deep as I pulled her arm higher, but she spun around me, wrapping her free arm around my chest, pinning my arms to my sides.

"Almost had me," Red rasped in my ear.

Stepping back, I bent forward and swiped my legs against the backs of her knees.

I wriggled out of her arms and let her fall to the ground with a thud. The watchers howled around us.

I stepped up beside her, fighting the urge to give her one last hit like she'd done to me. "Looks like I've got it now."

"Nope." She grabbed my leg and twisted it until I crashed down beside her on the concrete. "Never stop 'til you're safe."

"Why you wi—"

"Enough." Hawk appeared in the circle.

Muffled scuffling surrounded us as most of the onlookers scattered like rats back into the depths of the shipyards.

Hawk's shadow, tall and dark, loomed over us lying on the ground. "What's going on here?"

Red grabbed her knee and rolled herself back up to standing. "Teachin' the girl to fight."

"And why exactly?"

I jumped to my feet, pain shooting through my limbs, but I fought to hide it. "Because I told her to. You have a problem with that?"

In that moment, it's possible he might've exploded. Something inside him looked like it'd snapped and you could see it seething to get out, clawing and pulling on his muscles, but he managed to hold it back. My throat went dry, wiped clean with fear and regret, but it wasn't enough to stop me.

I put my hands on my hips, the broken skin on my palms stinging against the fabric of my shirt. "So do you?"

He marched toward me, his arms crossed behind his back, his eyes glued to my skull. I stared right back, barely able to see the flames creeping up his neck.

"Mercury. Inside and clean the infirmary floor, now." He scanned the crowd of bystanders and then flipped me a disgusted look, his face hardening as his eyes landed on mine. "By hand."

A collective groan, coupled with a few breathy whistles, erupted behind me.

His eyes burned, streaks of lightning striking in his stare.

Part of me ached to apologize, but another part, likely the one that got me in this mess, didn't give a crap.

"Fine." I stomped past him, hurling my shoulder into his and throwing him off balance for only the briefest moment.

SCRUBBING THE FLOOR. What kind of torture was this? Try to break me by giving me some menial task? Make the rich girl do some hard work for a change? I guess that's where they were wrong. All of them. I'd been in a lot grungier places than this and worked way harder than I would need to scrub a room this size. Joke's on them. I'd make this the cleanest floor they'd ever seen.

Starting in the corner, I took the scrub brush and made a few circles on the cheap linoleum. Dust and dirt darkened the water, but fortunately the dingy yellow coat had started to wear away to reveal an equally uninspiring off-white. That wasn't so hard. I'd show them.

Time passed. Shadows moved across the floor as the sun floated over the small skylight in the middle of the ceiling. With each arm stroke I'd gone back and forth between hating everyone and feeling terrible about how I'd acted, then every other color of confused in between. Fortunately, the manual labor wore down some of my fight. Unfortunately, I'd only finished half the room.

At the foot of one of the military-style beds, a dark brownish stain marked the floor. I gagged thinking about what disgusting human fluid might've caused it, but convinced myself it was just dirt so I wouldn't have to clean up my own vomit as well. After spraying some extra soap directly on the spot, I scrubbed at it, but it stayed as dark and dirty as when I started.

Stupid stain. Stupid floor scrubbing. I should be out there, doing something important, not in here, not like this.

I scrubbed harder and harder, but the stain wouldn't come out. I growled under my breath and fell back on my butt, not caring that the wet floor would soak through my designer leggings in about ten seconds. I wiped the back of my arm across my forehead and moved the stray hairs that had fallen in my face. My knees and shoulders ached from crawling around on the floor and being smashed into the concrete. My knuckles burned from the one good punch I actually landed. I spread my fingers and stretched my hand out in my lap. No marks, but definitely swollen.

This was ridiculous. I'd been in this room for what felt like hours serving out some punishment that I didn't even deserve—or maybe I did—from someone who had absolutely no authority in my life—but it felt like he did. *I could leave. I should leave.* But where would I go? Home, so I could creep around under my father's nose? That would only piss him off more, and I'd be grateful he'd only slapped me last night. Maybe I could take off again. I never did make it to the ocean last time. I'd always liked the ocean.

I leaned forward and scratched my fingernail across the stain. Not even a flake came off. I grabbed the brush and chucked it across the floor, leaving a wet, soapy streak across the grungy worn-out tile. Just before it crashed into the far wall, a black boot slammed down on top, pushing the bristles out into awkward directions. I followed the boot up its leg to the owner with my eyes, still refusing to raise my head and face whoever had come to mock me.

"What the hell are you doing?" Hawk said, far too calmly. I would've preferred yelling.

"Scrubbing the floor, as instructed." I smoothed my hair back over my ears and sat up as straight as I could for being hunched over on a floor. I wouldn't let him get to me. No one had that privilege.

"I meant out there." He pointed to the outside wall, as if I was incapable of following his line of conversation. "I'd really thought you were above petty yard fights."

"Me? She's the one who didn't fight fair."

"I don't mean that. I mean making a scene in front of everyone and then lipping off at me. I've spent way too much time building their respect to have you come in here and undermine me in front of them."

I had no response. It felt like the perfect thing to do at the time, freeing, but facing him with no one around, it suddenly didn't. But admitting that out loud wasn't going to happen.

"What were you doing going up against Red anyway?"

"I need to learn how to defend myself. I can't go walking around being a liability to everyone, now can I?"

"Doesn't explain why you didn't ask someone else. Tucker, Ratchett, even me. I would've helped you without smashing you into the ground."

"I won't be any help to you if I can't beat the best. Red's the toughest one here. I needed to take her on."

"Take her on? You don't even sound like yourself right now."

"Maybe I don't want to be myself. Maybe I want to forget who I am and just be someone who does something for other people. Maybe I don't want to be the outsider. I want to be all-in."

"All-in? This isn't a gang. We don't beat people up to prove they're worthy. If that's what you think, you should probably leave."

I pushed myself up, my limbs searing in pain worse than I tried to let on, and headed toward the door, taking one last look at Hawk as I passed. His face wasn't angry. I wanted him to be angry. Angry I could deal with. Instead, he gave me this look that made me think everything might be okay, even when I knew it wouldn't be. False hope and sympathy would only mess with my head. Why couldn't he just turn away like everyone else in my life?

"I know it's not a gang. I just ... I...." Swirls of doubt swept through my brain. I didn't really want to leave. That was the only thing I knew for sure. "Forget it. You don't understand what it's like."

He let out a heavy sigh. "So this is about what happened last night."

"Why would you say that? Can't I just want to be a part of something?"

"I don't blame you, but trying to take out your frustration on someone who could probably kill you with their bare hands is not the way to make yourself feel better."

"Then what am I supposed to do to feel better?"

He looked down, his silence answering me far more than any words could.

"Yeah, I haven't figure it out either."

"Why don't you tell someone?"

"I wanted to. I thought about it lots of times, but how do you turn the king in to the castle guard? You can't. Even if someone actually believed me, there isn't much they can do without sacrificing themselves."

"I would." He stared at me with conviction like he might actually be telling the truth.

"Thanks. But I think you've got enough reasons for my father to hate you without taking on my cause too."

"Then leave. You don't need to stay there and let him keep hurting you."

"Don't you think I've tried? Every time he hits me, I run

away, and every time I do, he drags me back. I won't be able to escape until he lets me."

"There's a difference between running away and making the decision to leave."

I crossed my arms and jutted out my hip. "Sounds like the same thing to me."

"Running away shows fear. Leaving requires strength. They're different."

The door creaked open. Ratchett poked his head inside and twitched when his face came close to mine. I backed away a few steps, but he didn't relax, his gaze darting from Hawk to me and back again.

"I found something. You need to see this," he said and retreated into the drama-free safety of the main room.

"I should go see what he wants," Hawk said. "You're welcome to stay if you still want to."

I nodded, the desire to keep arguing finally disappearing.

I turned around and reached for the doorknob, but Hawk grabbed my arm and tugged me back. Instinct tried to shake him off, but he was too strong, too determined, and from the look on his face, I knew he wouldn't try to hurt me.

"Don't go around trying to self-destruct, Mercury. I've been there. It's not worth it."

"And what happens if I do?"

"I won't let you." His grip relaxed on my bicep, his stormy eyes calm and clear like June blue skies. "I promise."

TWENTY-ONE

All that sparring and scrubbing had left me starving. I could've crept down to the kitchen, but figured I'd try the casual dining room so to avoid drawing too much attention to myself. Hopefully there should be cereal or something still from breakfast.

I'm sure I looked like hell after what I'd been through. I probably should've showered first, a damp layer of sweat gluing my clothes to my skin, but my stomach rumbled with a hunger so fierce my knees would've buckled and I'd have cracked my head open on the tile floor. Besides, I didn't have time for a run to the emergency room right now. I needed to get fed and get back to the Sanctuary before five o'clock or everyone would leave without me.

I stepped around the corner and stopped so fast I almost fell the rest of the way into the room. Mom and Christophe sat at the table talking in hushed voices, quiet enough that I hadn't heard them from the hallway. *Dammit.* They both looked toward the door and I ducked back into the hall, hoping they didn't notice me.

Heavy footsteps echoed on the other side of the wall. I turned to run.

"Mercury," Christophe called from behind me.

I froze midstride and exhaled. *Busted.*

"I didn't mean to disturb your conversation. I'll just come back later."

"Don't worry, it wasn't anything important anyway." He closed the gap between us, forcing me to face him. "What happened to you?"

My stomach clenched as I tried to look myself over without being too obvious. Did I still have gravel in my hair? "What do you mean?"

"The huge bruise on your face. Are you okay?"

I reached up and rubbed my cheek, the dull pain so minimal compared to getting my butt kicked by Red all day, I'd actually forgotten. I glanced around looking for inspiration, but the wallpaper and his charcoal suit jacket weren't providing any. "Punching bag. I was in the gym and it swung back and nailed me in the face."

He looked me over, his eyes serious, likely seeing through the weakest excuse I'd ever used. Then he laughed.

"You got hit by a punching bag. Since when are you into boxing?"

"It works for you, so I thought I'd give it a shot. Never know when it might come in handy one day." I put up my fists, giving him an awkward smile and a punch in the shoulder.

He laughed again and shook his head, amused. "All right, whatever you say. But next time call me first and I'll spot you." He reached up and ran his knuckles the length of the bruise, his skin hovering just above mine so I could feel his fingers without him actually touching me. "I don't like seeing you hurt."

"Thanks. But I'll be all right." How many times would I need to say that today? "But I'm sure you've got important business to attend to."

"I do, actually, and you should probably get in there since your mom saw you lurking in the doorway."

I groaned.

"Take it easy on her, okay? I know you guys don't always get along, but she's not feeling well."

"Sure." Being sick probably meant that she was crankier than normal. I didn't have the energy for that today.

He headed off down the hallway and turned back one last time with a wink. "And I'm serious. If you ever need me, just call."

I took a deep breath and considered walking away, but my stomach started making angry gurgling sounds. Hunger mixed with dread—a painful combination.

Mom stared at the wall as I walked in, a delicate teacup clutched in both her hands, inches from her lips. I glanced over at the wall. Nothing of interest, but apparently to her it was fascinating. I grabbed an apple from a bowl on the credenza and a box of oat cereal, then pulled up a chair across from her.

Midafternoon and she was still dressed in a lavender silk robe, her hair hanging in soft waves around her face. Honey and chamomile rolled off her skin and I let myself breathe it in for just a second, letting it spark the happy synapses in my memory. The edge of a bruise peeked out of her sleeve. She caught me staring and pulled the fabric into her fist and laid her arms on the table.

"The least you could do is try to cover up that unsightly mark on your face."

It came out so flat I wasn't sure if I should be offended or not.

"I tried, but apparently there isn't a makeup good enough. Maybe tell him to keep to inconspicuous places if he's going to leave bruises." I shoveled a spoonful of cereal in my mouth and reveled in how fantastic it felt landing in my stomach. "Or is that a privilege reserved for you alone?"

Her beautiful face twisted in disgust, her eyes narrowed to ugly, angry slits. "I'm tired of defending you. You have no appreciation for the amount of suffering I have to put up with for you."

It stung, deep in my muscles, like a dark black acid from my stomach trying to burn its way out through my skin. Of course I understood. I'd been on the other side of a hit too many times not to understand, but it didn't mean I couldn't still be pissed about it. "I'm sorry. I didn't realize this was all my fault."

Her hardened look softened a bit. The edges of her eyes crinkled in spite of the fortune of anti-aging treatments she'd had over the years. She didn't say anything, just watched me eat my cereal, watching her. Two different sides of the same problem, but neither of us had any idea what to do or say to make it better.

"It's only a matter of time before he goes after Matty," I said, finally breaking the awkward silence. "If he hasn't already."

She scoffed. "Mattias is just a child. He doesn't evoke the same sort of anger in him that you do."

"I was thirteen the first time Dad put me in the hospital. Was I not still a child then?"

She leaned back in her chair and drummed her perfectly polished fingertips on the tabletop, the hand-shaped bruise on her forearm completely exposed. Then, as if someone closed the blinds in her retinas, her stare went blank and shifted to the crown molding. "You've always been difficult."

I shook my head, snatched up the apple, and walked out.

TWENTY-TWO

"Is this wig really necessary?" I rubbed the mass of fake blond hair against my head, begging for the itching to stop. Even the cushion of my real hair between it and my scalp didn't help. Maybe I was allergic to it or something? Or maybe Red gave this one to me on purpose to see how much I could take before I went insane?

"Coulda stayed behind, Princess," Red said as she marched down the street, the rest of us struggling to keep up with her determined stride.

I considered arguing but bit my tongue instead. I wasn't going to miss out on this, even if it meant being uncomfortable and looking ridiculous.

Tucker leaned over and flipped some of the bleached strands over my shoulder. "I like it. Makes you look kind of edgy."

"Thanks, but I think this look is on an as-needed basis only."

And tonight was one of those as-needed times. While searching through The Five's computer system, under deep layers of confusing techno-speak security, Ratchett had found a list of addresses, each one cross-referenced by a date. Every address related to a different shelter or soup kitchen somewhere in the city, and although most of the dates had already passed, two addresses still remained on the list—tonight and next Tuesday. It didn't seem like much to me, but according to Ratchett, that was the problem. Why would someone hide an address directory unless they didn't want anyone to find it? And therefore, based on vigilante logic, if someone went through that much trouble to hide a list of addresses, they definitely all needed to be checked out.

So fifteen groups were hitting up fifteen different locations to see what might be lurking in the soup kitchen shadows. Hawk, of course, picked the location relating to today's date, then assigned Red, Tucker, myself, and some stocky guy named Duke to his team. He probably just wanted to make sure I didn't cause any more trouble today, which normally would've pissed me off, but heading into the unknown felt a lot better with him in arm's reach. Or more accurately, having Hawk within fingers' reach considering how close he walked beside me, I wouldn't need more than an inch to touch him, a fact that hadn't gone unnoticed based on the hammering pulse throbbing in my ears.

The only problem, however, with super-secret undertakings was they required a level of super-secret discretion, which required me to go in disguise and in the world's most impossible, completely hideous glasses and a platinum-blond wig. A horrible style combination I think they used to call hipster.

"Okay, maybe this really isn't your look. Plus, bangs don't really work for you," Tucker continued as we turned what I hoped would be the last of a million corners.

"Thanks a lot," I replied and nudged him in the shoulder.

He laughed and shoved me back, knocking me into Hawk for a brief moment until I regained my balance.

"Stop screwin' around," Red hissed. "We're here. Don't be causing a scene and gettin' us all noticed."

I straightened up and read the sign above the door. The Sunshine Community Mission was anything but sunny. A squat yellow building tagged with every color of an angsty rainbow and more boarded-up windows than stable ones. A tall man, who looked like he'd been on the losing side of a knife fight, stood with his arms crossed by the door. Some of the places we'd been before seemed rough, but this one felt like it might actually bite me if I tried to go inside.

As if reading my mind and outright defying it, Red marched up to the door, nodded at the scary doorman, and walked in, Hawk and Duke following close behind. I took a deep breath and shook out my hands, bracing myself for what I might be getting into, and started toward the door. A few feet away, I stopped and looked back. Tucker still stood on the sidewalk, staring up at the sky.

"Coming, Tucker?" I asked, part of me hoping he might be as unsure of this place as I was.

He didn't answer.

I jogged back the few steps and linked my arm with his. "Tucker. Everything okay?"

He looked over at me, his eyes empty and cold.

"Tucker?"

He flinched, then shook his head, the life coming back into his face. "Sorry, what?"

"Are you okay?"

"Yeah, fine. Now let's get this thing done so we can go somewhere a little less serial-killer chic."

I chuckled. "I know, right?"

Tucker's arm flexed around mine and he winked, giving me the little boost I needed to pull this off.

I straightened my dark-rimmed fake glasses and pulled the wig back into place. "All right then, let's go."

Only slightly more cheerful than the outside, the inside

seemed to try a little harder. Walls painted in icy shades of blue advertised hope through brightly colored signs with lame slogans trying desperately hard to be funny. Most weren't. A long line of tables where hair-netted staff served unrecognizable food with large metal spoons, blocked off what looked to be a large kitchen toward the back. Along a far wall, two doors speckled with chipped yellow paint—men's and women's— flanked a short hallway with a glowing Exit sign. Clusters of tables and people gathered in the center, way more people than I would've guessed, but fortunately the building stretched bigger than I would've thought from the outside. My perception must be a little off today.

Tucker yanked on my arm and pulled me toward the corner where the others stood watching the patrons, while trying hard to make sure they weren't caught staring. I doubted anyone around here wanted to be stared at.

"What exactly are we looking for?" Duke asked as we approached.

"Not really sure. Just anything that might be suspicious." Hawk took a quick scan of the room again. "If The Five picked this place for something, there has to be a reason."

"Demolition maybe?" Tucker suggested and received a side-eye from Hawk.

"Well that guy looks weird," Duke said, pointing to someone over by the bathrooms.

I rose onto my tiptoes to see him easier over all the heads in the room. The guy was big. Big arms, big shoulders, big tree-like legs and an all-black baseball cap pulled low enough to cover everything but his big square chin. He may have been trying to look inconspicuous, but he stood in a solid, commanding way that said otherwise. But the odd way he scribbled in a small black notebook seemed more suspicious than how he looked. He would write quickly, then look up for something or someone I couldn't tell, then scribble again. The same pattern over and over.

"Maybe we should split up," Hawk suggested. "I'll try to get closer to the guy over there and see what he's writing. Might just be some eccentric street poet, but you never know. Tell me immediately if you see anything else."

I wandered through the groups of people. One haunted face after another, but nothing looked out of the ordinary. Problem was, I didn't know what ordinary looked like in a place like this. I'd started getting used to seeing this side of society, but it didn't make it any easier. The more I understood, the worse I felt and the harder it became to ignore. The most sickening part, the part that pricked at the top of my spine, knew that who I was and where I came from was at least partially to blame.

I glanced over at Tucker and Duke chatting up some girl in camo by one of the intact windows and Red being Red, circling the room like a shark. I guess they hadn't found anything yet either.

Ow! My shoulder jolted backward as I pass too close to a guy with arms made of granite. I kept my head down and grabbed the sore spot, karma for getting lost in my own head instead of staying on task.

"Sorry," I mumbled, staring at the floor and his thick black military-style boots sticking out of a dirty pair of dark-washed jeans.

"Don't worry, my fault."

My limbs went rigid. That voice. I whipped my head up. Him. The guard who got in trouble for letting me into my father's office. The one from the Full Moon who'd ratted me out. By now I should've really made a point of learning his name; that way I could curse the right guy for constantly invading my life.

"Thanks," I said and moved to go around him. He bobbed, I

weaved, an all too familiar dance between us, and this time it didn't feel any better.

Finally, I managed to maneuver around him and darted across the room as quick as I could. What was he doing here? Did my father actually fire him and things had gotten so bad that he ended up in a place like this? Guilt crept in. Was this all my fault? Fortunately, he didn't seem to recognize me. I guess this stupid wig wasn't a dumb idea. I leaned against the wall and kept my focus on the guard, trying to figure out what went wrong. He mostly kept his head down, walking around tables of people, barely bothering to glance at them. More than once, my feet started to march me over to apologize for getting him fired, but my brain would eventually tell them to stop, and I would retreat back to my wall. When I'd convinced myself he had come here alone, the guard approached another guy, a little shorter, a lot broader, and seemed to have an intense conversation. I looked the new guy over. Nothing significant about him, except when I looked toward the floor and saw the same black boots. Not just similar, the exact same cut and style as the hazel-eyed guard.

Curious, I scanned through the room. One, two, three ... eight, nine, ten. Ten sets of identical black boots. This couldn't be a coincidence. There were at least ten guards in this room trying their hardest not to look like guards. I glanced over at the guy with the notebook still standing by the bathrooms. Another pair of black boots. Something was happening. Something bad. And we were very outnumbered. We needed to get out of here —fast. I pushed through a bunch of annoyed people until I found Hawk lurking in the corner near Notebook Guy.

"We need to go." My eyes darted around the room, expecting someone to be watching our conversation, but it didn't seem like it. "Like now."

"What's the problem?"

"It's the guard, the one who tried to keep us out of the office the other night. He's here with about ten of his friends."

Hawk ran his hand over his chin and clutched at his throat. "Are you sure?"

I nodded.

"Did he recognize you?"

"No, he didn't seem—" A terrible thought clicked in my head. "But he would recognize you. If he catches you here, he'll know something's up. You need to get out of here before he sees you."

"What if he's already seen me? Maybe I can get him to tell me why they're all here."

"And then what? Beg him not to turn you over to the cops, or worse, bring you straight to The Five?" I looked around again, trying to find a solution, my stomach twisting into quadruple knots. "You sneak out the back door and I'll tell the others we need to go."

"But I didn't find out what that guy was writing in that book yet."

"Trust me, he's a guard. You won't be able to get close."

"Which is exactly why I need to."

I crossed my arms and gritted my teeth. "Do I need to drag you out of here myself? We are outmatched. Staying is suicide."

"Fine. But you shouldn't wait around here either. As soon as I'm gone, you guys need to leave too."

"Deal. Now go."

He leaned forward and whispered in my ear, "Thanks."

Staying close to the wall, Hawk walked around the room toward the small hallway with the Exit sign, each step making it easier for me to breathe. If the guard had seen him, it would've been a complete disaster, but now we could get away without being noticed.

Except it was too late. Just as Hawk neared the exit, the

hazel-eyed guard stormed off in Hawk's direction. The guard's brow clenched and determined. My pulse pounded loud in my head. I had to stop him. If the guard recognized Hawk and word got back to my father, I wouldn't be able to get out of exposing everything without the world's most elaborate lie or a trip to the emergency room. Tucker loitered over by the door with Duke, too far to help, but Red, she was in the perfect spot.

"There you are, you boyfriend-stealing skank," I shouted as loud as I could, then charged through the crowd at her.

Confusion soured her face, but it quickly turned from wide-eyed surprise to venomous rage when my hands connected with her chest and pushed her with every ounce of strength I had. Her body soared backward, her arms and legs flailing, the lack of warning giving my shove an edge. She fell into a crowd of grumbling people, knocking over the guard chasing after Hawk. *Bullseye.* Bodies teetered and tripped out of the way, pushing more people over in the fallout. A woman lost her balance and leveled the guard by the bathrooms. His little notebook flew from his hand and sailed across the dirty, cracked linoleum into the far corner, his pen splashing into someone's soup.

"What the hell? Have ya not had enough today?" Red scrambled to her feet, every single head in the room tuned in to us.

I took a quick glance at the exit. Hawk had escaped, but every minute I could spare him would be vital.

"You heard me. You ... you...." Insults usually came to me easily when I thought of Red, but the captive audience threw me off and made my brain malfunction. "Hussy."

I wanted to crawl into a hole and die. Hussy? That's all I could come up with? This was officially the worst fake fight in the history of the world. If I survived the beatdown Red would give me for all this, maybe I could get her to help me up my insult game.

Red snorted. "Really? Did someone slip ya sumthin' toxic? 'Cause you're on one bad trip, girl."

She lunged at me, but two guards grabbed her arms and held her back. Interesting. If I ever doubted they were actually undercover, this proved it.

"We don't want any violence in here," one of the men at her bicep warned. "Can it or leave."

She jutted her chin at him, but he didn't back down. "Okay, jackass, just get your hands off me. She started it."

The two men let go but stayed close beside her.

Dammit. Getting kicked out would be so much easier than sneaking off, especially now. I considered running at her again and making sure we all got escorted out, but too many guards surrounded her to make a decent attempt.

Instead, I put my hands on my hips and used my next best weapon. "That's right. You and your annoying friends should just *run* off and get out of here. I really think you need to go."

"Us? Didja hit your head? We ain't got no reason to—"

Red looked left, then right, then back at me again, my eyes wide and screaming at her to get the message. Her eyes swelled back. Transmission received.

"Let's go, Tuck. She ain't worth our sweat."

She marched across the room and yanked Tucker's arm gruffly, pushing him toward the door. She nodded at Duke, then toward the exit. He hesitated, then followed behind her.

Tucker tried to pull out of her grasp and get around her, watching me over her shoulder. "What the hell, Red? We can't just leave her here. Besides, where's—"

"Enough," she barked at him. "Time to go."

"Since when did you become a bigger psycho than you already are? Let me go." Tucker pulled his arm up and then jammed it back down, breaking himself loose.

Red lunged for him again. The entire room shifted to watch,

the circle of guards closing in around them. I stepped backward slowly, letting everyone rush past until I'd tiptoed to the far wall and beside the black notebook in the corner. This wasn't part of the plan, but I'd take advantage of the added bonus. I slid down the wall, reaching down without looking until my fingers brushed the plastic cover. I slipped the book into my back pocket and stood up as inconspicuous as possible. Perfect. Now I just had to sneak out the back way and we'd all be home free.

I'd turned to go when Red's head snapped back toward me and nodded. Every set of guard's eyes looked too. Why did she suddenly start caring about me now?

The big guard in the black cap pointed a massive arm in my direction. "Stop her."

I put my head down and ran.

TWENTY-THREE

The loud bang of the door busting open and smashing against the outside wall echoed behind me only seconds after I turned the corner onto the street. I'd jammed my fake glasses in the door latch, buying me about thirty extra seconds, but the horrible wig flew off during my escape, leaving me completely exposed. Hopefully the guard chasing me wouldn't know which way I went. He had a fifty-fifty chance between being on my tail and giving me a clean getaway. Unfortunately, I couldn't risk waiting around to see what he'd chosen.

I'd already wasted time taking the long back way out of the alley instead of the shorter three feet to the front of the building. Everyone assumed people would take the easy way out, right? I hoped so. I'd just bet my entire escape on it.

I kept my feet moving, daring to look back once and almost tripping over a piece of broken sidewalk. I ran across the road. A car screeched as it slammed on its brakes, nearly flattening me, but I ignored it and ran faster.

"Stop," a deep voice yelled from behind.

I glanced over my shoulder. The guard had made the right choice, and he'd brought a friend.

They were still a distance back, but they'd soon catch up. This main street left me too visible, too vulnerable. Three blocks down I sidestepped between two buildings into an open alleyway. Every turn I took decreased the probability of being caught. Each option another game of chance. I ran to the end and turned left.

Wrong turn.

At the end of the alleyway—a dumpster, two fighting cats, and a wrought-iron fence. The fence stretched only about twelve feet, but it might as well have reached up to the sky since I'd never be able to climb over it, even with a running start. I looked back. No time to change direction.

I grabbed the side of the dumpster and pulled myself up. It would be a huge jump from here to the fence, but at least I might be high enough to get my hands on the top to pull myself over. I lined up for the biggest leap I'd ever made. Deep breath. Bent knees.

Wait. I stopped mid-start and nearly crashed back down to the concrete. Behind the fence wasn't freedom, but a bigger trap. A courtyard with three brick walls and no way out but through the building on the far side. A building with a giant metal door and a keypad on the wall.

For this to work, the door had to actually be unlocked, and I needed to slip through the building completely unnoticed. Chance of that happening—none, maybe less than none.

My pulse throbbed in my ears, and the nasty smell of rotting garbage mixed with my desperation stung my nostrils. Only one other choice.

I reached down and pulled up one side of the dumpster lid. A science class of bugs swarmed past my face as the true stench of human waste punched me in the gut. I shook off the dizzy feeling and swallowed. *It's this or get caught.*

"Hey," a voice called.

Too late. The lid fell from my hand and slammed back down.

An arm appeared above my head, hanging from the roof. I bit my lip so I wouldn't scream and backed against the wall.

"Up here," the voice said from above. "Quick."

Hawk's face peeked over the side of the roof, and my stomach fell back down into my abdomen. Never had I been more excited to see that set of blue eyes staring at me.

I grabbed his hand, and he managed to pull me high enough that I could wrap my other hand around the edge. Pushing my feet against the wall and Hawk pulling me with all his strength, I clambered over the side.

"Stay down," he said, as he lay on his stomach facing the alley.

I lay down beside him, watching the last light of day die in a hard red line behind a neighboring rooftop, the heat of it still holding in the concrete burning my belly through my clothes. The cats growled. Footsteps pounded close. My heart pounded harder.

The two guards appeared in the alley. They stopped halfway down, surveying everything. I cringed and pulled myself back from the edge. One of the guards launched himself at the dumpster. The metal boomed loud and echoed through my bones as he scaled up over the side and stood on the top, right where I'd been less than two minutes before. Seven feet down stood the end of us.

My breath came in short bursts. I clamped my palm over my mouth to hold it in, or at least slow it down. Hawk rolled closer to me and took my other hand, gripping it tight.

"It'll be okay," he whispered in my ear so quietly I wasn't sure if he'd even said anything out loud or if I'd simply felt the words flit across my skin.

"She couldn't have jumped. There's no way out over there,"

the guard on the dumpster yelled to his buddy, his voice far too close.

Metal rumbled under the guard's boots. Back and forth. Pacing.

Fingers popped up on the edge of the roof. Thick fingers with bulging knuckles and a crooked black star tattoo. I started to shimmy back, but Hawk squeezed my hand and shook his head.

What was he doing? We needed to get out of here. We needed to—

"We're chasing a girl, not a damn monkey. She probably went the other way," the second guard yelled from farther down the alley.

"I swear I heard noise coming from this dumpster. I know she came this way," the first guard responded.

"Then get down, check inside it, and let's go. I still have to go back and look for my book. My job will be on the line if I don't find it."

The fingers disappeared, followed by a metal bang. More footsteps and the creak of the lid opening.

"If she's in here, the smell probably would've killed her by now. I think I'm going to puke."

"See. You probably heard those mangy cats. Let's get out of here."

Two sets of footsteps faded into the distance. My lungs started breathing again.

Neither of us moved. We just lay there, still, listening to the noisy clamor of the city at nightfall. The dark, a blanket weighing heavy on our backs. The rush of the chase had drained from my body, but my mind still ran in circles at full speed. What were all those guards doing at an inner-city shelter? What would have happened to me if I'd been caught? Why was Hawk still holding my hand?

As if hearing the question in my thoughts, Hawk let go and pushed himself up to sit cross-legged beside me. "I think it's okay to move now."

I curled my hand into a fist and then flexed it wide, my skin feeling odd after being held so tight for so long. Now my hand just felt empty.

"What were you doing up here? I thought you'd be halfway back to the Sanctuary by the time I left," I said as I sat in front of him, a mirror, our knees less than an inch apart.

"You can see the shelter from the other side of this roof, and I wanted to stay close in case there was any trouble. That's how I knew you were coming this way and that you were being followed."

"I knew I was being followed."

"I hope so." He smiled, his white teeth making a line across his face in the dark. "Were you seriously going to hide in the dumpster?"

I nodded.

"Impressive."

A car horn honked, loud and close. I flinched, my head wobbling toward the sound. Hawk put his hand on my leg and grounded me again. I looked at him. He pulled his hand away.

"I'm sorry," I said, the words tumbling out of my mouth before I realized I was saying them.

His eyebrows furrowed, his stare laser-sharp. "For what?"

"For earlier today. I never really apologized."

"I understand. You don't have to."

"Yeah, I do." I dropped my head to stare into my lap and watch my hands as I linked and twisted my fingers around each other. "You need to know I'm not some selfish spoiled brat."

Silence fell over us as he processed my words and I bit down on the inside of my cheek for being foolish enough to say them out loud.

He let out a deep, throaty scoff. "Of course you're not. You're stubborn, reckless, and fight me on every single thing I tell you to do."

Great. It was worse than I thought.

"And you're smart, and brave, and I just saw you risk yourself on the chance that I might be recognized and saving my ass for the second time since I've met you."

"Third," I mumbled into my chest.

"What?"

"It's the third time I've saved your ass since we met."

I looked up, and a small gasp caught in my throat. Hawk had leaned toward me, much closer than I'd expected. So close I could see the tiny L-shaped scar on his chin where stubble wouldn't grow and breathe in the smell of him as it rolled off his skin, sweet and clean.

"Okay, three times, then," he said, glancing down and laughing, still so close. So dangerously close.

The air between us hummed. A sound I could feel. Bass notes playing on my eardrums and vibrating through my chest. Music, pulsating and hungry.

We locked stares, the familiar midnight-blue storm raging in his eyes again, and I held on as if I'd shatter if he looked away. He grabbed a piece of my hair and twirled it in his fingers. I swallowed.

"Hey, guys, all clear."

I jumped and let out of a pathetic yelp as Tucker bounded up beside us, out of breath and dripping sweat from his forehead.

"What are you doing here?" I blurted out.

"Hawk texted me to come get you when everyone was safe."

"Yeah, thanks, man," Hawk said, as Tucker gave him an arm and pulled him up off the ground. "Where are the others?"

"Red and Duke are waiting on the ground for us."

Hawk nodded and extended his hand to me, but I ignored it and pushed myself up on my own. He frowned. I steadied myself on my feet and followed Tucker back toward the far side of the roof, leaving Hawk behind me, the music fading out with every single step.

AFTER A NIGHT LIKE THIS ONE, seeing the dingy sprawling warehouse appear from behind the rows of rusty shipping containers felt more like coming home than returning to the penthouse after any of my self-directed vacations. A fuzzy yellow haze hovered over the infirmary skylight, like a secret beacon only those who knew about could follow.

I picked up my pace, heading toward the light and wanting nothing more than to be inside. Tucker opened the door and filed in, Duke and Hawk trailing behind. I followed, but maybe too closely, as the door slammed shut, almost taking off the top half of my foot.

"We're not done yet," Red said as she inserted herself between me and the door, a thick arm making sure it stayed closed.

I backed up. Whatever she had to say would probably end with me on the ground, so at least I could try to get a head start.

"Whatcha did back there," she said, matching my every step backward with a more aggressive one forward. "Ya did good."

I stopped, pretty certain I must've hit my head on the slamming door. "Really?"

She nodded, likely not wanting to taste another compliment in her mouth.

"Thanks. I would've warned you, but there wasn't enough time. Plus, I—"

She raised her hands and shook her head. "We're not friends. I just don't hate ya as much as this morning."

She opened the door and tweaked her head toward the inside. I let out the breath that had been trapped in my throat and marched forward. She jutted her hip in front of me before I could enter and stuck her pointed finger in my face.

"Do it again, I'll wear your kidneys for earrings."

I nodded, not doubting for a second that she wouldn't literally do that to someone, then hurried in with her nipping at my heels.

It looked like we were the last to return, everyone else standing in their assigned groups around the room as if we were picking teams for volleyball. I sidestepped around, weaving between the double-R creepy twins and a few of the others to stand with Duke and Ratchett.

Hawk paced in front of everyone, hands folded behind his back, recounting the story of the guards and the grand escape.

I leaned into Ratchett. "What did I miss?"

"Nothing," he whispered. "You're the only group who saw anything."

"—so what we need to find out is why there were over ten guards in disguise at this location. We'll need to talk to people who were there, people who know people who were there, and see if anyone saw anything unusual. We also need to see if we can find anyone who was at the other locations on any of the other dates." Hawk stopped walking and faced the crowd. "Make sense?"

Everyone nodded and agreed in a mumble.

"And if anyone hears anything about a guard with a black book, let me know."

Right! I slid the book out of my pocket and held it up. "You mean this black book?"

Hawk's jaw dropped and he rushed over, taking the book from me. "How did you? And you're just telling me now?"

I shrugged. "Sorry. I guess I forgot."

He smiled and shook his head, his eyes circling up to the ceiling. "Four times."

A familiar flutter tickled through my chest and warmed my cheeks.

Hawk returned to center stage and flipped through the pages, his index finger scanning down the center of every one.

"It's a list of names. Pages and pages of names."

"Do you recognize any of them?" Duke said.

Hawk's eyes stayed locked on the book. "Kind of. Not really. Maybe we can pass it around and see if anyone knows anyone listed."

"I could search all of them through The Five's network and see if there are any hits on the information, or any other links between them," Ratchett said, putting his hand out to Hawk.

"Good idea. And text a list to everyone so they can look it over." Hawk reached out to give Ratchett the book, but it fell from his hand as a high-pitched noise cut through the air.

A scream. A painful, stomach-twisting scream. One of the twins, her white blond head tipped back in a banshee wail as dark as midnight. I covered my ears. She pointed at Tucker, eyes wide and arm shaking, as blood dripped out of his ear and down the side of his face.

"What's with you?" Tucker said, his face warped with confusion.

The twin whispered in her sister's ear. The other girl gasped, a sound just as terrifying as the scream, then grabbed her sister's hand and pulled her out the door.

"What the hell?" Tucker shook his head and stared after them running out. "They keep getting weird—"

He coughed. Blood covered his hand. "What the?"

Another cough. Deeper. Stronger. More blood.

"Tucker. Are you okay, man?" Hawk called to him.

He didn't answer, his eyes the same blank stare he'd given me earlier tonight outside the shelter.

"Tucker?" Hawk rushed toward him.

"I feel kind of dizzy." Tucker closed his eyes tight and rubbed his forehead. He wavered on his feet and stumbled a few steps before collapsing in the chair behind him.

"Everybody back up," Hawk yelled as he squatted down beside the chair.

"I don't feel right, man." Tucker grabbed the neck of Hawk's sweater, his fingers awkward and limp trying to hang on. "Do you think it's—"

"I don't know. It could be anything. You'll be okay," Hawk said, but the clench in his jaw didn't agree.

"Good." Tucker let go of Hawk and covered his mouth with his hand. Suddenly, he lurched forward in a violent spasm. Blood spewed out between his fingers and across the concrete floor in dark crimson slashes. I gasped and crept backward, my hand clamping over my mouth to keep from screaming.

Ratchett rushed over with a towel. Tucker wiped his hands and stared at the splotches of blood on the cotton, as if they didn't make sense to him. He wrapped his fist in Ratchett's shirt. Ratchett tried to pull away, the fabric stretching between them.

"Where's Rai? I need to talk to Rai," Tucker pleaded, trying to pull Ratchett toward him.

"He's not here," Ratchett said and made a final tug to release himself from Tucker's grip, his face a shade away from puking.

Sweat beaded on Tucker's forehead. He raked his hands through his hair, his arms trembling. And his eyes, far away and desperate. "Tell Rai I need to talk to him."

Ratchett nodded and backed away, a haunted look on his face. "Sure thing."

Everyone stood and watched. A horror movie, but without a screen to save us. My stomach ached. I swayed, shifting weight from foot to foot, knowing he needed help, but not having any idea what to do. My limbs shook. So much blood.

"Everyone out," Hawk shouted.

Bodies scrambled toward the door. Words like X9, *dying*, and *death* rumbled through the crowd. I needed fresh air, my lungs suddenly feeling like they might burst if I didn't get out of here soon.

Hawk shouted again. "Red. Mercury. Wait."

We held up just outside the door, letting everyone else pass in a panic. I rocked back and forth on my feet as Hawk rushed over.

"Red, I need you to go to Iggy's and get a dose of the cure."

"Done." She nodded quick, then ran off, much more composed than me.

"What do you need me to do?" I asked, feeling completely useless.

Hawk looked around, stress creeping into his eyes. "Go with Red. Make sure nothing goes wrong."

He sighed, then closed the door. Three inches of metal separated everyone. Those of us on this side were safe, but those still inside were under attack with no weapon or army strong enough to save them.

TWENTY-FOUR

The night held its breath, leaving us in calm, eerie stillness while it waited for something to happen, the stars too afraid to come out from behind the clouds. Neither Red nor I spoke on the way to St. Ignatius, and even if she did, I'm not sure I would've noticed with Tucker's terrified face scorched into my memory, making my brain cringe.

The streetlight on the corner flickered. On, off, on, off in sporadic bursts of light and dark. It had done the same thing the first time I'd come here, but tonight it seemed even more ominous. On, off, on, off, sending out its message in Morse code, hoping someone would read it. Too bad Morse code wasn't a survival skill they taught at prep school.

"Do you really think Tucker has X9?" I said as we stood on the sidewalk across from the big wooden doors.

Red nodded. "That much blood ain't gonna be anything else."

She kept curling her hands into fists, then fanning her fingers out again, one by one. White knuckles. Black fingernails. White knuckles again.

"Only seen it once before. It's nightmare-type shit. Screws ya up in the head."

The horror she'd seen projected in her eyes under the intermittent streetlights. Her face blanched, white as bone. For once, she looked afraid.

Red caught me watching her and scowled hard, scaring the fear away. Fists tight, she marched across the street and up the stairs while I followed behind with short, quick steps.

The door creaked as she pulled it open, warm light glowing from inside. It was quiet, too quiet, and a musty, unaired smell lingered just past the doorway.

There weren't as many people here as I'd remembered. Hopefully they'd all recovered and moved on, but the unsteady feeling in my stomach wasn't so sure.

"And who's Rai?" I asked as we hurried past the rows of beds.

She didn't turn around. "Tuck's brother. Been gone for six years now."

"Oh." I'd hoped her answer would've made me feel better, but it managed to make the unsteadiness in my stomach worse.

"Well, good evening, girls." Mrs. O'Connell dropped a wet cloth on a freshly washed banquet table at the end of the room and scuttled toward us. "Wasn't expecting company tonight."

"Won't be long," Red replied. "Came for a shot of X9 cure."

Mrs. O'Connell's eyelids drooped, the soft, wobbly skin around them crinkling into sad, worrisome lines. "I see. Which one of you did the devil come for?"

"Tucker." I swallowed hard, trying to bite down the burn of tears from saying his name.

"The poor dear. We're running low, but let me see what we've got."

Mrs. O'Connell scurried away and disappeared through a blue door on the left-side wall. I looked at Red and she looked away, probably trying to avoid any more of my questions. This wasn't the time to push her. Never was really a good time, but now would be definitely one of the worst. I needed to talk. She needed not to.

Instead I leaned against the wall and looked around. Lumps of people covered under thin blankets lined some of the makeshift beds. Others peered at me with dark-rimmed eyes, staring while trying not to stare. It was late, people were tired, we'd disrupted their sleep. I shifted on my feet and readjusted myself against the wall, the heaviness of being watched tight on my lungs.

The front door creaked, and I gulped a breath as the weight slid off me and across the room. A woman walked in and scanned the place, her hand gripped tight on a little boy hiding behind her, his face resting against her lower back. She saw Red and me standing, clearly not patients, and rushed over.

"Excuse me," she said, her voice hushed and wavering. "Can you—"

"Mrs. O's in the back. We're just visiting."

"Okay." The woman backed away from Red, probably getting the warm, fuzzy feeling I got from being around her, and sat on the edge of an empty cot. The little boy, six maybe seven, crawled up beside her and kicked his dangling feet in the air. She looked over at him and smiled, but other than her lips, her expression screamed sadness.

I looked closer at the boy. Pained, sunken eyes and shaking hands, not the way a kid like him should look, at least not a healthy one. He began to cough, his body curling forward as each hack pulsed through his body. The woman ran her hand along his back until he quieted down again. He leaned against her shoulder and shivered.

I looked back at the blue door, hoping Mrs. O'Connell

would come back soon, my legs suddenly restless and wanting to leave. It remained closed.

"Mommy," the little boy called out. "It's happening again."

Blood dripped from his nose. Red droplets falling into his palms in messy, spiky splashes. The woman held his head close to her chest, her face pale as moonlight, the hard line of her lips telling me more than words. She ran her fingers through his hair, brushing it back from his ear where the black crust of dried blood still showed on his earlobe. She already knew; that's why they were here.

"You're in luck, ladies. One left." Mrs. O'Connell appeared behind us carrying the familiar Styrofoam cooler underneath her arm.

I leaned closer to Red. "We can't take it."

She jerked her head back. "Why the hell not?"

I nodded over at the cot. Her stare followed mine, the pieces clicking together in her head and turning into a deeper frown than she normally wore.

"Tough break, but we're here first."

"He needs it, Red."

"Tuck needs it more."

"Why can't we go find some more? There has to be more out there we can steal."

Red laughed. A scary deep laugh from the bottom of her stomach. "Ya think we just pop in and grab it? Takes time to plan. Tucker ain't got time."

Red lunged for the cooler, but I blocked her path. "We can't take it from a kid. I won't let you."

"Let me? What ya gonna do, Princess?"

"Whatever I have to." I lowered my voice to a whispered hiss. "Please. You can't let him die."

I looked back over my shoulder at the mother and her dying son, blood still dripping from his face. My heart beat faster and slower all at the same time, as if trying to maneuver around the sharp pain spreading through my chest. Tears streamed down the woman's cheeks. The boy coughed again, painting red speckles on the beige tiled floor. The pain spread to my throat, making it hard to breathe.

I stepped up into Red's face as close as I could. "There has to be a way to save both of them."

Red rose up on her toes, eager to remind me how dangerous of a line I had just stomped all over. Her glare pierced through me.

"Please."

She paused, waiting for me to back down, but I couldn't.

"Fine," she snarled.

I remembered to exhale.

Red threw her hands up and stormed out of the building into the street. I chased after her, but she'd already sprinted halfway down the block.

The streetlight flickered faster. On, off, on, off, calling after her.

"Thank you," I yelled into the night.

She didn't stop.

HAWK HELD Tucker's hand while he tried not to scream. His black hair created a sweaty helmet, with beads running down his face and dripping off his chin. Dark red spots dotted the cheap white cotton sheets of the infirmary bed and left a trail along the floor from the main room. If Tucker seemed terrible when we left, he looked six feet from hell when we returned.

Nausea rose in my chest, but I swallowed it down. There

had to be another way to save him. I just had to find it. Unfortunately, I'd need help.

I'd chased Red all the way back here, knowing I needed to be the one to tell them what I'd done before she could rat me out. She wouldn't acknowledge me the entire way, but at least she slowed down enough for me to catch up.

I tapped Hawk on the shoulder, and he turned, relief spreading across his face.

"You're back. Where is it?" he said.

I took a deep breath. "There was a problem. We couldn't—"

Red pushed herself in front of me, smashing me with her shoulder, and pulled a small vial out of her sleeve, handing it to Hawk. "Here."

"You didn't?" Rage built up from the bottoms of my feet, my thoughts too jumbled to form words. She played me. She lied and played me and let me leave that kid to die, thinking he was safe.

"I did what needed to be done," she said as sure as nightfall and twice as dark, her head snapping on her stump of a neck

My entire body wound up, ready to launch at her. "You're ... you're a monster!"

"Ratchett, get them out of here," Hawk shouted, throwing an arm toward the door.

Ratchett passed Hawk a syringe and grabbed us both by the arm. I squirmed out of his grip but agreed to follow. Too late anyway; the cure disappeared from the syringe into Tucker's shaking arm. Red turned to me, a hideous snarl-like smirk stretched across her wicked face. I wanted to smack it off her so badly, but she wouldn't think twice about pummeling me into the ground for it.

"Stay out until you calm the hell down," Ratchett barked and slammed the door to the infirmary closed, leaving Red and me alone in the deserted main room.

"I can't believe you. You took medicine from a dying kid. Do you know how disgusting that is?"

Red shrugged. "Sometimes you got to make decisions for the greater good."

"But you let a little kid die."

"Lots of kids gonna die if Tucker don't get better."

There were no words. I could argue with her all day, but it wouldn't matter. She didn't care. She wholeheartedly, one hundred percent believed in what she'd done.

I muttered under my breath, "Heartless witch."

"Ya think I wanted to do that?"

"Yeah, I do." Without thinking, I pushed both my hands into her shoulders, knocking her back a step. "You had a choice. You picked Tucker."

"Choices suck. But it's what we do." She pushed back harder and with better aim. I fell backward and slid across the floor, my head smashing into a table leg, a pile of cell phones falling in a series of reverberating plastic clicks.

The infirmary door burst open and Hawk stood in the entrance staring us both down. "What's going on out here?"

"Your recruit done lost it." Red pushed past Hawk back into the infirmary. "You deal with her."

He looked at me, then shook his head, the stress of the situation heavy in the wide circles around his eyes and the ashen color of his cheeks.

Tears streamed down my face, but I couldn't speak. How could she be so horrible?

"What happened?" Hawk asked.

"There was a kid ... he was sick ... she just took it from him." I tried to form complete sentences, but I couldn't breathe. Between sobbing and trying to hold back from all-out crying was all my lungs could handle at one time.

"It's okay. She made the right decision. It's all right."

I jumped up from the floor, rage still pumping hard in my veins. "Right decision? How can you defend her?"

"If you saved the kid, you only save the kid, but if you save Tucker, you save his family, his neighbors, and his friends tomorrow."

I rubbed my skull and shook my head. This couldn't be happening. Things weren't supposed to be like this.

Hawk came closer and rested his hands on my biceps. His face was haunted and tired, but he still tried to keep upbeat. Still tried to take charge. "Sometimes being a hero means you need to make the right decision, not the one you want."

Tears came harder. I didn't want them to. I tried to be as strong as him, but I couldn't.

He slid his thumb underneath my eye, wiping away a few of my teardrops. "Come here."

He put his arms around me, tight and solid, but his hands stayed oddly gentle as he ran his knuckles along my spine. "Honestly, I wouldn't hold something like this against you. You have a good heart. You care about people. I never want that to change about you."

"But you would have made the same decision as her. Wouldn't you?"

He sighed, his chest deflating into me and answering for him.

I backed out of his arms and made some much-needed space between us. "Then I'm not sure I can do this."

He rubbed the back of his neck and stared at the floor. "I'm sorry."

Tucker howled from the other room. Pain and fear and anger all in one terrible animalistic sound that rumbled through my rib cage. It hurt.

"Go help Tucker, he needs you," I said, then turned and walked straight out the front door without looking back.

I SCRUBBED my skin until I thought it might bleed, then leaned my forehead against the cold tile wall of the shower and let the hot water wash over me. It burned against my raw flesh, almost more than I could stand, but I needed to feel clean again. To feel okay. Every inch of my body trembled like something creepy was crawling all over it, and on the inside, I felt even worse.

I wasn't completely sure how the virus spread, but I couldn't take any chances. I'd been in contact with two infected people tonight, one who probably wouldn't survive until sunrise. My stomach churned at the thought. I'd always heard of making life-and-death choices, but I never thought I'd have to. And in the end, I guess I never did make a choice. Red did, dealing out death like a losing hand at poker.

After the shower, I lay down on my bed, the soft mattress suddenly feeling like a trap I could never escape. Instead of sleeping, I crept down the hall and tiptoed toward Matty's room, resting my cheek against the lacquered door. My hand twitched on the doorknob, wanting so badly to run in there and see him, but the risk of spreading Tucker's virus kept me rooted in place. I closed my eyes and pictured him lying in his bed, his dark lashes painting lines along the tops of his cheeks, and the curly ends of his hair a tangled mess on his pillow. An image of the dying boy flashed across the thought of Matty, merging and fusing together in one horrific thought. I grabbed on to the doorframe to avoid falling over, my legs quivering. What if that boy was Matty? What if someone sacrificed him to save someone else? Would I make the same choice as Red or the others? Could I?

My hand tightened on the wooden frame until the feeling

passed and I could see again. Lucky for me, the dying boy wasn't Matty—at least not today. I ran back into my room and slammed the door, collapsing against the wooden panels as terrible thoughts consumed my brain again. What if someone chose to let me die? I closed my eyes and slid to the floor, then curled my knees into my chest and fought myself to sleep.

TWENTY-FIVE

Six days, seventeen hours since the night I'd left the Sanctuary. Since the night Tucker might've died.

I thought about him several times a day, wondering if he survived or if the cure wasn't enough and hoping that it was. But when I thought of Tucker, I thought of that kid. The little kid sacrificed to save someone else. I paced outside my father's door that first night, wanting to tell him I knew about the cure and to get it down to Mrs. O'Connell. I'd convinced myself I could sit through whatever punishment he'd give me if it could save the kid, but a more rational part of me argued that it would risk everyone at St. Ignatius, and worse, force me to expose Hawk and the others. Even through my anger, I knew New America needed them to stay hidden. Needed them to keep fighting.

And then I would think about how bad I wanted to be a part of that again. To do something better than sit up in my penthouse and watch the world fall down around me. Then I'd think of Hawk. Then the sad look on his face as he watched me leave the night Tucker might've died.

After that, everything would spin through my head again,

around and around like a carousel, until vomit rose in my throat and I begged to get off.

But I promised myself today would be different. Today I would let everything go and try to get back to the life I had before, even if I hated it.

I opened the door to the Drake family study. A strong whiff of lavender almost knocked me over, but Kendall launching herself at me actually did. We fell into a pile of legs, arms, and hair on the plush white carpet.

"You came," she said as she rolled over onto her back beside me. "I feel like I haven't seen you in forever."

She giggled, and I jabbed her in the side with my elbow, which only made her laugh harder, and I found it impossible not to laugh with her.

"You too."

"I was starting to think you were abducted by robots that sent me random messages every so often so I wouldn't try to look for you."

"Being abducted by robots is only half as ridiculous as we probably look lying on the floor right now."

She propped up on her elbows, a wide, amused smile across her face. "Who cares. No one's home but the house staff today, and they're paid not to notice."

Kendall planted her feet and swung herself forward until she stood upright again, then put out her arm to help me up in a much less graceful way. I tugged my shirt down and straightened my skirt before I noticed two large leather chairs in the middle of the room, each with its own tub of water and an aproned woman kneeling on the floor.

"So I was thinking pedicures today," Kendall said as she flopped over the arm of the left chair, her feet dangling over the side. "Just like we used to do. Unless you've just been for one."

"No. It's definitely been a while."

She clapped her hands twice and let out a short squeal. I laughed at her and shook my head, but she simply tapped the arm of the empty chair beside her. I slipped out of my shoes and melted into the soft leather of the chair, sliding my bare feet into the water. Of course, already the perfect temperature.

"And I stole us a bottle of champagne." Kendall twisted an arm behind her and produced a green bottle, dripping water all over her lap. "You know, for fun."

"You stole it? Would your parents even notice or care that you took it?"

"No, but it makes me feel like a badass saying it that way." She ripped off the foil and clenched her face as she pushed on the cork. "Ready?"

Pop.

The cork flew into the air, barely missing the skylight in the vaulted ceiling, then plunked back down in Kendall's foot bath, splashing all over the woman massaging her feet.

"I'm so sorry, Greta." Kendall tossed the woman a towel and gave me a wide-eyed glance as she clamped her hand over her mouth.

Greta wiped the droplets off her arms and continued back to work, not caring to make eye contact with either of us. My throat went thick watching her work.

"What's been up with you?" Kendall said as she passed me a fluted glass filled more than polite with bubbles.

I took a sip and enjoyed the funny way the champagne felt as it trickled down into my stomach. "Lots of stuff, I guess. Running errands for my mom and her society stuff. It's taken up a lot more time than I'd expected. You?"

"That's funny, Christophe said he's barely seen you around the house these days."

Dammit, Christophe. What was Kendall talking to him for anyway?

"Well ... he gets so busy at work, I try to stay out of his way."

"Oh, okay," she said, although her narrow, slatted eyes told me she wasn't even close to believing me. "I've been doing a bunch of stuff too. Nothing too exciting, just trying to enjoy the summer as much as I can before my parents ship me off to college."

"Sounds fun."

"It'd be more fun if you came out more." She reached over and playfully pushed my arm. "You're going to turn into a troll boarded up in that big house of yours. You need to go out and see more of the world sometimes or you'll go crazy."

I chuckled. I'd probably seen more of the world in the last little while than she'd ever know. But we weren't really talking about the same worlds anyway.

"Anyhow. Remember when I sent you that invite to Bridget's? You definitely should've come out then, we...."

I could still hear her voice, but it slowly seemed farther and farther away. Something about Mick's parents' new beach house and some embarrassing thing Alexandra did at a party last week, I think. I did my best to force myself to listen. Kendall always had the best stories. Even if you were with her, it was way better to hear her tell it later, but I just couldn't do it today. My mind still preoccupied with thoughts about people and things that I came here to try and forget.

I tried to focus on my pedicure. The just-slightly-less-than-unbearably-ticklish way the woman in the apron scrubbed my feet. The warm soothing calm of the water. The scratch of the salt scrub. But then I started to wonder who the woman working on my feet really was. Where did she live? Did she have a family? Was she happy? Did she ever need help from Hawk and the others? Would she one day? Was there anything I could do?

"So, when were you planning to tell me about your new boy toy?"

"What?" I lunged forward in my chair and choked on my champagne, the carbonation burning in my nostrils.

"Oh c'mon. The new guy who's been keeping you too busy to call me, instead of the super weak excuse you gave me earlier. The one you tried to pass off as my fictitious cousin Martin, or something like that."

I forced a cough to clear my throat and regain breathing. "His name was Max, and how do you know about that?"

"Good. Max is a way better name than Martin." She wrinkled her nose and twitched as the name rolled out of her mouth. "Your dad told my dad about some ill-dressed relative of mine coming by your house, and I knew it had to be a lie. You're crazy lucky I was there to remind them about my distant cousin, who neither of them seemed to remember, because he doesn't really exist."

My heartbeat slowed back down from its kick into overdrive. After what happened I never thought my father would tell anyone about Hawk being at the house. "Thanks, Kendall. I owe you."

"You bet your butt you do. Now spill. Who is he?" She leaned her elbows on the arm of the chair, staring at me with full attention. This Kendall was dangerous. This Kendall needed details and would commit every one to memory.

"I don't think you know him. He's been ... out of the circuit for a while."

"So how did you meet him, then?"

"I met him at the last party my dad threw. He was just standing around by himself and we started talking."

"And his name is?" She flipped her hands in the air, patience never being one of her strongest qualities. "Obviously not Max."

I squirmed in my seat, the soft cushiony chair suddenly

feeling more of a trap than a comfort. "It's Harley. His name is Harley."

"Hmmm." Her face scrunched up, and I saw her brain turning, flipping through the mental images of every guy she'd ever met to find a match. "Don't think I know a Harley. What's wrong with him?"

"What?"

"You're making me drag out every little detail and you didn't even tell me about him in the first place. There has to be something you're hiding. I know you too well for you to pull something over on me."

Of course she did. That's exactly why I never told her anything about what I'd really been doing.

"There's nothing wrong with him. He's just different from everyone else I've met, you know?"

I struggled to find words to tell her what had been going on. She could never know the real truth, not without getting myself into a world of trouble, but I knew enough that she'd keep digging until I gave her something.

"He and his friends are a bit idealistic. They see things differently than anyone I've ever met, and it's kind of ... I don't know ... like I found something that has meaning to me. Stuff makes sense. Like even though they aren't perfect, I feel like I get it."

Kendall's face blanked. "Intense."

"Kind of. Yeah."

"When are you going to stop hiding him from me? My parents are hosting a brunch thing next week you could bring him to."

"They, I mean—he's not really into all the society stuff."

"Look at you, rebel. No wonder you kept him to yourself. You know your mother will lose it if you don't pick someone she can parade around to her galas."

"Yeah, he's definitely not that guy."

My mind drifted back to the first time I'd seen Hawk at the party. He could blend in if he wanted to. The way he carried himself in that tuxedo, no one noticed he didn't belong. Not even me.

"Doesn't matter anyway. I don't think I'm going to be seeing him again." I shifted in my chair as a small twinge of pain sparked in the bottom of my stomach. For some reason, saying it out loud made it feel real, and apparently at least part of me didn't like that.

Kendall let out an irritated sigh. "How long are you going to be gone this time?"

"What does that mean?"

She lowered her forehead and raised her perfectly arched eyebrows. "You know I love you, but running away is kind of what you do. Whenever things get bad, you just bail."

"I do not."

"Of course you do." She grabbed her glass and swallowed the entire contents in one gulp, then sat back in her chair. "At least you were nice enough to come see me before you skipped town, instead of leaving me some cryptic message like all the other times."

"I'm not going anywhere." I smacked my hand on the armrest, but she didn't even flinch.

"Really? Are you just going into hiding, then? Like when you broke up with Christophe last time and avoided him for almost three months, which, although masterful since he practically lives at your house, was kinda obnoxious."

"That was different."

She rolled her eyes and leaned over the arm of the chair toward me. "M, you always talk about how trapped you are in your life, but if you go around acting like a spoiled princess, that's how people are going to treat you."

Ugh. That stupid nickname again. Why did everyone have to keep calling me that?

I opened my mouth to argue, but she kept going. "You're my best friend and I know you're way smarter and way better than you or anyone else gives you credit for. You are just so damn scared of anyone actually seeing it that no one ever does. So you can hide out from this guy for the next month or two, or you can try to make him see how great you really are. If you try, and he doesn't, then he's an idiot, but you can stop hiding and know he just wasn't good enough to keep up."

Words, so many words, built up on the tip of my tongue, but I kept them trapped by keeping my mouth shut. I'd always run away from my father, but I never thought I'd run away from everyone else too.

"When did you get so wise?" I asked quietly, my heart hurting as I thought about all the ways I'd let people down. How I'd let Kendall down.

"Since always. You just don't hang around long enough to notice." She refilled her glass and sunk back in her chair, staring off at the wall.

TWENTY-SIX

"Well, looky who showed up."

A ball of paper bounced off my head and landed in the middle of the floor. Red howled at her impeccable aim and clapped her hands like she'd just landed the winning shot in sudden-death overtime. Luckily, she'd only thrown paper at me and not something sharper.

I took a deep breath and walked toward her. "Nice to see you too."

She sported a gray knit skullcap pulled down over her ears that made her big hair slightly less intimidating. The rest of it ballooned out around her face and seemed to be even brighter crimson than I remembered. Maybe she'd dyed it while I was away, or maybe it was always more obnoxious than I'd realized.

"Where's Hawk and Tuck—"

"Hello there, gorgeous. I'm germ-free. How 'bout a hug." Tucker ran over from the far end of the room and held me tight, lifting me off the ground with a grunt. "I've been having to listen to Captain Grouchy Bird and the Scarlet Miserable all week. Never leave me again."

I laughed as he put me back on the floor, happy beyond

words to see him still alive. "I'll try. But don't you have Ratchett to keep you company?"

"Geek Squad never talks to anyone. You know that."

Ratchett flipped Tucker off without looking away from his computer screen in the corner.

"Are you really okay, though?" I looked him over thoroughly, not knowing what to look for, but thinking it needed to be done. "I worried about you a lot."

"That's sweet, sugar, but yes, I'm one hundred percent. Nothing to get distressed over."

I pulled him in for another hug, holding on too tight to be respectable. He patted my back like a little kid, but I didn't care.

"I'm okay, really. Believe me, there's a shitload of trouble I'm still planning to get into before I'm done," he said, pulling me off him and giving me a playful wink.

Red choked. "Like what? Playing Go Fish with your grams?"

He responded by mocking her silently, his head bobbing back and forth.

"And how's everything else been?" I wasn't sure how to ask what I really wanted to know—was everyone else still alive? And, the selfish question, did Hawk hate me for leaving?

"Not gonna lie. Things have been rough. The plague's getting worse. Mrs. O'Connell says the cases are doubling every few days, and she doesn't have room for them anymore."

"So you've been busy, then? Stealing more medicine?"

Tucker crossed his arms and his smile sunk into a frustrated scowl. Even though he said he'd recovered, he looked thinner. His cheeks appeared more defined, in a sunk-in kind of way, and his clothes seemed to hang heavy and wide on his lanky body, more than they normally did. My heart ached knowing he'd probably never be exactly like his old self ever again.

"That's the problem," Tucker said. "Supply's drying up. We

can't keep up and there isn't enough out there to help everyone, at least not that we can find."

"Sorry. I hadn't heard." I looked at the floor, guilt for not keeping up with the world creeping into my bloodstream.

"Of course not. No one wants to talk about entire neighborhoods getting obliterated just down the block. The news won't cover that stuff."

"So what are you—I mean—what are we going to do?"

Tucker lit up and gave me a punch in the shoulder. "Not wasting any time, huh?"

Red's throat let out a disgusted click. "We're meetin' a guy of Tuck's who has info on X9. Just leavin' actually."

"Did you want to come?" a deep familiar voice said behind me.

Hawk stood in the doorway, his hand still on the doorknob and his face blank, unreadable.

"Definitely." I smiled. He didn't. Just kept staring at me in confusion.

"You actually came back."

I wasn't sure how to read that. Was I wrong to think I would still be welcome here?

"You sound surprised."

"A little, yeah. But I should know to expect the opposite of whatever I think you're going to do." He gave me a smirk. An almost smile.

My shoulders relaxed, even though I didn't realize I'd been holding them so tightly until they dropped. "Is that a good thing?"

Hawk released the doorknob from his grip and joined us, standing just a little too close. The odd sensation I'd felt on the roof came rushing back, almost knocking me over.

He looked down at me and laughed, all light and teeth. "I'm not sure yet."

I'd honestly thought the night I walked out of here I'd never see him again, but looking at him standing there made me realize how much that fact truly bothered me. It might've been the thing that had been rolling around the back of my brain, even though I couldn't seem to place it. Like when you feel like you've forgotten to do something but can't remember what it is.

Tucker tapped his wrist. "Hate to break up this little reunion, but my guy's waiting for us."

"Of course. Let's go." Hawk backed up a step, his posture straightening to a sharp edge.

"She can't go like that." Red tossed her hand at me and I flinched by instinct. "Better luck bringing a pig to a BBQ and makin' it out alive."

I looked myself over. "Did you just call me a pig?"

She rolled her eyes and groaned.

"Here." Hawk grabbed the edges of his Lincoln-green hoodie, pulled it over his head, and tossed it at me. "Wear this."

I pulled it on. Only three sizes too big, but if I rolled up the sleeves, I could manage. At least it wasn't another itchy wig. I tucked my hair down the back and tugged the hood over my head. A soft smell of soap and Hawk lingered in the fabric and drifted into my face. I think I might've actually missed that smell.

"Better," Hawk said, looking me over. "I doubt anyone will recognize you, but if they do, we could be in for a lot of trouble."

"Hood up and head down." Red stepped in front of me and adjusted the hood down over my eyes as we headed out the door. The most helpful thing she'd ever done for me.

"Thanks," I said, giving her a smile.

"Whatever. Don't wanna have to come rescue your scrawny ass."

TWENTY-SEVEN

"Couldn't your guy have met you someplace, you know, less hostile?" I said as we turned the corner into the middle of a full-scale protest. Upset faces holding signs with hateful messages spread out almost a full city block. Messages that at best demanded changes, at worst my father's head.

It looked just like the news report that played in the dining room every morning. The one that never had a happy ending, except now I couldn't close my eyes and pretend it wasn't really happening. Now I stood right in the middle of it. Standing among the protesters. Feeling their heated breath on me. Knowing what Red already knew—I wasn't welcome here.

Tucker pushed himself up on his toes and scanned over the crowd before us. "Didn't have time. When Rooster crows, you get up or he'll be gone."

"Your informant's name is Rooster?"

His face twisted like I'd asked the dumbest question in the world. "And?"

"Never mind."

Spotting what must be the infamous Rooster, Tucker headed deeper into the crowd while Red and Hawk trailed behind. I pulled my hood as low as I could get it without completely blocking my sight and took a deep breath before chasing after them.

I kept my head down and followed the heels of Hawk's green sneakers past hundreds of sets of feet as we weaved through the bodies. Dark spots stained the pavement where we walked and I hoped it was oil, not leftovers from last week's public protest turned massacre. If I'd even dared to look up, it probably wouldn't have mattered, but I suddenly felt very exposed, very accessible. I plunged my hands deep into the hoodie pocket with my elbows out, trying to send a keep-your-distance kind of vibe.

In the thickest part of the horde, Hawk's feet stopped moving.

"Tuck. Wasn't sure you'd show." A skinny guy with a bright purple mohawk, gold shoes, and leather gloves appeared out of the mob. Not exactly what I'd thought someone named Rooster would look like, but it kind of made sense.

"Hey, man," Tucker said, his arms wide and a smile on his lips. "Been a long time."

Rooster pulled Tucker close and the two hugged with a very bro-like tap on the back, then Rooster reached into his back pocket and slid something into Tucker's hand. "Everything's on here. Emails. Internal docs. The works."

"Thanks. I owe you one."

Rooster winked. A strange smirk cut across his face, making Tucker's cheeks redder than the midday sun could be responsible for. "I know you always pay up."

Tucker shifted his gaze away and cleared his throat loudly. "Seriously, though. Thanks for this."

"Just get things taken care of. Enough's enough."

Tucker nodded.

"Besides," Rooster said as he shoved his hands in his pockets and his eyebrows knit. "We all miss you down at the Raleigh."

Tucker smiled. "I'll be back. Stuff's just been a little too real lately."

"Yeah. Lots been going down around the old neighborhood too. Could use your crew to help clean it up."

Hawk stepped in, taking charge. "We'll get on it."

Rooster gave him a sharp nod and disappeared back into the crowd.

"Okay, let's get out of here." Hawk patted Tucker on the shoulder as he stared after Rooster.

I turned around, wanting nothing more than to be away from here, when someone turned up the volume on the noise. Shouts morphed into full-out screams. Anger dialed up to rage. My muscles tensed. Something buzzed through the crowd. More screams. Arms and elbows crashed my direction, knocking me around. I looked up.

"What's going on?" I yelled, but no one heard me.

Then a sound. A whistle, but more mechanical. Something high-pitched and distorted ripping sharply through the blurry mass of voices. I slammed my hands over my ears, trying to shut it out, but it didn't help. I looked at Hawk. He shook his head without me needing to ask, terror streaking through his eyes.

So I ran, or at least moved the fastest I could to get out of there. The whistle noise stopped, but the yelling grew louder. I kept my head down and my feet forward, trying not to get distracted or, worse, attacked. A boy flew into my chest, knocking me back. I pushed him to standing. He turned and glared at me, then swung a punch at the guy in front of him.

Everything around me had exploded. Fists and feet, knees and elbows smashed into my body as my heart banged at me from the inside, but I kept running.

Finally, the bodies thinned. I pushed hard and willed my

legs to go just a little faster. My shin slammed something solid. Pain shot up my thigh. My stomach dropped, weightless. I was falling.

I crashed on my knees as the mob above me blocked out the sun. A sharp hit to the head knocked me one way. A kick to the ribs pushed me the other. I screamed, but I couldn't hear my own voice.

I crawled forward, stepped on and fallen over, but I refused to give up. I reached for an empty spot ahead of me, hoping there would be enough room to stand, when a hand grabbed my wrist. It yanked me forward, and I prepared myself for a fight. I pulled back my free arm, hoping to get a head start, when the sight of flaming red hair shocked me out of it.

"Keep moving," Red barked as she muscled her way out, me following close behind.

We finally reached the edge of the riot, Red blasting through like a rogue tank. I grabbed my knees and gulped air, choking and sputtering on it as it hit my soon-to-be-bruised lungs. I glanced back over my shoulder. Tucker emerged from the crowd, stopping suddenly instead of running away like he should.

"Tucker, over here," I yelled, waving my arms at him, but he didn't notice. The sun glinted off something in Tucker's hand. Something metal and shiny.

I called after him again, louder this time, but he still wouldn't look. I ripped my hood off, hoping he'd recognize me. No response. Something was off. I'd started to run toward him when Tucker wretched his arm up and back. The metal object came into focus as I got closer. A knife. Tucker had a knife and he was ready to use it.

Hawk appeared out of the fray and I stopped in my tracks. Tucker lunged the knife at Hawk. Hawk jumped back and pivoted to run. Tucker swiped at his back. Hawk's shoulders fell back as he shouted to the sky. His mouth open, the sound lost in the chaos.

"No." I rushed forward, elbows up, trying to get there as quick as I could.

Hawk grabbed his side and twisted around, his face dark as he raced into the protest after Tucker. What the hell was happening?

"Tucker," Hawk yelled after him.

Tucker spun around, the knife swinging through the air and nearly slicing three people in the process. His hands, his sweater, the blade all dripping red. His eyes as wide as I'd ever seen as he stared at Hawk. My stomach turned as Hawk neared him. This would not end well. I could feel it.

Red sped past me and grabbed Tucker's arm, wrestling it behind his back and forcing him to drop the knife. He fought her grip, but she wouldn't let him go, hauling him away.

"Got him, Hawk," Red yelled across the square. "Get the hell out of here."

Hawk turned and a new fear burst into his expression as he saw me standing behind him. He grabbed my hand and ran, pulling me through the crowd, my feet stumbling over themselves, trying to keep up. His fingers laced tight with mine, and for a second, I almost felt safe. Almost.

"It's a Masters," someone shouted.

Solid tree-trunk arms locked around my waist and lifted me in the air. Hawk's hand broke from mine as the arms carried me away. I screamed, kicking and punching at the arms as we ran, but they wouldn't let go.

"Put her down," Hawk yelled as he caught up.

The arms didn't listen.

"I said put her down."

Hawk pulled on the body behind me and my captor lost their balance. Suddenly Hawk went flying into the crowd, knocking over at least five people who tossed him to the ground as the arms hauled me away. I slammed my head back, trying to catch a piece of the person behind me. He groaned loudly and something behind my skull cracked. A nose? Glasses? Whatever it was made him loosen his grip for a split second, the ring of flesh and muscle holding me sliding up across my chest.

I leaned forward and bit down, the salty tang of sweat and dirt in my mouth, but I wouldn't let go until they did. A male voice cursed behind me. I bit harder. Metal taste. I'd broken the skin. He yelped and the arms fell away. I spit out the flavor and rubbed the back of my hand over my mouth. Without looking back, I ran toward Hawk. He grabbed the edge of my too-long hoodie sleeve and pulled me forward so I was in front of him.

"Run. Don't stop," he shouted.

I had no idea where to go; every street looked exactly the same as they streaked by in my periphery. Steps pounded loud behind me and I hoped it was Hawk still following, but I wasn't sure. I couldn't think, only move, adrenaline and fear making it too hard to concentrate on anything else.

The voices faded into the distance, but the tension still coursed heavy through my blood. I heard sirens. Loud screeching sirens heading toward the chaos, as red-and-blue lights reflected in the windows of the buildings as we ran past.

"Turn here," I heard Hawk call and my feet obeyed without a thought.

We swerved into an alleyway, the path so narrow that we could only run in single file. A fence blocked the end of the alley. Chain link. Nothing I couldn't climb.

"Wait," he called.

I turned around, my pulse hammering in my temples. Hawk tapped a security code into a panel on the wall and held open the door to a staircase. "In here."

TWENTY-EIGHT

This place had been alive once. An art studio. Maybe a gallery. But whatever soul it had died a long time ago, leaving behind a stuffy, unaired smell. The faded squares where paintings might have hung on the brick walls were covered with layers of dust. The exposed wood floor desperately needed refinishing, and the large arched windows were clouded in a sad shade of brownish-yellow dirt.

I pulled my sleeve over my fist and wiped a clean circle, or at least a cleaner circle, onto the window closest to the wall and peeked out. Three stories down, people were still running in the street. Pushing, shoving, hurting each other. Wild animals. How had everything gotten out of control so quickly? It was as if the protesters didn't know what side they were on.

My body ached, now that I let it, my breath only starting to get back to normal. I bunched up my sleeves in my fists and clenched my muscles, hoping it would help me relax now that I'd survived the chaos below. It didn't.

Hawk sat in the middle of the floor, one leg bent up and the other stretched across the dusty wooden planks, staring into the far end of the loft. I twisted to see what had interested him, but saw nothing.

"What went wrong?" I asked, but he didn't answer.

I stepped closer, the floorboards creaking and echoing under my feet. He didn't move. Kneeling beside him didn't spark a reaction either. If his eyes weren't open, I would have thought he'd fallen asleep.

A thin slice in his shirt ran along his shoulder blade, the fabric around a darker shade of black than the rest. I brushed my finger across it. Red and damp.

Hawk snapped out of his trance and flinched, jerking away from me. "I'm fine."

"I think you're bleeding."

He shrugged, wincing as he moved his shoulder.

"Can I look at it? Make sure you're all right?"

Again no words, but he pulled the torn shirt over his head and held it at his elbows.

A dark red line snaked across his back. It wasn't wide and didn't appear to be deep. A few smears of blood appeared to be fresh, but most had already dried to a thick crust. A faint smell of sweat rose off his warm skin.

"Did Tucker—"

I didn't need to finish my question as Hawk's defeated sigh already answered it. It must've been an accident. What other reason would Tucker turn on him?

"You need to get it cleaned up, but I don't think there's much damage."

Uncomfortable silence again.

I felt like I should do something, but I wasn't sure what, or if he'd even want me to. When I was mad I pushed everyone out, but I doubted anyone else acted as irrational as me. Besides, I didn't know where we were and from the shouts outside the window, it probably wasn't safe to leave.

A cool draft whispered through the space and Hawk's bare arms quivered, drawing my attention again. I already knew he was physically strong, but now I could see how fit he really was. My eyes took their time running over each sculpted ridge, from his collarbone to his hips at the edge of his low-slung jeans. Lean, defined muscles started in his broad shoulders and rippled into his chest and arms. He wasn't bulky, just clean and toned and functional. Almost militant. Absolutely sexy.

But a surprising tattoo peeked out from underneath his arm and traced down his ribs. A picture of a robin. It wasn't fresh, but the color of the bird's red chest beamed bright enough to say it wasn't old either. Every shape, every contour of the bird flowed, fluid and beautiful. Every detail perfect. The edges of the feathers looked soft enough to be real. Like one day it might free itself from his flesh and fly away.

Without thinking, I ran the tip of my finger along the back of the bird. Hawk twitched as our skin connected, but he didn't tell me to stop.

"Why a bird?" I asked as I traced the wings, his exposed skin pebbling into goose bumps under my touch.

"My mom...." He turned his head to face me. The fire in his eyes had burned out. Only ashes left. "She always called me her little bird. That I reminded her of springtime. I got it for her."

"She must be very proud of you."

"She's dead." He slid his shirt over his head and stood, then wandered over to the window.

"I'm sorry. I didn't know," I said, still on my knees in the middle of the floor.

Hawk stayed quiet and sat along the window frame, looking out onto the street. I wasn't sure what to do. Was he mad at me? I couldn't tell. From the second I'd met him, he'd been in charge. He controlled every situation, every person with the precision of a professional. To see him retreat like this unsettled me.

I moved to stand, but stopped when I heard him whisper. "Why are you here?"

The question didn't make any sense. "Hiding out?"

"That's not...." He turned away from the window and put his head in his hands, staring down at the floor. "I mean, why are you still here? Why did you come back? There's no reason for you to have to go through this. You have a life anyone around here couldn't even think to dream of, but instead, you're here. For what?"

"Maybe I just want to make a difference. Is that so unbelievable?"

"No. It's just, after you left, I never thought you'd be back."

"Me neither." I paused. I'd done a lot of thinking over the last few days, but I'd never actually had to put words to anything yet. I'd just come back because I knew I needed to, which sounded completely illogical, but it's really what it came down to. "I couldn't get everything you've shown me out of my head. I still don't agree with what you did, letting that kid.... All I know is that I want a world where no one ever has to make that choice. Coming back was my best chance at seeing that happen."

"I tried to save him, you know." He shifted in his spot and kept staring at the floor. "After you left, I did everything I could, but it was too late. He was already too far gone. I'm sorry."

My ribs felt two sizes too small around my lungs. I'd known what would happen, but I'd convinced myself that maybe the kid got better. Maybe he'd still be okay.

"Thanks," I said, but I wasn't sure if I really meant it. "What about you? You gave up your life for this. Why are you here?"

He sighed. "It's not a good story. You don't need to hear it."

"Way to deflect, Corbin. Guess those years of private school weren't a waste of money."

His face soured at his real name. "What's that supposed to mean?"

"It means that you swoop in all do-gooder superhero and tell me about how to live my life, but no one knows anything about yours. You're so quick to make people earn your trust, but have you even tried to earn mine? I'm risking a lot being here. You know what will happen to me if I get caught."

Hawk looked back out the window, drawing thick lines in the dust. "You're right."

He brushed his dirty hands off on his jeans, leaving gray streaks across his thighs, and slid down to the floor, his back against the wall. "I'm here because I had nowhere else to go."

I sat up straighter. Definitely not the answer I'd expected.

"I was fifteen or so, and I was into a lot of bad stuff. My parents were gone, my guardians didn't care as long as the trust-fund check kept coming, and I hated everything. A lot of money and a lot of anger make a lousy combination.

"I tried everything to feel something. Drugs. Alcohol. Letting roided-up frat boys try to kick my ass. But what I really loved was stealing stuff. I'd break into anything with a lock just for something to do. For the rush of it. The high. It was cheaper than drugs, didn't hurt my fists, and I was good at it. Really good. A natural thief. Plus, I could sell whatever I stole to keep up my other habits.

"One night, I stole the wrong thing from the wrong guy and he wanted it back. He beat me with a golf club and left me to die under a bridge in the park. I was so high I didn't even feel it until I was too messed up to fight back. And that's when Ratchett found me."

"Ratchett saved your life?"

"Yeah, he was one of the guys I ran with sometimes, but he was always chirping about some grand scheme he had for something better. He agreed to help me if I helped him. I had means, he had a plan."

I got up and brushed myself off, then sat beside him near the wall, the empty space suddenly feeling more menacing. "So you quit, just like that, because you owe Ratchett a favor?"

"No. I struggled, and there are plenty of nights I still regret, but Ratchett stuck with me. Once you've been to a dark place like that, it's really easy to find your way back. It's something I still have to work on every day, so I don't slip. But eventually I got better, I cleaned up, and we recruited some others, then things just started rolling. Helping people gave me something to focus on other than my own problems." He gathered his left hand into a fist and wrapped his right over it, cracking his knuckles with his long fingers. "It made the hurt stop."

I held my breath and slowly let it back out. So this was it. He'd said everyone had a story, and this was his. I'd been lucky that my father left all my scars and bruises on my skin, but Hawk's wounds were deeper, internal. Holes no one else could see. The look he'd given me after I'd been hit wasn't pity, it was understanding. He knew what it was like to feel lost, fractured, just like me.

"I'm sorry about your parents," I said. "Did they ever find out what happened to your dad?"

"No. I tried to find out, but I never got anywhere. I'll probably never know now."

"Oh." Not a great response, but the only thing I could think to say. Instead, I slid my hand against his palm and laced my fingers between his. He rolled his head toward me and tried to smile, but it looked too sad. Too broken.

"My mom used to be an artist and this was her studio. I should sell it, but I can't. They blamed her for the murder. Said she was the only one who would have had access to our apartment when it happened. But it wasn't true. She loved my dad and he loved her. They were happy." He paused. "She killed herself six months later."

He shuddered. Just once, but so violently that I felt the aftershocks up my arm.

"When I close my eyes, I can sometimes still see their faces. Like I could reach into my head and touch them. But most of the time it's just their bodies. Blood splattered across the kitchen and down the hall. Like it all happened at the same time." The ghosts of his dead family floated across his face, draining his cheeks of color. "I still don't sleep much."

He traced his thumb over my fingers, drawing lines like he had on the window. "Only you and Ratchett know about this, and you can't tell anyone. No one else would understand."

"I wouldn't. You kept my secret, I'll keep yours."

He nodded and let out a breath that deflated him to the point he almost melted into the wall. One thing I understood was secrets. The heavy feeling in your chest, the pain in your stomach from carrying them around. But sometimes survival meant suffering a little pain. I understood that too. The problem with secrets was that sharing them gave other people power over you, and I wasn't sure if he could afford to give any of his power up.

The sun still shone bright through the window, and I watched the dust motes dance in the drafts as Hawk's hand rested in mine. I looked around the studio and tried to picture what it used to look like. What kind of people used to come here. How often Hawk still did.

"I missed you when you were gone," he whispered, so quiet I thought I'd imagined it. "I didn't know I would. But I did."

He flopped his head toward me, his face pressed beside mine against the wall. So close we shared a breath. He pulled my hair back, his fingers knotting in the strands as he held on to my head.

"There were so many times I would be planning, or thinking, or anything, and I'd wonder what you would say if you were there. What your opinion would be. Every time the door opened, I wished it was you."

All the nerves in my body fired at once. He'd missed me. Even after all I'd put him through, Hawk had actually missed me while I was gone.

"Well, I'm back now," I said, not being able to fight the sides of my mouth from edging up. "And I'm not planning on going anywhere unless you make me."

He gave me a crooked smile, the worried crease in his forehead disappearing and his eyes switching from stormy skies to deep blue with no end. "Good."

I pulled myself over him and straddled his legs so my thighs made a triangle over his. Face-to-face, his hand still tangled in my hair.

"I missed you too. More than I should have."

I put my hand on the side of his face, and he closed his eyes, resting his tight jaw deeper into my palm. The pain in his expression seemed to drift away. Falling into my hand like rain.

My pulse pounded steady in my ears. His lips less than an inch away. I ran my finger over those lips. Soft and full and just a slight bit dry that made me suddenly thirsty. I leaned forward, for the first time unsure of what to do. Kissing other guys had never made me nervous like this before. Kissing other guys had never made me shiver.

I brushed my lips against his. Testing. Waiting. Then he kissed me back. Slow. His mouth closing around mine and pulling me in. Dragging out every second.

It was the kind of kiss that felt like forever. Every touch, every taste, stretching out and lingering, lazy as if time didn't exist. His tongue running along my lips. My fingertips brushing against the ends of his hair at the nape of his neck. Every sensation, a swirling heat under my skin, winding me higher and higher.

And then I fell. Down, down, down into all those emotions I'd dismissed because in this world there were no happy endings. Futures here were never certain. But right then, with his teeth grazing against my tongue and his hands gripping tight on my hips, everything seemed possible.

And then his lips vanished.

He gasped and turned his face away. "We should get back."

"What?" I asked breathlessly, remembering to inhale again, my head still spinning.

Without an answer, he wrapped his hand around mine and pulled it away from his face, placing it on my leg. Then he rocked forward and brought us both back up to standing in one smooth motion, leaving whatever had happened between us back on the floor.

He ran his hand over his head, grabbing the back of his skull, and walked over to the window. "The streets are clear. It should be safe now."

Without a word, or even one last look, he headed straight to the stairwell. I sighed and followed, my heart still in extreme danger.

TWENTY-NINE

Silence. That's how we walked back to the Sanctuary, in complete silence—save the soft thuds of our feet on the pavement. We moved beside each other, close enough to feel the summer sun bouncing off Hawk's skin, but never actually touching. Near and also very far away.

For blocks I wished he would say something, because I didn't have any words to describe how foolish I felt. Everything he'd said about missing me, the way he looked at me, I thought…. It didn't matter what I'd thought. In the end, I'd kissed him and he'd pulled away. Coming back here wasn't about him, but part of me knew it was. That part screamed at me right now.

At the door, he inhaled deep. His shoulders heaved, and he popped his neck before reaching for the handle. But instead of storming in, he turned and grabbed my hand. I wished he hadn't. His grip had a steady stillness, but I was anything but still. Yet another thing I'd never been good at. Before I had the chance to argue, he let go and disappeared through the door.

Inside buzzed with life. More people had crammed in here than I'd ever seen in this place at one time and, for once, it didn't seem so big. Except instead of keeping busy, they all stood waiting by the door.

"You're safe." A tall girl I remembered as Galaxy gave me a quick hug and patted me on the head with her fingerless-gloved hand. "You were both gone so long everyone was getting worried."

"We're okay," I said, giving her a genuine smile.

I tried to move farther into the space, but met with more greetings and high fives and special handshakes that I had no idea how to do. I hadn't realized we'd been away for so long, but everyone seemed to be concerned. I looked over at Hawk in the middle of the same welcome, but amped up to the nth degree. I knew this wasn't all for me. I could see it in their faces. The relief. The adoration. They'd be lost without him.

And then I saw another face, lurking in the corner away from everyone else. Hood up, staring at the floor. At the same moment, Hawk saw him too. The mood in the room changed like the wind before a hurricane. I tried to stop him, but too late.

"You tried to kill me." Hawk barreled across the room, hitting Tucker square in the chest and knocking him to the ground. "What the hell were you thinking?"

The entire room stopped and suddenly silenced except for Hawk's heavy breathing as he stood over Tucker with a homicidal look that must've come from the dark place he'd talked about.

Tucker scuffled backward, out of striking distance, and climbed back up to his feet. "I don't know what happened. I don't remember hitting you. I must've blacked out or something."

"You didn't hit me, you knifed me in the back." He lunged forward and slammed his hands into Tucker's chest again, pushing him back a few steps. "What's the number one rule around here?"

"Trust," Tucker replied, staring at the floor.

"Say it again."

"Trust," Tucker yelled louder, finally able to meet Hawk's eyes.

"Now how am I going to trust that the next time we leave here, I'm not going to end up with a knife in my gut? I would never do that to you, man. Never."

"I swear I didn't know it was you. The crowd started freaking out, and then there was that sound, and then I was running down the street with blood on my hands."

"My blood on your hands."

Hawk stepped closer. Tucker shuddered. I couldn't watch.

"Hold up." Red pushed herself between them and thrust her hands into Hawk's shoulders to keep him from lunging again. "It's true. Boy's head ain't right since we came back. He didn't know what he was doing. Honest."

Hawk looked at Red, then glared over her at Tucker, but eventually backed down, his hands still in tight white-knuckle fists.

"That virus still got him messed up. I'll keep an eye on him," Red continued as Tucker straightened himself out, still smart enough to keep his distance.

Hawk rolled his shoulder back and fought against the pain-induced wince, the cut on his back starting to drip red again. He pointed at Tucker and scowled. "Never again. Got it?"

Tucker nodded three times, quick and sharp, likely knowing he'd barely escaped a long and painful death.

"Can you all stop yelling?" Ratchett spun around in his chair to get our attention. "There are way more important things to deal with than Tucker's latest screwup."

"Hey," Tucker said in his own defense, no one else willing to jump in, at least not right now.

Ratchett rolled his eyes. "Whatever. Based on the information Rooster gave us, we now know two things. First, the vaccine is ready for distribution, and second, the virus isn't some random freak of nature. It's manmade."

"What does that mean?" Hawk asked.

"It means this isn't some animal mutation or some old plague coming back around. Someone cooked up X9 and, either by accident or on purpose, they let it out of its test tube."

Someone behind me released an airy whistle. The vibe in the room actually managing to get grimmer.

"That's messed up," Red said under her breath, but loud enough to hear in the sudden silence. "Any clue who made it?"

"Nothing yet," Ratchett replied. "But I'll keep looking."

Ratchett's words raced around my brain. Something about this felt painfully familiar. I raised my hand, the quiet making me feel ten years old in crabby Mrs. Raintree's math class. "I think I know."

The weight of a hundred eyes fell on my head.

I cleared my throat. "With all the bad stuff going on, The Five think other countries are looking to start a war. They've been trying to rally support, but what if whoever it is already struck first?"

"You mean like bioterrorism?" Ratchett said matter-of-fact, although red splotches crawled up his neck and dotted his cheeks, the fear and intrigue of the prospect battling for supremacy over his limited emotional responses.

"I guess so. Do you think it's possible?"

"Of course it's possible. I'd even say really friggin' likely." He clapped his hands together and turned back to the computer. "This blows things wide open. So much to do."

"Ratchett?" Hawk said, but he didn't turn around. "What about the vaccine? What did you find out?"

"Right." His chair spun back around, his fingers still flexing like they were tapping an invisible keyboard, his brain running a thousand times faster than anyone else's in the room. "The vaccine has been ready for about two weeks, but it's not rolling out to the public for at least three more."

"What? That doesn't make any sense. The virus is getting worse out there."

Ratchett shrugged. "Plus, it's being phased in by social class. No one around here will have access to it for at least another month."

Hawk ripped at his hair and let out a growl, but with a lot more gravel to it. "Don't they know how many people are dying?"

He grabbed a chair and chucked it across the room. I jumped as it slammed against the wall with a loud crash. No one spoke. No one moved. Every head turned to stare at the empty plastic chair like it was the center of the universe.

"Enough. This can't wait," Hawk said as he threw his hand through the air. He started to pace, back straighter, steps solid and determined. A strange air of confidence fell off him and emanated through the room.

I'd seen this before. I'd felt it. The reason armies marched into the impossible, searching for victory. The reason my father was the *One* among The Five. The reason this room of the city's most notorious street kids hung on whatever Hawk would say next. He was their leader. Without question. No confirmation needed. They just knew.

"If we're being attacked and The Five won't do anything about it, we will," Hawk said.

The room erupted with cheers and Hawk paced faster, fueled by the energy. A plan was clicking in his head like lock tumblers falling into place, each calculated move flashing through his eyes.

"We'll run a blitz. Hit every location all at once and collect everything we can. Cure for the suffering and the vaccine for everyone else we can reach. Who's in?"

"Hell yeah," someone shouted and the excited murmur continued.

"But, this will be extremely dangerous." Hawk waved his hands and everyone quieted. "There is a serious risk of getting caught. If anyone wants out, I suggest you leave now."

Nobody moved.

Hawk nodded at his makeshift soldiers. "All right. We'll wait until nightfall. Everyone go see your families and check in. Get rest if you need it. Anyone who still wants to do this, meet back here at nine o'clock for instructions and assignments."

He turned back to the desk along the wall.

"Ratch, can you find out where they're holding the vaccine?"

"Sure thing."

"Red, make a list of all the locations that might still have vials of the cure left."

"What about me?" Tucker said.

Hawk eyed him closely, the decision on whether to let Tucker help splashed across his face. "Split everyone into groups. Make sure each has muscle, a smith, and a ghost.

"Also," Hawk shouted over the noise of everyone shuffling to the doors, "no phones or electronics that emit signal. We'll give everyone burners when you get back."

Within seconds, everyone drained out the exits, leaving only Hawk and his elite to their work.

I shifted from foot to foot, half wanting to stay and half knowing I needed to go. "Is there anything I can do?"

Hawk frowned as he realized I hadn't left yet. "You should probably go home."

"Oh." So that was it. One kiss and I'd been tossed back to the other side. Tucker had actually stabbed him and I—

"Mercury," Hawk called.

"What?" I snapped as I kept plummeting down my shame spiral, barely managing to keep myself from saying everything out loud.

He chuckled at me and smiled. "You'll be part of this. You just need to check in at home so no one suspects anything. If anyone came looking for you, it would be a disaster."

"Oh," I said again, but less harshly, my vocabulary suddenly significantly lacking when confronted with reason.

I walked away, pausing for a second at the door and looking back at Hawk.

"Trust me," he said, his knowing stare the only sure thing in the world right now.

I sighed and closed the door. The city was in crisis. A war was coming. What I had to say would have to wait.

THIRTY

I filled a backpack with anything I thought I might need, but I had zero idea of what to bring to a heist, so basically I'd packed a pile of tight black clothes, a knitted skullcap, and a pink diamond-covered swiss-army-knife-looking thing I'd found in the pile of graduation gifts I hadn't earned. It probably wasn't even sharp enough to cut thread, but it might pass Red's concealable-weapon test.

"Where are you going?" a voice asked behind me.

I jumped with a yelp and dropped the bag to the floor, my heart slowing down when I saw it was just Christophe.

"I'm going to spend the night at Kendall's," I said as I scooped up the backpack and tossed in a couple of hair ties from my dresser.

"You can't leave. There was a huge riot this morning. X9 cases have tripled. It's not safe out there."

I laughed, but it came out a little too nervous to be natural. "It's just Kendall's. Her building has a security detail, and we'll be there all night. It's not like I'll be out running through the streets or anything. I'll be fine."

"But what if...?"

He grabbed the back of his head and sighed, craning his neck up to the ceiling. I'd never seen him this worried or agitated before, like one wrong move and he might explode all over my carpet.

"I'll be okay." I pulled him into a hug. His arms clenched tight around my body and I feared he might never let me go. I couldn't blame him. After all, he didn't know everything that was happening. He wouldn't know that the virus was some kind of foreign terrorist plot. He was the same as the rest of the ignorant city.

"I couldn't stand it if anything happened to you," he said.

"I'll be careful."

I gave him a pat on the back, hoping he'd get the hint to ease up and let me go. He didn't.

"I don't think you understand how much I care about you, Mercury."

"Of course I do. And I care about you."

"It's not that. You're not just any girl to me. You're important. The only person I can talk to."

I turned my shoulder into him and pushed myself back until his arms finally fell away, his face sinking into his chest.

"What is going on with you tonight?" I said, Christophe's weird behavior making me suddenly nervous too.

"You don't even wear the necklace I got you," he continued, either ignoring or refusing to answer my question, his frustration seeming to grow exponentially by the second.

"I didn't want to wreck it."

I walked over to my jewelry cabinet and pulled the necklace from a small velvet-lined drawer at the top, doing my best to keep watch over Christophe as I did. I slipped the arrow around my neck and threaded the head through the leather loop. A lightness appeared in his expression as I settled it against my collarbone. "Happy?"

He nodded.

"Okay. Can we talk more tomorrow? Kendall's waiting."

"You don't need to show me how strong you are. I know that already. Just don't do something reckless that you'll regret to prove some point. I would rather have you caged than dead."

What? Did he hit his head or something? "You're being a little dramatic, don't you think?"

He didn't answer. Instead, he sat on the bed and ran his palms over his thighs. His eyes fell to the floor and his brow crinkled with worry. This wasn't just his normal overprotective concern. There was something bigger.

"What aren't you telling me, Christophe?"

He took my hand and pulled me onto his lap, resting his forehead against my shoulder, the cologne smell of his hair product mixing with whatever secret hung in the air.

"We're going to catch them tonight."

I pulled his chin up to face me. "What are you talking about?"

"The vigilantes. There's a trap set."

My body went rigid in his arms, but I forced myself to breathe. "How do you know it'll work?"

"It will. The vaccine for X9 is ready. We know they know. They'll come for it and we'll be ready."

"What?" I tried to stand, but he wrapped an arm around my back and pulled me down. I gripped his wrist and yanked him off, freeing myself and putting a few feet of space between us. "If the vaccine is ready, why aren't they giving it out to people? Why are they letting people die?"

"Once the vigilantes are caught, the vaccine will get distributed to everyone. We just have to wait."

Absolutely disgusting. The Five weren't discriminating about who received the vaccine first. They were holding the lives of the entire city ransom to catch Hawk and the others. To catch me. The warm taste of acid built in mouth, but I choked it down. If I puked on Christophe now, he'd likely have me quarantined.

"Do you even know how sick that is?"

He frowned. "Believe me, this isn't what I want to happen either, but the sooner the vigilantes are stopped, the faster the vaccine can get to the people who need it."

"Why do you care? Isn't this exactly what you wanted? Take down the infamous vigilantes?"

He stood and tried to step toward me, but I backed away. "I'm not that arrogant. I know once the people's heroes go down, the riots will get worse. There will be more violence. It won't be safe for you or anyone out there."

"Then maybe stop killing people and things might get better."

He sighed and shook his head, the pained look on his face showing his frustration because I didn't get the grand plan. But I did understand; I just didn't agree with his logic.

"It's already done, Mercury. The teams are in place. It ends tonight."

"Then I guess there isn't anything left for me to say."

Christophe reached toward me, but I ignored him and grabbed my bag from the floor, then swung it over my shoulder. "I have to go."

"Please just stay home tonight—" He stared at me, wordlessly pleading with his wide, sad eyes. "—for me."

A sharp pain rippled through my stomach. "I can't. I made a promise. I have to keep it."

I pulled open the door and took one last look at Christophe standing in the middle of my room, his face in his hands. Maybe one day I could explain that I never wanted to hurt him. No. One day I *would* explain it, but right now I had to stop Hawk from walking into a trap.

THIRTY-ONE

The Sanctuary seemed different with no one around. No sniping comments, no sneers from Red, not even the monotonous tapping of keys from the computers. It seemed kind of eerie and oddly more in line with how I would have considered a sanctuary to actually feel. An open and empty space where an overwhelming feeling of reverence would make it necessary to whisper.

Hawk looked like the only person still lurking around, his head down, staring at a large sheet of paper that spilled over the sides of a table. It must've been important, as he didn't even flinch when the door clicked closed behind me and made a faint echo through the room.

For a moment, I stood still and simply watched him. He'd cleaned himself up. A fresh shirt, and his dark hair damp, almost black. His thick shoulders peaked and hunched as his hands pressed down on the tabletop. The sharp edges of his jaw clenched tight to match his narrowed, scrutinizing stare. His neck slanted forward and made it seem like the entire world rested at the top of his spine in that very moment. And it probably did.

I'd imagined bursting in and shouting everything I knew, but I could barely find the motivation to walk across the room and disturb him. In the dim overhead lights and the shadows creeping in from the corners and across his face, my mind kept wandering back to places it shouldn't go. Places where, for the briefest of seconds, I felt exposed in both terrifying and freeing ways. Places where his lips burned against mine, and where he pulled away from me, leaving the entire incident on agonizing repeat in my brain.

My hand reached out and knocked on the wall behind me, although my brain wasn't ready to make my presence known yet.

Hawk shook his head and jerked it toward me as if being woken from a dream.

"Hey," he said, then rubbed his hands over his face and made an unnatural groan. "I wasn't expecting you yet. No one's going to be back for a few more hours."

"I know, but I needed to talk to you."

I walked over to him. His dark, bloodshot eyes followed my every move as I sat on the table next to the large piece of paper, my feet dangling an inch too short to touch the floor. I glanced at the page. Some sort of building drawn with 3D rooms spliced from the larger structure. Detailed blueprints, maybe.

"What are you doing?" I asked as I traced my finger along what appeared to be an outside wall.

"I'm trying to figure out how I'm going to pull this off. It's a lot of responsibility, you know. Putting everyone in danger like this. They all count on me to keep them safe."

"I know. But they would only follow you if they trusted you, and they do. Anyone here would follow you anywhere."

"Would you?" His ashen face wasn't asking me to fall in line. He wanted to know, as if he honestly didn't know my answer.

"Of course." I rested my hand on his arm for a second, then pulled it away and laced my fingers in my lap. "You're a great leader, Hawk."

"Maybe. But sometimes they all forget I'm just some guy. I don't want them to regret putting their faith in me."

"You're not just some guy. To most everyone here you are *the* guy. The way they all look up to you. How they stand at attention when you walk in a room and hang on your every word. Win or lose, I doubt any of them would regret trusting you."

He exhaled hard, pushing every last bit of air from his lungs. The warmth brushed my shoulder and I shivered. "You're always so good at giving me hope, you know that? I need that, more than you know."

I dug my fingernails into the backs of my hands, my throat suddenly dry. "You need to call off the mission."

"What?"

"Someone arranged for you to get the information about the vaccine and knew you would try to steal it. It's a trap."

"Seriously?"

It came out loud, and short, and sharp, and I jumped. He struck his hand across the table and the blueprint crashed in a pile on the floor.

"How did you find out?"

"Someone told me. Someone reliable."

He looked me over, searching for a better answer, his hands gripped tight to the back of his neck.

"Trust me. They know what they're talking about. You need to call this off."

He began to pace, turning his face to the ceiling, his eyes shut tight. "But there's no time. If we don't do this, more people will die."

"And if you do, you all might as well walk into the nearest police station with your hands tied behind your backs."

"Then I'll just have to go alone." He kneeled and started to roll up the crumpled blueprint with quick twists of his wrists. "It's the only way."

"Are you insane? Look at me, Hawk."

He kept rolling.

"I said look at me." The harsh shout caught his attention and he finally turned. "That is probably the most ridiculous thing I've ever heard you say."

"Well what am I supposed to do?"

"First, you're going to stop panicking. Then you're going to tell everyone that plans have changed, stay put for tonight, and then tomorrow when the trap doesn't work, I'll do what I can to convince my source their trap will never work while you tell the world The Five are letting their own citizens die by withholding lifesaving medicine."

He sighed and stared at the floor, letting the paper unfurl in his hand. "Why does all of this keep getting worse no matter what I do?"

My face scrunched up.

"The virus is getting worse. The Five are doubling down. Everything I do, everything I try to do, gets smacked down by something bigger. And then there's you—"

"Me? What did I do?"

"Nothing." His head hung lower toward the floor. "You're just a distraction."

"A distraction?" I launched off the table, my feet slamming against the floor and echoing around me, my heart doing the same thing in my chest. "That explains everything, doesn't it?"

He stood at the sound of my feet pounding toward the door. "What? No, I ... that didn't come out how I meant ... what do you mean, 'that explains everything'?"

"I mean everything." My arms flailed, hard and wild. "Why you're always going out of your way to make sure I'm okay, like I'm some sort of delicate ornament that might break if you aren't careful. I bet that wastes a ton of time."

"That's not—"

"And why one minute you tell me you miss me, and then I kiss you and you're kissing me back, and then you just … just stop, like nothing even happened. But I guess that's my mistake, because I didn't realize I was only getting in your way."

"Mercury, stop." He held up his hands, either for surrender or safety, I wasn't sure. "I didn't do any of that to hurt you. I've tried, been trying, to keep my distance from you, but I haven't been doing a very good job. I have to focus on this battle with The Five, and being too close to you makes everything cloudy."

I still wasn't sure what it meant, but deep down, it stung. "So why didn't you tell me instead of cutting me out?"

"And say what? That you've gotten in my head so bad it makes it hard to think? That I worry about you when you're at home and I can't be there to stop anyone from hurting you? Or that when you're here, all I want to do is pull you close to me and kiss you until I can't breathe?"

I shook my head, trying not to let his words sink in too deep. "That doesn't make any sense."

He inched forward and took my hand. "When you're around I forget about trying to be everyone's hero. I just want to be yours, and I know how risky that could be."

"I don't need someone to rescue me. I need someone who'll be there when I finally figure out how to save myself." The words tumbled out like they'd always been there, just waiting somewhere behind a tonsil until it was safe to come out. "Can you be okay with that?"

He ran his index finger slowly along my jawline. Earlobe to chin, tossing gasoline on the slow-burning embers that had been smoldering in my stomach since this afternoon. His eyes burned through mine, intense with something I couldn't explain. Stormy. Thunder. Lightning.

"I don't know how to be with you without losing myself," he said, his thumb tracing slow circles on the back of my hand.

"Stop trying so hard."

My throat tightened as he leaned toward me. His forehead rested lightly against mine. The warmth of his breath fell on my cheeks.

"May I?" he asked, his voice a low whisper rumbling in his chest.

I nodded into the kiss. His lips, soft and tentative, like his body were as unsure as his request. Like I might say no.

Pushing my mouth harder against his, he pulled away.

Not again.

He stared at the floor, his breathing deep and haggard as his chest heaved slow in the dim lights. I tilted my head to meet his gaze. His eyes locked on mine and followed as I raised my head back up. Why wouldn't he say something?

Then he did. He lunged forward, his mouth crashing into mine. The force knocked me back, but I wrapped my arms around his neck to steady myself. The backs of my thighs hit the edge of a table and I pulled myself to sit before my knees gave out. His lips parted, his tongue searching, urgent. I ran my hands up the back of his shirt, grasping at his warm skin under my fingertips. Bunched cotton over solid shoulders. He left my mouth and kissed a trail down my neck to the small space before my shoulder, making me quiver in my shoes.

I brushed my hand under his chin and guided his mouth back to mine. I needed to feel his lips again, to give my head time to put all the pieces together. And then they were, shifting and sliding into place. The clean smell of him in my nose. The soft groan in the hollow of his throat as his lips pulled on mine and asked for more. The flex of his biceps against my sides, holding me tight to him like he might never let me go. And suddenly everything made sense like this was how a kiss was supposed to be. Like every other kiss before now didn't matter because this one was it. This was the kiss I'd been waiting for and I didn't know it until I'd found it. This was real.

"Something's happening." His lips had managed to escape mine again and traced across my ear. "I don't know for sure. I'm not sure of anything right now, but I might be falling in love with you."

"What?"

I put my hands on his chest and pushed him back so I could see his face, and saw terror. The full-out fear of being stripped to your bones and having nowhere to hide. His words were dangerous, and he knew it. If used wrong, they were weapons that could cut us both and leave scars.

"Please stop staring at me like that," he pleaded. "Say something."

I opened my mouth, but the words I pictured in my brain weren't the ones that came out.

"Oh no. Christophe."

THIRTY-TWO

"Mercury." Christophe stood in the doorway, looking at me, then Hawk, then back at me again. His face looked pale, colorless, with a grimace like he'd dropped something on his foot and desperately tried not to show the pain of his clumsiness. That or he was cataloguing ways to kill the both of us without leaving a trail.

I grabbed Hawk's arms and pushed him back so I could stand, both of us frozen in place the second we were interrupted. "What are you doing here?"

"I followed you."

"You told this guy where you were going?" Hawk dug the heels of his palms into his eye sockets.

"Of course I didn't. I'd never do that." I put my hand on his chest, hoping he'd look at me and know I was telling the truth.

"You don't have to keep lying to him anymore." Christophe tore across the room and grabbed my arm, yanking me away.

I twisted my fingers in Hawk's shirt and he held my hand.

"Let her go," Hawk yelled and pulled Christophe backward by the collar of his suit jacket.

Christophe turned to face Hawk and pushed me behind

him, sidestepping in front so I couldn't get past, his hand still roughly attached to my arm. "You have no idea the damage I could do to you."

"Get the hell out of my building before I rip your smug face off," Hawk threatened back and stepped directly in front of Christophe, using the inch of height he had on him to leverage his scowl.

"Fine, but there's nowhere for you to hide now. We know everything. Mercury has done a great job reporting back every little thing you do. We have your picture, your name, your past, everything. We'll take you down piece by piece."

"That's not true," I yelled, trying to pull from Christophe's grip. "He's lying."

But too late. Doubt had already crept into Hawk's face, and I couldn't get any closer to keep it from spreading.

"Why would I lie? Or did you actually think a girl like her would get involved with a pathetic street punk like you without an agenda?"

"It's better than being with a douchebag like you."

"Nice inner-city vernacular. Is that supposed to be an insult?"

What was he doing? *Just shut up and walk away, Christophe.* I would claw his eyes out for this. Then I heard it. A quiet clicking behind the door. Heavy footsteps. The door rattled in the frame. Christophe was stalling.

"Run," I yelled, squeezing past Christophe, my arm pinned awkwardly behind me. "He brought guards. You need to get out of here."

Hearing my warning, five guards rushed in the front entrance. Hawk's eyes widened as he turned and ran toward the back door.

Bang. Bang. The back door burst inward and another group of guards ran in.

Hawk slid through the infirmary door and slammed it shut, the lock clicking into place. The guards banged on the door and my knees quaked with every pound. Hawk was trapped in there. He had nowhere to run.

I yanked on Christophe's sleeve. "You need to stop this."

"Get her out of here," Christophe ordered.

One of the uniformed worker drones took my arm and tried to pull me out the front door.

"Let me go." I struggled against his firm grip but couldn't get loose. "Do you know who I am?"

"Yes. And you are to be removed from any hostile situation at all costs," my captor said as flat as if he were reading the line from the world's dullest textbook.

"Christophe," I snapped as the guard forcibly dragged me from the room. "Make him stop. Tell him to let me go."

He mouthed *I'm sorry* and turned away from me.

Slam. The guards rammed the infirmary door hard enough it burst open. A hatch flapped from the skylight, the room empty except for moonlight cutting across the floor. They were too late. Hawk was gone.

The front door of the Sanctuary closed in my face.

I THREW OPEN my door and stomped across the room, rubbing the tender spot on my arm where not one but two of my father's men had manhandled me today. Another bruise, courtesy of The Five. Bad thoughts and black feelings swirled through my head; fury at Christophe, and terror over what might happen to Hawk if they caught him. Prison would be the least of his worries. My father would make an example of

Hawk. A hero of the people brought to his knees to prove a point. Disobey and die.

I put a hand to my mouth. I could still feel his lips on mine. The hard pressure from him trying to tell me things that words didn't cover. Part of me had been falling for him a lot longer than my brain had realized, and best of all, I could see myself getting stronger, being better because of him. Being around him pushed me. It was scary and messy and wonderful, and for the first time I felt like a version of myself that I created, instead of someone else's. And then Christophe screwed everything up.

As if drawn to my seething, Christophe knocked on the door and timidly entered the room, his head drawn down into his shoulders.

I crossed my arms and jutted out my hip, hoping he would be smart enough to keep some distance. Preferably enough that I couldn't be tempted to take a swing. "What do you want?"

"I came to see if you were all right."

"Are you kidding?" I yelled, loud enough to make him twitch. "You actually think I'm going to be all right after what you did?"

"Keep your voice down."

He walked back to the door and glanced down the hallway before closing it completely.

"I've kept your name out of the reports, so unless you want me to tell your father and everyone else what you've been up to, you should talk quieter."

"Are you threatening me?"

He stretched his head toward the ceiling and let out a frustrated sigh. "No, I'm not threatening you. I never did any of this to hurt you, but you being in that place makes things complicated. For both of us."

"What were you even doing there?"

"I was following up on a lead about the vigilantes threatening your father."

"That's fine, but what were *you* doing there? You're just an intern."

"I wanted to make sure you were okay. You'd been disappearing so much lately that I had you tracked—"

"You did what? Get out."

"I was worried. I didn't want you to run away again. I didn't want to lose you."

"So you had me tracked? How did you even?"

He paused and stuffed his hand in his pockets, staring at the floor. "Your phone. I used the GPS."

"But I didn't bring my phone with me. I wouldn't be that careless."

His face burned a telltale shade. Christophe was accomplished at many things, but lying wasn't one of them.

"Then how?"

He didn't answer, but his eyes exposed his deception as they stared at my throat, the necklace he'd given me suddenly tight as a noose around my neck. I grabbed the leather cord and tried to rip it off. It stretched, but didn't break. With angry, shaking fingers I undid the clasp and chucked it at his feet.

"I can't believe you. You're no better than any of the villains you work for."

He cringed but didn't bother to dispute it. "I'm trying to keep you safe. Kendall told me you might have gotten into trouble and I put the rest together myself. I set up the trap to save you."

What was with everyone needing to save me all the time? Did I come off that helpless? "Did it really look like I needed to be saved when you walked in?"

"No, it just hurt. To see you with him like ... like that." He turned his face away from me. "It wasn't what I expected."

"You need to leave."

I pointed at the door and his eyes followed down my arm, but he still didn't move.

"I'll go, but tell me one more thing. Why?"

"Why what?"

"Why you would go against your family, your friends, and everything they stand for?"

Now it was my turn to pause.

"Because they're all standing on the wrong side."

He nodded, not in agreement but in acknowledgment, then slowly walked out, the door closing with a soft thud behind him.

I exhaled, and it stung. Sharp and bone-marrow deep. I collapsed onto my bed and let all the ugly I felt crash over me in dark, pounding waves. I reached for my pillow to bury my face in, but a familiar crème-colored paper sat with black wings widespread on my pillowcase. Hawk had been here. I closed my eyes and inhaled, hoping maybe I could still sense him here. If I could breathe deep enough, part of him might still be floating around. But nothing.

The card read:

Trust is something you earn.
You broke mine.

THIRTY-THREE

Hawk had escaped. For now.

Christophe's guards searched most of the night, but he managed to stay hidden. Now I couldn't help but see him everywhere I went. Every light post, every wall, every blinking television billboard with the same photo I'd seen all over the internet, all over my house, all over everywhere. Hawk was a fugitive. Not like he wasn't before, but now they had proof. Wanted posters with a bounty rich enough to sway almost anyone, like in those old Wild West movies the kitchen staff watched when they thought no one was looking.

I'd gone back to the Sanctuary, but it was empty. Nothing left but bare wires and light fixtures. The guards had seized everything, then trashed the place for good measure. I hung around for a while anyway, hoping maybe someone would come by and tell me something useful in tracking Hawk down, but the morning turned into an afternoon, turned into a night, and no one came.

For the thirtieth time, thirty-two to be exact, I dialed the anonymous number Hawk had given me. Instead of ringing endlessly like it had before, there were three distressing beeps and then nothing. Cut off. Gone.

The next day I tried St. Ignatius. I couldn't just walk up and ask where everyone went, especially since I doubted even Mrs. O'Connell really knew, so I lurked outside like an anxious ghost haunting the place. After two days of waiting, I finally saw a flash of crimson hair as I paced the street corner out of view from the wooden doors. I crept closer and after about a half hour, Red reappeared outside, all spit and snark like I remembered. I ducked behind the large stone railings as she scanned the street, either sensing someone watching or simply being smart enough to keep cautious. When she moved, I moved, inching after her like a shadow instead of just a stalker. I hated that she was the one to follow, expecting her to turn on her big black heels and curb-stomp me. She'd enjoy it more than the others, I was sure of it. But she kept moving instead, stopping only twice to look back. Except she never saw me, or at least didn't make it known that she had.

Eventually, the streets started to look familiar again. Dark semi-tall brown brick buildings. Streetlights that looked like they were transported from another time. A building with large arched windows on the top floor. Hawk's mother's studio. I smacked myself in the forehead for not figuring this out before. Of course they would come here.

Red punched in the security code and disappeared through the side door. I should've tried to talk to her, but by the time my brain switched from stealth mode to speak mode, she'd vanished. I looked at the security panel and tried to filter out any memory of Hawk entering the correct numbers. No luck. I hadn't known to pay attention then. Only one more choice. I swallowed hard and took a deep breath, then raised my fist to the door just as it creaked and came flying at me. I jumped toward the wall, barely missing getting my face crunched, and held still.

A lanky, hooded figure leaned out and looked back and forth down the alleyway. Seeing nothing, he slammed the door behind him, staring toward the street and not noticing me pressed against the wall. He dug his hands in his pockets and walked away.

"Tucker," I shouted after him. "Tucker."

He turned around, his entire body rigid and his feet planted, ready for anything.

"Hey, Tucker. I'm so glad it's you."

I stepped toward him but he recoiled, pivoting his long leg back as far from me as he could get.

"Don't come any closer, traitor." He crossed his arms, making me stop in my tracks. "You're not welcome here."

"But you don't understand. I didn't do anything."

"Oh really? That's not what I heard. I heard you've been feeding information to The Five about us, then led their designer-suit-wearing lackey boy and his band of violent-ass mindless monkeys to capture my boy Hawk and then all the rest of us in one giant two-faced betrayal. Or am I missing something?"

Whoa. Tucker's words tore through me and couldn't make me feel any worse than if they were actually true.

"That's not what happened."

"Doesn't matter. He doesn't want to see you. Nobody does."

So this wasn't going to be easy. It looked bad. I knew it did. And all those things that Christophe said would be enough to make anyone question my loyalty, but I thought Hawk would be different. I thought he'd know I wouldn't ever do that to him. To any of them.

"It doesn't matter anyway. Hawk was just using you the same way you were using him."

I snapped out of my self-deprecating thoughts. "What are you talking about?"

"He only wanted you around to get back into your dad's secret stuff, then he was supposed to bounce you, but for some unknown reason, he kept you around. Bet he's kicking himself for that."

"You guys were using me?"

He raised his eyebrows and tilted his head to the side. He didn't need words. I already felt foolish enough.

"Honestly, Tucker, I thought you were my friend."

"And I thought you weren't going to sell me out. In the end, the only person you can trust to watch your back is yourself."

Blood boiled at my temples. I balled my hands into fists and screamed, "I didn't sell you out."

He shrugged. The door creaked open behind me and Red stepped out into the alley, her hands on her hips and a sinister smile across her lips.

"Ballsy move coming here, Princess. Didn't peg ya for the daredevil type."

I stepped away from her, but the chill coming off Tucker as I edged closer frightened me more.

"She was just leaving. Weren't you?" Tucker said.

"Not until I talk to Hawk. I know you don't believe me, but he will. I know it."

"Don't think so. He never wants to see your double-crossing face again. Listen to me, Your Majesty, Hawk used you and now that he has what he wants, he's done. Go back to your castle and leave him the hell alone."

Tucker tried to stare me down, but I wouldn't let him. I stood as tall as I could, my muscles tense.

"Ya gonna stand there all day or ya gonna make me make you leave?" Red said and started after me.

I jumped back a step and she laughed. No, cackled. This was pointless.

"Fine, I'll go. Can you at least tell him I was here?"

"Yeah," Tucker said, his stance suddenly more intimidating with Red by his side. "I can give him a warning before you send the troops in again."

I opened my mouth to argue, but decided against it. They didn't believe me. No matter what I said, it wasn't going to get me any closer to getting in that door. I waved my hand dismissively and walked toward the street.

"And before you think of coming back again, remember—" I looked back, regretting it instantly. Tucker's face had turned into a sneer, darker than I thought he was capable of. "—snitches get stitches."

I cringed and walked away slowly, hoping maybe Tucker would change his mind, or at least feel sorry for me. But what would it matter? Why should I apologize for something I didn't do when I was the one being tricked all along? Or was I? My mind replayed everything on loop in my head. Every touch, every word, that last kiss. Could it really have been a lie? Every day I'd felt a little bit worse about the whole thing, but here, standing in the tight and dirty alleyway, knowing Hawk was on one side of the wall and I was on the other, it was finally clear that I shouldn't have come back. I didn't belong here anymore. Maybe I never did.

THIRTY-FOUR

"Wake up, sleepyhead," Christophe said from the doorway.

I groaned and pulled a pillow over my face. "Don't you know how to knock?"

"I did, but you didn't answer." He ignored my complaining and sat in the armchair beside my mirror. Something seemed different about him today. Something I hadn't seen in forever and honestly didn't think I'd ever see again. Instead of his future-leader power suit, he wore jeans and an actual T-shirt. Even from my bed, it still looked way too expensive for a T-shirt, but the cut of it looked really good on him. Dark blue, rolled up slightly at the sleeves, pulling against his thick arms, but looser through the torso so he could move. He almost looked comfortable.

I sat up and made sure my pajamas hadn't shifted inappropriately in my sleep. "Why are you waking me up? Go away."

"You can't stay in this room forever."

"Why not? There isn't any reason for me to leave."

"And rob the world of your pretty smile? That would be a tragedy."

I threw a pillow at him, but it missed and bounced off into the corner.

"I thought you had better aim than that. Maybe you should head downstairs and shoot some targets?" He laughed, then reached over and tossed the pillow back at me, hitting me square in the head and knocking my hair in front of my face.

I spit out a stray strand that had snuck its way into my mouth. "What do you want, Christophe?"

"You can't keep moping around, so I took the day off and we are getting you out of this house."

"I thought the world was too dangerous for me?"

"I'm sure we'll be okay. Plus we can bring guards."

"Great. Just what I need. More babysitters."

He rolled his eyes and shook his head, but kept his mouth shut. Smart move. After all, I was still mad at him for following me to the Sanctuary and then lying about me to Hawk. It'd been a week since I walked away from Tucker and Red in the alley. A week filled with me trying to process what to do next, if I could even do anything. A week full of a thousand apologies from Christophe. Neither of these things had made me feel any better. But at least Christophe kept up his promise to keep my name out of the reports on the raid. My father would've exploded if he'd known about that.

"And where exactly are we going?" I asked, still not convinced to get out of bed just because he asked.

He raised an eyebrow and smirked. "You'll see."

"And why now?"

The smirk disappeared. He leaned forward, his elbows on his knees, his fingers woven tight together. "You haven't given me a fair chance. That Hawk guy had an opportunity to show you his world. Why can't I get a chance to show you mine?"

"This isn't some competition, Christophe."

"Everything's a competition. I just don't give up as easily as he did."

That stung. Mostly because he was right. I hadn't heard a word from Hawk. He told me he was falling in love with me. I guess it was just as easy to fall out of it, if it wasn't all just one big lie.

"Fine. But I have to get dressed."

"I can wait." His lips curled into a devilish smile.

I pointed at the door. "Outside."

"WE'RE ALMOST THERE," Christophe said as he reached across the backseat of the car and squeezed my hand.

I really wished he'd told me where we were going. Instead, I sat staring out the window, analyzing every intersection, every street corner, to try to figure it out before we arrived. I wasn't in the mood for a surprise. I'd been craving certainty and assurance these days.

"And I wanted to say again how sorry I am about everything," Christophe added, his tone dropping to a more somber, sorrowful pitch. "I was only trying to—"

"Protect me. I know. You've told me a hundred times already."

"But it still doesn't seem like it's enough for you."

I sighed and looked over at him sitting there, staring at me, his face all twisted and distorted with regret.

"I don't need any more apologies. Just don't give me any more reasons to be mad at you."

He nodded. "I can try."

The car slowed and pulled into a large parking lot that looped around past a series of glass doors in the front of a large steel-and-glass-style building. A sign near the roof read *Nott Health Center* in bright orange letters.

"What are we doing here?"

"You wanted to be a part of something that was making a difference, so here's something that doesn't involve getting into trouble with dangerous people." He opened the car door and jumped out, then leaned back inside. "Are you coming, or is this too much of an adventure for you?"

I helped myself out of the car, a knot of worry building in my stomach. I wanted to ask more questions about what the heck we were doing here, but Christophe had already bounded up to the front entrance and held the large glass door open for me.

He waved politely at the receptionist behind a plain-looking desk at the front. Her cheeks flushed at the attention as she smiled back and nodded to hide her eyes that followed him closely as he continued marching down the hall. I couldn't blame her. From this angle, Christophe did know how to rock a T-shirt, and he definitely didn't look half bad from behind either.

Three sharp turns, two more doorways, then we emerged in a large open room with comfy couches, small little tables, and sunlight streaming in through the windows.

"Christophe," a little girl squealed as she jumped up from the group of children sitting on the floor and rushed over to grab his hand. "We already started."

"C'mon," Christophe said as he motioned with his head toward the group and sat on a rainbow colored, poly-blend mat. "You don't want to miss storytime."

I blinked, not sure which dimension I had accidentally found myself in, then sat next to Christophe since standing made me feel twenty feet tall with everyone sitting on the floor.

Christophe grinned while a nurse at the front pulled out a

book about a misplaced puppy and began to read in an animated voice. The little girl who'd met us at the door curled up beside Christophe, listening intently with her head resting against his shoulder, a fuzzy yellow robe covering her thin blue-green hospital gown.

"What are we doing here?" I whispered in Christophe's ear, trying not to call attention to myself.

"Volunteering. Today is the day I help in the children's ward."

The answer seemed unsettling for some reason. I thought I knew everything about Christophe. Maybe I wasn't the only one leading a secret life.

"How often do you come here?"

"At least a couple times a week, sometimes more when I can. My mom used to volunteer here before she...." He still couldn't say it out loud, even in a whisper. "They were having financial trouble a few years ago, so I convinced your dad to buy the place and it's been my own private project."

"How come you never told me about this?"

He shrugged. "Didn't seem like the kind of thing you'd want to hear."

I sat back and looked around the room, not really seeing anything as my sense of thought was suddenly more dominant than my sense of sight. How could I have not known about all this?

"So my dad really owns this place?"

"Sort of. Technically The Five does. Nott is the corporation they use when they want to keep things separated from the government operations."

"And they all lived happily ever after," the nurse said, closing the book and settling it in her lap.

The kids clapped their small hands, then erupted into chaos. Tiny people scattered all over the room, playing, making noise, laughing, and being kids. It kind of looked like fun.

Two boys, a tall scrawny one with a shaved head and a shorter, even thinner-looking one, reminded Christophe he'd promised last time he would play with them.

"Can Mercury play too?" he asked as he pulled himself up off the floor and offered me a hand.

They nodded with matching toothy smiles.

Christophe followed them toward a basket of cars and trucks and looked back at me with a wink. "Welcome to my world."

AFTER FIVE ROUNDS of some game I didn't fully understand, which might explain why I lost every single time, I flopped down in a small blue plastic chair three sizes too small for me. Christophe continued playing, laughing and crawling around on his knees, blending in almost too well with the blue-green–dressed kids. The color made my heart hurt for a minute, a small squeeze reminding me that life wasn't always fair.

To my left, a little girl sat drawing a picture. Long dirty-blond hair stuck out of two messy braids hanging off either side of her tiny head, and the tip of her tongue peeked out of her mouth as she concentrated on her work. I leaned over and watched her.

It looked like the top of a building. A stick figure with wings stood on the edge looking down over a city drawn in crooked black crayon lines.

"What are you drawing?" I asked.

"It's the hero that flies around the city and watches over us. The one that's on all the posters outside. His name is Hawk," she replied with a smile, still shading in the lemon-yellow sun she'd drawn in the corner of the page.

My stomach flipped at hearing his name, and I immediately hated myself for it. "I'm not sure he's a superhero. I think he's just a real person like you and me."

Her little face scowled and a big pink lip stuck out at me. "How do you know?"

I paused, waiting for the right words to appear in my brain. How was I supposed to tell her that sometimes getting our hopes up was just a way for us to get hurt later? Just another trick for us to fall for. "I met him once."

"Really?" She perked up and dropped the yellow crayon in her pudgy hand. "Was he wonderful like everyone says? And is he nice and kind and handsome?"

I laughed to myself for a second, then realized there wasn't any way I could lie to her. "Yes. You're right. He's all those things, but maybe he's not really the hero you think he is."

"Of course he is. Maybe *you* just don't know what a hero looks like."

Christophe appeared behind me, trying hard to catch his breath. "Hey, Ainsley, nice picture."

"Thanks," she said as she slid it off the desk and looked at me with her big eyes and know-it-all smirk, then walked across the room and hung the picture on the wall.

"Cute kid," I said as Christophe took her seat, his knees almost up to his shoulders in the preschool-sized chair. He reached over and hooked his index finger with my pinky.

"Having fun?"

"Yeah. Do you seriously come here every few days?"

His phone buzzed in his pocket, making a dull rattling sound against the chair.

"When I can. They could always use more volunteers if

you'd like to come with me next time. There are other areas that need help here too."

"I think I'd like that. But you know this isn't the same, right? It's really great what you're doing, but there's still so many other bigger things going on out there."

"I know. But I wanted you to see that not everything has to be a fight. Figure out what means something for you and use your connections and resources to make it meaningful. If you're going to turn your back on your family, you should really make sure it's worth it first."

His phone buzzed again. He frowned and pulled it out, frowning even harder when he looked at the screen.

"I'm sorry, but I really need to get this."

I sat back and let him take the call, his words bouncing around inside my head. Ainsley gave me a smirk from across the room. I looked away.

"No, no, no. That can't be right ... well check again ... I see ... thirty minutes." Christophe smashed his finger against the screen and let out a frustrated groan. "I hate to do this, but I have to go."

I pushed myself up from the chair.

"If you want to stay I can send a car back for you. It shouldn't take too long."

I looked around the room. Maybe I should stay. For a few hours I actually felt normal again. Forgot about all the things pulling at my insides. But I didn't need to stay. I would be back. "It's fine. We can go."

We waved goodbye and headed back out through the large glass doors, a car already waiting for us by the curb. I glanced back at the building as we drove away, heavy gray clouds hanging from the roof. The dark hollow crept back into my stomach. I understood what Christophe was trying to do, but he didn't really understand the enormity of what was really going on, what we were really up against. Someone was poisoning the country with X9. Maybe I needed to tell him what I knew.

Christophe's fingers flew over his phone screen, his eyebrows knit together, and his arms and shoulders clenched so tight I felt the tension in the air from his muscles all the way across the backseat.

"Hey," I said. "Thanks for doing this."

He didn't look up. "Uh. Yeah. You're welcome."

Splashes of drizzle spread across my window and I ran my finger along the lines as they got thicker and pooled along the glass. I took a deep breath, letting it fill my lungs and hoping the air would carry out the nasty feelings of cowardice building in my blood as I exhaled. It didn't, but it didn't change what I needed to do.

"Christophe, I need to tell you something."

"Just a second."

A second passed. A minute. Five minutes. Now that I'd decided what I had to do, it suddenly became urgent in my head. My hands shook, the waiting making me feel like I might explode.

"Christophe."

He raised his hand in my direction. "One more minute."

I let out a frustrated sigh. He didn't notice. The rain picked up and plunked against the roof of the car. I lowered the window a crack and grabbed his phone, hovering the device dangerously close to the outside.

"Don't," he yelled. A deep, terrifying yell I'd never heard from him before, and I shivered.

I raised the window and lowered my hand. "It's important."

He snatched the phone out of my fingers so fast I thought I might lose a knuckle.

"I wasn't really going to do it." However, now I kind of wished I had. "Relax. It's just a phone."

He ran his open hand through his hair, his face clenched in an uncomfortable scrunch. "I'm sorry, but you don't understand how important this phone is."

I crossed my arms and looked out the window. "Clearly."

He exhaled loudly, then put his warm palm on my shoulder. "Can I trust you with something?"

Trust. A deadly, loaded word. But trust was exactly what I needed from him as well. I just wasn't planning to be bold enough to ask for it by name. I nodded.

"This phone is the switchboard for all private communications for The Five."

"What?"

"All emails or other communications for the main officers are directed through me and I route them to where they need to go. Anything noncritical to national security is pushed through, but anything really important goes to a secret address on a private server located across the country."

"That doesn't make any sense. You're just the intern."

"Exactly. Because who is going to suspect the intern to have all the key information? Hackers can get information so easily now, they had to be smarter. Security software isn't enough. This phone isn't connected to any of the other networks so it can't be accessed by any other computer or device in the organization. Haven't you ever noticed that I'm the only intern they've ever had?"

"But what about my dad? The office at the house must have access."

Christophe shook his head. "The main office is a front. Sure, we meet there and discuss things, that's why there are no cameras, but nothing important actually gets kept there. It's the obvious choice for anyone trying to get information."

So that's why Ratchett didn't find anything on my father's

computer. There wasn't anything to find. They were looking in the wrong place.

My mind started firing with so many questions. Did The Five know Ratchett was watching the computer system? Did they care? What about the information he did pull? Was it planted for him to find?

"Doesn't that seem ... dishonest?" It wasn't the right word, but it was the only one I could think of. To me this whole thing felt like one giant lie.

He looked puzzled. "No, it's about safety. There's a lot the public would be better off never seeing. Sometimes you need to make a decision between what people need to hear—"

I bobbed my head, this discussion seeming all too familiar. "And what's right."

"No." His face scowled. "What's best for The Five."

The car pulled up in front of the building and Christophe jumped out so fast I wasn't sure we'd come to a complete stop. He leaned back in his open door, rainwater dripping down the side of his face.

"As soon as I'm done, I'll come find you and we can talk. I'm really sorry. It's just something important. I swear."

"Stop wasting time apologizing to me and go deal with what you have to do." The need to tell Christophe about X9 had fizzled as my brain tried to put together what he had just told me. He was a lot more connected to The Five than I had ever expected. Maybe I should figure out what Christophe knew, instead of telling him what I did.

"Right." He nodded awkwardly. Whatever the emergency, it weighed heavy on his mind, as he didn't even look back as he walked away.

THIRTY-FIVE

The room was freezing. My skin shrunk and stretched tight against my bones as if trying to hide from the cold breeze circling through my space. The long burgundy curtains flanking the window by my bed blew and danced in the current. I rushed over and slammed the window shut. The chill in the early evening air declared that fall was definitely coming, although it was always cooler this many floors above the world.

I grabbed a sweater from the closet and pulled it on, hoping to stop my shivering. Small specks of light bounced around the walls as my white paper lanterns kept swinging on their strings. I twisted one in my hand and it spun a carousel of shooting stars around my room.

"I guess that means you like them."

Christophe stood in the doorway watching me. His quick work thing had taken him the rest of the day, but he'd found me just like he'd said. He always kept his promises. Unfortunately, he'd also changed back into his suit, but at least he'd left the first few buttons of his dress shirt undone and he'd skipped the tie. A reasonable compromise.

"I never did thank you for them, did I?" I said, giving the lantern one last spin.

"It's okay. I didn't do it for the credit."

"Then what did you do it for?"

"That look on your face right now."

He walked across the room to stand across from me. Slow, careful steps.

"Did you finish whatever it was that was so important?"

"Yeah. For now. The X9 vaccine is getting dispersed from the central lab that makes it tomorrow and I needed to get a few last things in order."

"Really? Not planning on using it as bait for Hawk anymore?"

Christophe cringed when I said his name, both of us stinging a little from hearing it out loud.

"No. Vigilante activity has died off and we really need to get the vaccine out to the public. We'll have to draw them out some other way."

I dug my toes into the thick carpet and tried to keep my breath steady. It would only be a matter of time before The Five found them again, but at least this time they wouldn't be able to use me to do it.

He stepped closer and tilted my chin up to look at him. He tried to smile, but he probably sensed what I was thinking. "I know these are your friends, and I will do everything I can to get them leniency. I swear."

"Thanks," I said, but it was little consolation.

"Merc, I saw how you looked at him. I saw how you...." He shuddered instead of speaking. "I know I'm not the one you want. But I could be. There are so many things I could give you that he never could."

"Doesn't matter now. He's done with me. They all are."

"I can't figure you out. Why is that such a bad thing?" He shook his head and stared out the window into the fading light, his jaw tightening against his cheeks. "I would never make you earn my attention. I would never make you question how I feel. What's wrong with me?"

Every word pierced through my skin and swam through my blood to sit at the back of my throat, making it hard to swallow. I put my hand on his shoulder and he looked down at me, his eyes unsteady, his confidence stripped.

"There's nothing wrong with you. You're smart and ambitious and kind and thoughtful—" I let my gaze wander over his chest, the lump in my throat getting bigger. "—and you're pretty hot too."

He laughed, his teeth peeking out of the smile he tried hard not to show.

"You're exactly what any girl would want."

"Any girl but you?"

"I didn't say that. You mean way more to me than you think. You always have." I moved my hand from his shoulder to his palm, awkwardly twisting my fingers around his. "You're one of my best friends. You're more than that. You're one of the only reasons I always come back here."

"I just want to make you happy. I might not be perfect, but I could be good to you, if you would just let me."

He curled my hand up to his lips, his eyes never leaving mine, the heat from his hand stopping the chill still coursing through my body. "I would do anything for you."

"Christophe ... I...."

But I couldn't finish. His hand had moved up against the back of my head. His fingers laced in my hair and his lips pressed against mine. My body tensed, my mind protesting, but why? Here he was willing to try and make things work. He had waited for me to figure things out, and even though I hadn't, he'd still been here. Where was Hawk? I was just a complication for him anyway. He'd made that very clear. He had his work to do, and maybe I could find a way to do my part in my own way. Maybe it was for the best.

So I let go. My fingers traced up Christophe's arms and linked around his neck. He responded, pulling me tighter, my feet coming off the floor. My lips pushed back against his as I remembered every other kiss we'd ever had and falling into the slow, familiar rhythm from memory. Kissing Christophe was easy. Simple. Gravity.

"We could be happy," he said between soft kisses near my ear.

"I know."

I wasn't sure if it was true, but in that moment it felt like it could be. Like some kind of secret I'd just uncovered that could change my world. I closed my eyes, trying not to think. I could do that later when his strong fingers weren't tracing down my back. When he wasn't trying to kiss away everything I couldn't seem to forget.

His lips found their way back to mine. Slow, careful kisses.

"You're the one thing I've always wanted," he whispered low against my skin, sending a ripple through my chest.

He let me back down to the ground and pulled my arms off him, enclosing my hands in his.

I opened my eyes. "What's wrong?"

"Nothing."

He smiled, the uncertainty still lurking in a slight twitch of his upper lip, and reached into his jacket pocket, pulling out a small folded square of black satiny cloth.

"I know things haven't been great for us recently, but if we could forget about the past, I think the future could be amazing." He started unfolding the cloth. "We could be amazing."

As he pulled back the last fold, the lantern lights caught the contents and fractured it into a million sparkles. In his palm lay a small emerald-cut ring with a border of tiny diamonds. Vintage and classic, but somehow clean and modern at the same time. Simple, beautiful, and perfect.

"This is crazy. I'm only seventeen."

I tried to pull my hands away, but he held them tight.

"I know that, and we can have the world's longest engagement if you want. Years, even." He squeezed my hand. "I just can't keep guessing with you. I can't stand back and watch you slip away from me because I'm waiting for you to tell me how you feel. I know what I want. I know I love you. And I know you love me too, even if you aren't ready to admit it."

"Chris ... I don't know ... I...."

"You don't need to say yes, just please don't say no. I can handle a maybe, as long as you will seriously consider my offer."

He let go of me and closed the ring in my fist. "Take your time. I can wait."

I shook my head and held the ring out to him.

He waved me off. "Keep it until you decide. Maybe it'll help."

Brushing my hair back over my shoulder, he leaned forward and kissed my cheek, then turned and disappeared out the door before I could bring myself to move.

I swallowed hard. Marry Christophe? The whole idea was insane. But I knew what he was really asking. He was asking me to choose. To pick him and this life. Except he didn't know the other life had already kicked me out.

I opened my palm and stared at the ring. I liked it. He either had taste or he paid enough attention to really know mine. I slid it on and held it up. For something so small it seemed heavy and foreign. One hundred pounds balancing on my finger.

Christophe had been right. I did love him. I always had, but likely not in the way he needed me to. But maybe I could, if I let myself. And maybe I could find a way to make the world better from the inside. Without Hawk.

I closed my hand into a tight fist. Before Christophe got any answers, I needed some of my own.

THIRTY-SIX

I drew the arrow back. The diamond glinted under the gym lights, luring my eye away from the target, and the weight of the setting on my finger made the motion of the draw feel off. Something that used to come as natural as walking, now felt wrong—or was it all in my head?

Coming in here was supposed to clear my mind. Make it easier to think. But instead, all I thought about was Hawk—the one thing I shouldn't be thinking about. Until today, I'd honestly believed I stood a chance. A chance to be part of a team, to make a difference, and maybe for us to be together. But I guess I was just a mark, like Tucker said. A line of communication to The Five, far better than any hacking job could obtain. I was a means to an end, and telling me that he was falling in love with me was some sort of ploy for information. But it didn't seem right. In that moment, the moment before Christophe stormed in and changed everything, the look on his face seemed so real. The worry of uncertainty creeping in at the sides of his eyes. The slight quiver of his bottom lip as he watched me react to his words. It couldn't have all been a lie. Could it? And even if it wasn't, did it matter? Christophe offered me the world if only I'd be willing to take him with it. And why shouldn't I? Kendall or any of the other girls I knew wouldn't have hesitated to say yes to his proposal, so why couldn't I?

I released a deep breath and tried to focus. I let loose the arrow. It swerved and hit to the left of the bullseye.

"You seem a bit out of practice."

Lowering the bow, I turned to see Mom standing behind me. At least she had the courtesy to wait until I had made my shot before speaking.

I shrugged. "More like out of sorts."

"Which one, your head or your heart?" She took a step closer, and the faintest smile curled on her lips. Her real smile, not the one designed for company.

"Both, I think. I'm guessing Christophe told you about his proposal."

She nodded. I sighed, having actually thought he might keep this a secret until I gave him an answer.

"Let's see the ring."

I held out my hand, fingers crooked at an awkward angle. It felt strange, like it wasn't really me.

"It's pretty. I tried to talk him into something bigger, but he was right, this is more your style." She nodded, eyes locked on the ring, or simply refusing to look at me.

"You knew?"

"Of course I did. He's been carrying that around for a while now."

"So you think I should marry him?"

"I'm not going to tell you what to do. You never listen anyway." She let go of my hand and laced her fingers in a tight knot, holding them at her waist. "But what I will tell you is that he really does love you."

"I know that." I swallowed hard, then placed the bow back

in its place in the cabinet. Gently. Taking my time. "It's just a lot to think about."

"You're young. Figure out what you need to figure out. If he's it, then I'll be happy for you both, but if he's not, that's something only you can know for sure."

"How'd you know?"

"Love isn't just something you feel, it's something you do. Even at the worst of times, it should never feel like a chore."

"Is that still how you feel? Even after all he's done."

The smile vanished, replaced by a glare that bore down on me cold as ice. The softness in her voice disappeared, and she replaced it with a clipped, irritated tone. "You're my daughter, and you are my priority, but I love Christophe like he was my own son. He's grown up in this house from a charming little boy to a noble young man. A good man. If you decide not to accept, please have the courtesy to let him down easy."

"I will," I said, not sure if I was responding to a request or a command.

The door across the room opened. Christophe froze when he saw us, his face void of color, rightfully knowing that we were talking about him. "Sorry, I didn't realize anyone was in here. I'll go."

"No need. I was just about to leave," Mom said as she cast one last knowing look at me.

I exhaled, relieved this conversation would soon be over. She turned back toward me and stepped closer. I tensed, expecting the worst, but instead she wrapped her arms around me, so quickly and out of character that it took me several seconds to hug her back. I inhaled the smell of her perfume as my face disappeared into her hair. Her signature scent, sophisti-cated like an exotic flower. It never changed. For the briefest of moments, I was six years old again and safe in her arms.

"Do what you feel is right, but remember, if you walk away from a proposal it may not come around again."

She let me go and left me stunned as she glided across the room, graceful and poised, stopping only once to squeeze Christophe's arm before leaving. He stood there and stared at me, me staring back at him, neither knowing what to say. I hadn't given him an answer yet, and he was smart enough not to ask again.

"I can come back later if you want," he said, finally breaking the awkward silence.

"No, it's okay. I wasn't really into it tonight anyway. I...." What was I supposed to say? *I'm not sure. I don't know what I want.*

"You don't need to tell me." He shrugged out of his suit jacket and hung it on a hook by the door, then rummaged through his gym bag for his shorts and T-shirt before chucking it on the floor. He pointed toward the hall. "I'll just go change and give you a minute."

I nodded as he slipped back out of the gym, never once daring to look my way.

As the door clicked shut, I took a deep breath and gasped against the strange thickness in my chest. The room seemed to close in around me. Tighter. Smaller. Suffocating. I ran toward the exit, but stopped, my hand frozen on the doorknob. Beside me, Christophe's suit jacket hung slightly heavier on the right side. I hesitated for a second but then dug my hand inside, my fingertips brushing against the phone weighing his pocket down. An unassuming square of plastic that held the secrets of an entire country.

Opening the door a crack, I peeked down the hall. Empty. I pulled the phone out of his pocket and held it in my hand. So many things could be on this device. Information that thieves like Ratchett and Hawk would give up everything to get their hands on. But was there anything on here that I might want to know? Things I might need to know?

I clicked the tiny Power button at the top of the device. A bright red, white, and blue lock screen popped up. Now what? I closed my eyes and searched my memory for anything I could think of. Christophe's birthday, 1107. The device vibrated and the screen cleared. Nope. I thought again: 2356. The screen cleared and opened to the main navigation page. Seriously? He still used his locker combination as his cell phone password? Kind of funny. However, the only people that would've known it were likely me and the filing clerk in the Charlotte Hall administration office.

I stared at it again. If I'd ever actually marry him, Christophe had to be able to trust me. I needed to be someone he could trust. But how could I even consider his proposal without being certain of what I was getting into? I'm sure he'd understand.

Sliding the phone into my sweatpants pocket, I flung the door open.

"Whoa," Christophe said, as I ran directly into his chest.

I stepped back, flustered and face red, the phone feeling like a brick in my pants, the weight surely noticeable.

He chuckled and moved to the side of the doorframe. "Make sure you keep your head up."

"Sure. Thanks." I forced a smile as I slipped around him, then sped down the hallway.

My mind raced, trying to find somewhere to go that the cameras wouldn't see. Somewhere I wouldn't get caught. At least not right away. I dodged into my room and looked around. No cameras in here, but also the first place Christophe would look for me. I ran into the bathroom, climbed into the shower, and crouched in the corner farthest away from the shower head.

The dampness of the tile seeped through my sweats, but at least I had privacy.

As I typed in the passcode again, my heart pounded in my chest. I had the secret email of the entire country in my hands. I clicked on the Mail icon. Reams and reams of emails filled the screen. Names I'd never heard before with references to things I didn't know anything about. What was I even looking for exactly? Where to start?

I scrolled down page after page when something finally caught my attention.

An email sent from Christophe with the subject *X9 Vaccine Project*. I hadn't realized he really did any real work around here. I clicked on the message.

Preliminary testing on the vaccination program has been a success. We will be halting the infection process in expectation of the rollout of the vaccine. Any undesirable factions will be targeted and eliminated prior to the vaccine being provided to the public at large.

Eliminated? Infection process? The X9 virus wasn't some foreign threat. The Five knew about it. They were the ones spreading it to their own people.

Clicking in the Search function, I typed in X9. Emails from various personnel over the past three years popped up. The oldest ones from Hawk's father, Eldrin Locksley.

Thank you for the grant provided for our research. However, we will not be able to accept it. The X9 project has taken an unexpected turn and we have decided to table the project indefinitely. We have developed the technology you expressed interest in regarding brain functioning and impulse control, but feel the applications for this technology are not within our corporate ethical framework. If you are still interested in donating, I would be available to discuss the other meaningful projects in our research portfolio.

This didn't make any sense. This X9 didn't sound like the same thing.

I typed *Locksley* into the search. The prior email showed up in a shaded hyperlink. I scanned through the list. So many emails about X9. It would take me days to sort through this information. Then one stuck out. I clicked on *Purchase of Locksley Chemical,* dated two weeks after the last email from Eldrin.

Negotiations with Locksley have stalled.
Still refusing to give up formulation for X9.
Please advise.

Then a response from Vincent Masters himself:

Use alternative measures.

I fell against the tile wall as I furiously ripped through every email I could, each one filling more blanks in my head. Hawk's father developed drugs to affect brain functioning and wouldn't give them to The Five. Then Eldrin wound up dead. The Five were infecting people with a virus with the same X9 name, hid a known cure from the infected, then announced a miracle vaccine to save everyone. It didn't add up. Why spend so much time poisoning people just to save them in the end? I thought of Tucker and all those people who suffered because of The Five. All the blood. All those lives. Tucker still wasn't the same after taking the cure.

All the disjointed information swirled around in my head

trying to come to a logical conclusion. My vision blurred as the shower stall seemed to spin. I dropped the phone into my lap and held my head in my hands as the pieces finally started to connect and fall into place.

It was all a lie.

Everything was a lie.

The virus wasn't really a virus, it was a marketing plan for the vaccine. And the vaccine wasn't meant to control the illness, it was meant control the world. The government the people thought protected them was poisoning them, executing them like lab rats that had passed their usefulness, just to turn on anyone who survived. My father would kill anyone who stood in his way. He already had.

There was only one thing left that I could do.

I had to warn Hawk.

THIRTY-SEVEN

The lights were on. Shadows of figures moved across the arched windows while I stood watching them from the street below. In my pocket, the phone vibrated again. Longer this time. I pulled it out and glanced at the little screen, my finger itching to hit the Answer button from reflex but my brain smart enough to let it keep ringing. I didn't recognize the number, but that didn't mean it wasn't Christophe trying to track me down. He was probably losing his mind without his phone, stalking the halls and ripping his hands through his hair, cursing me for betraying him. The guilt in the pit of my stomach grew a few more inches and I gagged. Even after the things he'd done, I didn't want to hurt him. There had to be a good explanation for why he never told me the whole truth; there just wasn't time for me to find out what it was. Christophe had to be another victim in this whole crazy screwed-up plan, but things just got too big for him to get out. At least that's what I'd been telling myself over and over on the way here.

I stuffed the phone back in my pocket and took one last deep breath. *Go time.* I drew back the arrow, careful not to knock off the note tied to the shaft, and aimed just above the window to compensate for the extra weight. I only had one chance to get this right.

Exhale. Release. *Smash.*

The noise echoed louder than I expected. Shards of glass fell from the sky like razor-sharp rain. I ducked toward the side of the building, eyes down and head covered with my arm. Now I just needed someone to find the note. I looked around the corner into the alley. Seeing no one, I slung the bow over my shoulder and walked to stand next to the door, hoping.

Leaning against the wall, I closed my eyes. The rough surface of the bricks scratched at my head and snagged my hair as I stretched my chin toward the sky. They'd probably be pissed about the broken window, but I couldn't think of anything else to try. Tucker told me never to come back, but I couldn't let this go. They needed to know what they were up against. Hawk needed to know who killed his father. He may never forgive me, but I couldn't let him go on not knowing. I would never hurt him like that.

The door opened with a screech. I jerked upright.

Tucker's angry face popped out toward me. "You've got your fifteen minutes. That's it."

EVERYTHING HAD CHANGED since the last time I'd stepped into this loft. It already felt like that day happened in a past life or an alternate universe instead of last week's reality, and looking around now didn't help the feeling that it had never happened at all. The dirty floor had been scrubbed clean. The walls and windows thoroughly washed to a grime-free finish. Lights hung on wires and chased away the shadows that used to live there, and the hollow emptiness now had tables and chairs

and couches and all the things that belonged in the Sanctuary—
the one that no longer existed because of me.

"Your note said you had information," Tucker said as he
retreated as far from me as he could get while still being able to
hear my response.

"I did ... I mean, I do."

My carefully planned words jumbled in my brain. The
shock of seeing that they had moved on so quickly without me
had sucker-punched me in the gut and I had trouble bouncing
back. In my head, I had also pictured—hoped—that more people
would be here. People to distract me from Tucker and Ratchett's unimpressed faces, from the death stare Red burned
through my skull or, worst of all, from the fact Hawk wouldn't
even look at me.

I cleared my throat and concentrated on Tucker, the least
threatening of the crowd. "It's about the virus. It's a huge lie.
They are infecting people on purpose."

"Knew that already. Thanks for wasting our time." Red
stood and tried to push me out the door by sheer force of fear.

"That's not it. It's not some other country attacking us, it's
this country, we're attacking ourselves. The whole virus thing is
supposed to scare people into taking the vaccine, but the
vaccine won't help anyone. The virus isn't real, it's a poison."

Blank stares. Snarled lips.

"The vaccine is really a mind-control drug. They're
building an army of zombie soldiers."

"Could you not come up with a more convincing lie than
that?" Tucker rolled his eyes and laughed. "Besides, the zombie
trend dropped out a long time ago. Try something fresh next
time."

"Not real zombies." I stepped forward to make my point and
regretted it instantly as the temperature in the room dropped,
and not from the smashed-up window swirling an evening

breeze around us all. "The virus, or poison, or whatever it is, was supposed to threaten people into taking the secret 'cure,' but the cure was actually an antidote for the poison mixed with the X9 mind-control drugs to see if it would work on real people. Since it did, they're going full-scale with the vaccine."

"Okay, that doesn't make any sense. First of all," Tucker said, counting off on his fingers, "X9 is the virus, not the cure. Second, if they needed guinea pigs for the drugs, why wouldn't they only infect those people instead of killing off whole neighborhoods? Third, who are they? And fourth, last, whatever, why should we even consider believing you?"

"Because I'm telling you the truth." I pulled out Christophe's phone and waved it in the air. "It's The Five. I have emails, texts, all sorts of things from my dad's inner circle that talk about the X9 drugs and the testing they've been doing. I don't know why they called the virus the same thing as the actual drugs, but it's all part of one big deception. They used the soup kitchens to poison people and create a fake plague so no one would question when they rolled out the fake vaccine. They created a sample of people to test X9 mind control on, used the media to frighten everyone else into wanting to take the vaccine, then let the poison kill off protesters and anyone who rebelled against The Five.

"But they never planned on you guys getting in the way. Instead of stopping you, they've been using you by letting you steal the cure and giving them a real-life, uncontrolled test sample. When protests get crazy they flip some kind of trigger that makes everyone affected turn on each other. That's why you went all homicidal, Tucker. You didn't do it on purpose. You did it because you couldn't stop yourself."

"Nuh-uh. No way." Tucker waved his arms in the air and started pacing back and forth. "I'd know if someone was controlling me."

I narrowed my eyes and stared at him. "So you stabbed Hawk in the back on purpose?"

"Of course not. But...." His face twisted as my words clicked in his brain. "They couldn't do that. Could they?"

"That's what the emails say. Now that they know the mind control works, they mass-produced it and called it a vaccine so people will volunteer to be shot up with this stuff and The Five doesn't look responsible for the virus. Once it was ready to launch, they tried to use me to finally get rid of you. It didn't work, but once the vaccine is given to everyone, you'll never be able to hide."

Nobody moved, but nobody argued either. The whole thing sounded ludicrous. I knew it with every word I said. Every word that had come spewing out of me like a broken sewer pipe of conspiracy theory. Every word one hundred percent true.

"And you're telling us 'cause?" Red said, hands on her curvy hips, looking dangerous.

"Because we need to do something. Stop them before it's too late."

She dropped her forehead and snickered. "We?"

"Yes. I can't let this happen and I figured you wouldn't either. If you don't care, I'll deal with it myself."

Red burst out laughing. A loud amused laugh that made me doubt myself, but I shifted on my feet and held my head up.

"Thanks, Princess, but we can take it from here." She waved her hand in two quick bursts to dismiss me.

"No. I brought you the information that none of you have been able to get. I'm staying."

Red charged up in my face, but I refused to back down. "Screw that. After what you did to us? Hell no."

"You have no idea what happened."

"You ran to Daddy. That's what happened."

"No, I didn't."

"Quiet." Hawk stood and stared at Red, not even willing to give me a dirty look. "You two can fight about this later. Right now we need a plan."

Red shut up except for one loud huff.

"Now, we need to—"

"There's more." I bit down on the side of my cheek and took a deep breath. "The X9 mind-control drugs were created by a scientist at a private downtown lab that was bought out by Nott Chemical."

Hawk's head whipped toward me, no expression on his face, except the fear in his eyes that couldn't hide the question he wanted to ask. *Bullseye.* Every word had hit right on target.

I stepped forward and lowered my voice. "Can we talk about this somewhere else?"

"Whatever ya gotta say, just spit it out," Red said.

I ignored her and tried to keep Hawk's gaze, letting everything and everyone else in the room fall away. "Please."

The corner of his mouth twitched like he might say something, but he kept silent and headed past me to the stairwell. I followed quickly, not wanting to miss my chance.

As the door clicked closed behind me, Hawk crossed his arms and planted his feet in a firm, ready stance, his face still lowered and refusing to meet mine. Was he really that mad that he couldn't even look at me?

The hallway light flickered and buzzed on the wall as I stood there trying to piece together the words to tell him the bad news. I thought it would be easy to spill everything if I could get him alone, but instead it brought up the last time we were this close, when the last thing on my mind were words. The clean, unmistakable smell of him filled the tiny space, creating a sting in my lips and a quiver in the soft spot behind my knees. That wasn't helping either.

"Did you know your dad's lab was developing X9?"

He shook his head and finally looked up with a dark midnight stare on the edge of a breaking storm. "They killed him to get it, didn't they?"

I pulled out Christophe's cell with my father's email displayed and held it up for Hawk to see. "It's from the day before he died."

He took the phone and fell back against the wall as if he'd been pushed, hard, his shoulders crumpling into his chest.

"He figured out what The Five were going to do with it, so he refused to hand it over. He tried to stop all this. He tried to do the right thing."

"But he's still dead." His voice wavered on the last word and a shocked, vacant look spread over his face that shot a chill down my back. I'd seen the same look after Tucker stabbed him. The look he had when he talked about his mother. The look that wasn't Hawk the hero, but Corbin the lost boy.

I stepped closer and he didn't move. I raised my right hand and cautiously placed it on his arm. "I'm sorry."

He blinked and snatched his arm away, knocking my hand off. I backed up. I'd crossed a line. I should go.

I turned to leave, but his arm wrapped around my waist and pulled me against him, my head suddenly swimming. He buried his face in my neck and held tight, the heat of his skin seeping through my tank top.

"Thank you," he whispered.

"I thought you needed to know the truth."

I reveled in his hands spread across my back, his head against my cheek, the needy tightness of his grip around my ribs, then sighed and peeled myself away.

"And you need to know I never betrayed you. Someone figured out I was involved with you guys and stuck a GPS tracker on me that night. I'd never do something like that to you, and I tried to tell you but Tucker said you didn't want to see me, and then I found out everything and I knew I needed to tell you, and—"

Before I could finish his mouth pressed against mine, devouring my chaotic apology. His lips tasted so much better than I'd remembered a hundred times since the last time he'd had his arms around me. His kiss embodied everything he was—strong, hopeful, and had a way of making me want to do anything he said for the rest of eternity. I kissed him back, hoping he would understand all those things without me having to trip on words to say them. He put his hand on the back of my neck, pulling me in as far as he could without swallowing me whole. A strange feeling rushed through my stomach and tingled up my spine. He believed me. It was all going to be okay.

He pulled away too soon, both of our breaths mixing together in heavy, frenzied gasps.

"Every single day I'd hoped you'd come back. I wanted you to stomp in here and tell me how wrong I was about what happened, but you never came." He put his hands on my cheeks, holding my head like I could actually turn away. "I wanted to tell you I was sorry."

"I'm sorry too. I swear I didn't know about the raid."

"I know." He let me go and took my hand. "Just promise me you won't leave again? I was a complete wreck with you gone."

"Never."

He smiled. The confident, carefree, sexy smile. The one that made my knees tremble. He leaned forward and kissed me on the forehead, giving my hand a squeeze. I winced as metal pinched between my fingers, sending a painful jolt up my arm. The ring. I'd completely forgot I was still wearing it.

"What's wrong?"

"Nothing," I said, but my hand twitched in his, giving me away.

He pulled my hand up into his sight, the diamond sparkling

in the dim lights even brighter than I ever thought possible, or maybe I'd just imagined that it was.

His smile disappeared as his jaw fell open. "Is that—"

"It's not what you think."

"So it's not an engagement ring?"

"It is, but—"

"It's that guy." He dropped my hand and backed away. "The one that tried to have me arrested. Isn't it?"

I nodded.

"You're going to marry him?" It sounded more like a statement than a question. "He's one of them, Mercury."

"No, I'm not marrying him. I don't want to."

Hawk grabbed the sides of his head and spun around, punching a white-knuckled fist into the brick wall behind him. He shook off the pain, his jaw clenched and a spot of red pooled against his skin where he'd made contact. "Maybe I wasn't wrong about you at all."

I put my hand on his chest, but he pulled away like my touch burned. "That's not fair. I thought you'd given up on me."

"So you just gave up on me instead?"

"I was never going to marry him!"

He stopped and stared, hard as stone. I missed when he'd been mad enough to ignore me.

"If you never considered marrying him, then why are you wearing the ring?" He closed his eyes and shook his head, then rammed his hands through the air. "It's your life. Don't let me stand in your way."

He ripped open the door to the stairwell and marched back into the main room. "Tucker. Red. I feel like setting a lab on fire tonight. You in?"

"Hell yeah," Tucker said as he gave Red a high five. "Matches or explosives?"

"Whatever. I just need to leave now."

Hawk turned and brushed past me back to the stairs. I ran behind him, but he stopped and turned to me. Whatever he'd felt five minutes ago had evaporated and been replaced with a blank emptiness.

"Oh no. You're not coming," he said, stopping so I couldn't pass.

"But I'm the one who told you about the lab."

He huffed as reason started seeping in. "Don't you have a wedding to plan?"

"What?" Red hollered behind me and then laughed so hard she snorted.

Hawk continued down the stairs followed by Tucker and Red, both looking me over as they passed, amused smirks on their faces. I leaned against the wall and let myself sink to the floor as the outside door slammed shut with a smack.

How could I be so brainless as to not take off the ring? And he wouldn't even listen to me. I'd risked everything by coming here and telling him what I knew. My father was going to be so pissed when he found out about this. Christophe had probably already told him about me stealing his phone. *Dammit.* His phone. Hawk still had it. *I'm good as dead.*

"If you're just going to sit around, you could at least clean up the glass from that window you smashed into my workspace."

I snapped out of my own thoughts and stood up to see Ratchett watching me from his corner. He'd been so quiet, I'd forgotten about him.

I walked over and leaned against his desk. "I guess I'm useless now that Hawk has the information he needs."

Ratchett shook his head and made a sound that could have been a laugh or a grunt, then turned back to his keyboard and hammered a series of keys too quick to follow. What was his problem? I sat there staring, hoping he would fill me in on the joke, but he didn't look up.

"Tucker said that's all he wanted from me anyway. Information."

"Just like you're trying to get out of me by lurking here instead of going away?"

I sighed.

"Of course he was using you for information. You're Vincent Masters's daughter. Who wouldn't want to use that connection? Why do you think he would let you into our operation so quickly?"

So it was true, and it stung somewhere under my rib cage. They used me the whole time. Tucker had accused me of using them—

"Doesn't mean he didn't actually fall for you. He definitely didn't plan for that."

"And you think I did? Honestly, all I want to do is march out the door and never come back, but here I am." I whipped my hand through the air toward the door, partly to make my point, partly to do something aggressive to start burning off the anger building up in my chest.

"Calm down. This is why I don't like getting involved in these types of things. People are too messy and my systems don't give me snark." He ran his hand gently across the keyboard. "I've known Hawk for a long time and he doesn't let people in. Every other girl who—"

"Every other girl?"

He lowered his forehead and stared at me as if I'd dropped IQ points by breathing. "You honestly think you're the only girl he's made out with? You obviously didn't know him back in his hardcore party-boy days."

I gasped, not knowing how much I should let on. Not like it mattered; he didn't think my loyalty existed anyway.

"Don't get your firewalls in a fury. I know he told you about his past."

"Not about the swarm of girls in it."

"Look. You're not the only girl on his list, but you're the only one who's mattered."

"I don't think I matter much right now."

He swiveled in his chair and faced me with an irritated expression.

"Don't you understand? He actually let himself fall in love with you and you broke his heart. Don't think because you didn't see him that he wasn't around. Every night he'd disappear and come back a bigger disaster than the night before," Ratchett said as easily as if he were ordering a coffee. "He gave you the only real thing he had left, and you broke it. Badly."

"I broke *his* heart? I tried to explain, but he wouldn't listen and just took off. He didn't even try to fight for me."

"He's got enough to fight for. What he's doing, what we're all doing here, is important. I know you know that. Maybe what he really needs is someone willing to fight for him once in a while."

I pushed myself away from the desk and stormed across the room. Ratchett was right. A little harsh, but right, and sitting here wasn't going to accomplish anything.

"Where are you going?" Ratchett yelled after me. "You haven't cleaned up your mess yet."

I glanced over my shoulder. "Actually, that's exactly what I'm going to do."

THIRTY-EIGHT

The bow and quiver banged against my back as I ran, but I didn't care. It didn't even matter when people chucked awkward stares and muffled swear words at me as I weaved through the streets like an escaped prison inmate. Maybe when this was over I would take Red's advice and find a more concealable weapon, but right now I had somewhere to be.

Everything that had happened came bubbling up through me, making me vibrate with words to say and things to do, and I knew I couldn't sit around waiting at the loft. Sitting back and waiting had got me to this point, and if I wanted anything to change, I'd have to go after it. I didn't fight for what I wanted. I gave up. I ran away.

I deserved to be part of this group as much as anyone, and I was going to tell Hawk that. I'd tell him they all needed to give me another chance. *No!* I shook my head. They were going to give me another chance, because this was all a massive misunderstanding. Even if it meant earning every single person's approval. Even if I had to be nice to Red. Even if I had to forget all about Hawk's lips on mine.

My feet fell out of rhythm for a second and sent me sideways. I struggled against gravity, not wanting to waste any time falling, and managed to keep moving forward, but it was too late to keep my thoughts from crashing into the memory of that kiss in the stairwell. It was all still there. Every feeling I'd tried to purge since the night Christophe hauled me away. Every uncontrollable tremble in my stomach when he looked at me the way he did when his hands were in my hair and brushing against my skin. The look that lit up, no matter how hard he tried to be nothing but angry. The look that remembered me the way I remembered him.

But I could let that go if I needed to. I could. There was a lot more at stake than something we might've had, and I'd be willing to give it up if it would make things right again. I would tell him that too. If I could just find him.

The streets had disappeared into dark buildings, warehouses, and widespread factories that looked like they'd gone to sleep for the night. I slowed down, looking at signs and addresses, trying to make sure I hadn't accidentally passed the lab. As I rounded the corner of a particularly run-down packing-supply warehouse, I heard voices. I stuck close to the walls, listening for a moment, but the glowing red head bobbing in the distance let me know I'd found the right place.

"Hey," I yelled with difficulty as I ran as hard as I still could manage.

"Shut up." Tucker charged forward and ran into me palm-first against my mouth and an arm wrapped around my back. I struggled under his grip, but he refused to let go. "The least you can do is not turn us in again."

I shook my head under his hand, not understanding what he was talking about. He stared me down and slowly pulled his hand away.

I dropped my voice to a whisper. "What the hell are you talking about, and where's Hawk?"

"One of your buddies has him. He ambushed us."

"What are you talking about?"

Tucker pointed. I ducked behind a dumpster and looked out. The eerie glow of the building's exterior lights lit up the parking lot. Someone stood, right arm extended at a heap of someone kneeling on the concrete. From here I couldn't tell the faces, but I knew the stance. Christophe, and the person on the ground had to be Hawk. But what was he doing? Why wasn't Hawk fighting back?

As if reading my mind, Tucker pressed himself close to me. "He's got a gun."

What? My mind spun. Where would Christophe get a gun? Did he even know how to use one? By now he would know I'd stolen his phone. He would know I'd betrayed him. But maybe I could still talk him down.

The figures moved. Christophe took a step toward Hawk. Every muscle in my body tensed. Horrified, but powerless.

I couldn't hear it, but I felt it as Christophe smashed the gun against the side of Hawk's face. A shiver ran through my gut as his head flopped to the side. Darkness clouded Hawk's cheeks. Might be blood, might just be hate. A faint breath of relief escaped my lungs. At least he didn't shoot him.

I turned away. There wasn't much time.

"I can talk to him," I said. "I can convince him to let Hawk go."

"And why should we believe you?" Tucker said, scanning me over like I was wearing last year's shoes.

"Christophe is my friend. This isn't like him, I swear."

"Christophe?" Tucker's mouth dropped open and he rubbed his forehead. "You mean that monster over there is the guy you picked over Hawk? Wasn't he the one you sold us out to last time?"

"I didn't. He just ... and we're not...." I shook my head. "There's no time for me to explain."

Headlights illuminated the parking lot and everyone turned to see a vintage cherry-red convertible ease in. I grabbed the side of the dumpster and edged forward on my toes. The driver cut the engine, which distracted Christophe enough to finally stop and look. The door opened. Under the menacing yellow lights, my father stepped out of the driver's seat. I gasped. I couldn't remember the last time he'd been behind the wheel of a car. This situation clearly needed the utmost discretion. As if I didn't already know something bad was about to go down.

"This is so not good." I grabbed my head, pulling at my hair, and paced in the small space hidden by the bin, hoping something genius would suddenly come spilling out my ears.

"No shit," Red said with a snort. "Thanks for screwing us —again."

"I didn't do this." It came out louder than I'd hoped. Red's eyes popped out like she might choke me where I stood. I lowered my voice. "I know you guys don't like me, and right now I really don't care, but you're out of choices. If you want to help Hawk, you need to help me."

"What do you care?" Tucker grumbled.

"I just do. I always did, even though I'm sure you don't believe that, but he's in huge trouble right now and we don't have a lot of time. Can you please just trust me?"

Tucker pulled his hood farther over his eyes and backed away.

"Still don't trust ya," Red piped up. The only one willing to look at me. "But we'll help. Right, Tuck?"

He glared at Red. She glared back harder.

"Whatever," he huffed, clearly outranked or afraid of being beaten with his own limbs. "But if you get any of us killed, you're so dead."

I TOOK a deep breath as I watched Red and Tucker disappear into the shadows. My turn now. Fortunately, I hadn't heard any shots, but I didn't think Christophe would really shoot him. I knew him too well. He wasn't a killer. But I'd never betrayed him like this before. And since when did he get a gun?

Leaning against the cold metal of the dumpster, I surveyed the situation. Everyone had stayed in the same place. My father talking to Christophe. Christophe pointing the gun at Hawk. Hawk on his knees.

Whatever move I made had to be quick. If they were waiting for the police to take Hawk away, I would only have a few minutes. If they weren't waiting for the police, if they actually ... I would have less time than that. I grabbed an arrow from the quiver and loosed it as fast as I could. Aim didn't matter now. I just needed a distraction.

It flew inches from Christophe's face into the brick wall and bounced back onto the ground.

My father leaned over and picked it up, running his fingertips over the shaft. He raised an open hand to Christophe and stared in my direction.

Bullseye. I'd got their attention. But now what?

THIRTY-NINE

I held my breath as I nocked the arrow. No turning back now. They knew I was here.

"Mercury," a voice called through the dark. I couldn't tell who called through my own pulse ringing in my ears. But it didn't matter. I was being summoned.

I stood. Arms raised and arrow aimed at Christophe's chest, I sidestepped my way closer.

Nobody moved as I approached. Set pieces. Like walking into a painting. My father, strong and official to the left of the frame. Christophe to the right, gun raised at an injured Hawk kneeling on the ground. Still-life figures in brushstrokes of fear and power and blood. Each one of us brought here for our own reasons. Each one of us standing our ground, locking us in a stalemate.

Christophe struggled to keep his arm straight, but I could see the tremble in his hand. Either he wasn't prepared to shoot, or he was wound up enough to kill us all.

I drew the bowstring back and gripped the feathers tight. "Drop the gun."

No response. Was he even listening to me? His stare was fixed on Hawk. Nothing else existed outside the two of them.

"I said drop the gun."

"I can't." He murmured, not looking at me. "I can't let him walk away."

"Yes, you can. He won't hurt you." A promise to Christophe, an order to Hawk. I couldn't stand to see either of them hurt in this.

"Don't listen to her." My father's booming voice cut into our conversation. "She's trying to get you to back down. He's a dangerous criminal. He's right there, Christophe. Do it."

The tremble in his arm progressed to an all-out shake. He wasn't a killer. I knew Christophe. He wasn't ready for this. But I didn't know how much of a push it would take to put him over the edge.

"Don't." I lowered my voice and took a slow step toward him, keeping my eye firm on my target. "If any part of you cares about me, you won't do it. Please, Christophe, I'm begging you. Don't do my father's dirty work anymore. He's making you like him. Cold. Vicious. Don't go there. You're better than that."

"But ... I have to. He's messing everything up."

Christophe repositioned his hand on the gun and my entire body flinched.

"He's the enemy, Mercury. Don't you see that? Why can't you see that?" He rubbed his free hand over his face and growled. To me? To himself? "It wasn't supposed to be like this, Merc. I only wanted to make things better, but he keeps getting in the way. Everything I want he takes from me. He's ruining everything."

Hawk raised his head, blood oozing down the side of his face, and stared straight down the barrel at Christophe. "Because what you're doing is next-level evil."

"Shut up," he yelled, spit flying out of his mouth as he

jammed the gun farther into Hawk's face. "You don't get to talk."

"Christophe, this needs to stop. Hawk isn't hurting anyone. He saves people ... he saved me." It was the wrong thing to say. I knew it the second it passed my lips, but it was truth, pure and unfiltered. "Please don't do this. For me. Please."

For the first time, he looked away from Hawk and stared straight at me. His glassy eyes burned across the distance between us, drunk on testosterone, laced with a cocktail of rage and fear. This would not end well. "You know I'll do anything for you, but I can't let him get away this time. I'm sorry. I'm so sorry."

The bottom of my stomach dropped out and I used all my will to fight the urge to run over to him. I would never be fast enough. I wouldn't be able to save him that way.

"Wait." I pivoted on my heel, re-aiming the arrow at my father. "If you shoot him, I'll shoot my father."

"You can't," Christophe barked, shaking his head.

"I can and I will. Now drop the gun."

His gaze turned from me to my father. He wavered. I still had a chance. Hawk's head hung down, staring at the pavement. Was he admitting defeat, or was he willing to let his death take him as it came? He couldn't give up if he had any chance of escape. *Look up, Hawk. Look up.*

"Mercury, enough," my father shouted. "I can order Christophe to shoot him faster than you can hit me."

"But if you do that, then you'll be dead."

"My life is not up for negotiation." He unbuttoned the cuffs on his dress shirt and rolled them up his forearms as he stepped toward me. No fear. No trepidation. Calling my bluff. "Besides, you can't kill me with that thing."

I tightened my grip on the bow and raised it higher. "Depends where I aim."

He stopped, his puzzled expression showing that he didn't understand or he was weighing his options carefully.

"After all those lessons you paid for, you know I can make this shot. One clean hit is all I need."

The tip of the arrow vibrated as I tried to keep calm. If my father saw any sign of weakness, he'd know he'd won. There was no room for hesitation. If I shot my father, Christophe would shoot Hawk. If I didn't, he might still shoot Hawk, and possibly me. If I shot Christophe, my father would shoot Hawk. Only a minuscule chance existed that Hawk would walk out of here alive, but I couldn't back down now.

"You would shoot your own father for this boy? What a pathetic waste you are." The words stung. Standing in front of him with an arrow at his chest and he could still cut me deeper than a switchblade.

"Why wouldn't I? He would never hurt me the way that you do. Consider it payback for all those black eyes, the fractured wrist, and the broken nose."

His eyes flared. Even facing death, he had decorum. One should not talk about such things. One should never call out her father for being a monster, especially in front of staff and strangers. One should keep her mouth shut and know her place. I guess I wasn't socialite material after all.

"Or maybe I should do it for Mom? All those bruises you gave her. I don't know why she never left you."

"Because she knows better. She would be nothing without me. Sometimes people make sacrifices for the life they want. And who wouldn't want the life of a queen?"

"What are you talking about? What is she talking about?" Christophe started losing his grip. He looked at me, then my father, then me again, the anger melting away to complete chaos. For the amount of time he spent with my family, I would've thought he'd have noticed the scars.

"He hits me." It felt odd to say it out loud. "He hits me, he hits my mom. People that you love, that care about you, he hurts them because he can."

"What?" Christophe's face contorted in disbelief. All this time and he had never put the pieces together. Never considered that the bruises weren't normal.

"Just shoot him, Christophe," my father yelled. "She's just trying to distract you. Remember, there is a bigger plan at stake here."

"Every time I ended up in the hospital. Every time I ran away from home. It was because of him."

"No. No. No!" Christophe shouted. "This can't be true. Why didn't you tell me?" His head darted between me and my father again, unsure who had let him down more. "I could've helped. I could've been there. How could you not tell me?"

"I didn't want anyone to worry about me."

Hawk turned his head to look at me for the first time since I arrived. The skin around his eyes had already puffed up from the hit Christophe had laid on him, but even through whatever pain he felt, I could see his lips turn up at the edges. A broken smile.

"But you told him, didn't you?" Christophe's anger came flooding back, watching Hawk look at me. "Didn't you?"

He lunged forward and kicked Hawk square in the chest, winding him enough that his breath echoed through the night sky. Hawk's body twitched back, but he stayed upright like a high-end punching bag. But being tough wasn't going to help him if I couldn't get Christophe to put the gun down.

"You don't tell me everything either. You didn't tell me about the X9 experiments. All those people you stood by and let my father and his lackeys poison. All those people you were going to let them inject with that vaccine we all know isn't going to save them from anything. It's going to make them zombies,

Christophe. People who trust you and this country, only to have that same government enslave them without them even knowing. How is that not worse?"

"I wanted to tell you ... and it's not as bad as it sounds. This country is going to war. You know I would do anything you asked me to, but I can't let him walk away. He needs to be gone. Don't you understand that we have to do something?"

"I don't want to understand. You've let innocent people die. There is nothing to understand."

"Enough," my father bellowed, his face looking like it might explode. "This is not the time or place to discuss this."

"Because this is all your fault," I screamed. "You had a chance to do something great with this country. Instead, everyone is scared and angry and suffering and you don't even care."

"Of course I care. It's my job to care. You don't know what it's like to be in my position. The pressure. The stress. It's more than someone like you can comprehend. I make choices for these people every single day. Do you know the sacrifices I've made for this country?"

"I do know. You sacrificed your soul. I've seen what your choices have done to the people you say you care about. Those people who don't share our zip code. I've had bones broken because of your pressure, your stress. I've watched my mother cry night after night. I've hated myself every single day for the past five years because of what you've done to me." Hot tears pooled and burned down my cheeks. *Not now. I didn't have time for a breakdown now.*

Then for a moment, so fast I almost missed it, I thought I saw something shift. Something in my father's face that wasn't anger or disappointment, something that looked a lot like somewhere in there he might actually feel sorry for what he'd done to me. Might actually regret the choices he'd made. But then it disappeared. The smooth publicist-approved image for the world slid back into place.

"I'll shoot him myself." My father started toward Christophe. I followed him with the arrow. I didn't want to shoot. No matter how much I hated him in this moment, I didn't want him to know he'd completely broken me. Shattered to the point where I would even consider shooting my own father. But I couldn't let him hurt anyone else.

My fingers started to go slack. The sting in my muscles from holding the bow made my arm twitch, but the sight never left my mark. I swallowed hard against the lump growing in my throat.

"I'm sorry," I whispered into the night.

Something moved in the window behind them. I tightened my grip on the arrow fletching. Another movement in the background.

A flicker.

A flash.

A spark.

Then ... *boom*.

FORTY

The ground rumbled. Tremors vibrated up through the soles of my feet and fought against the already-present quiver in my limbs. Smoke and flame burst from the building at weird angles. Shards of hot glass seared my skin as they ripped through the air, hundreds of tiny knives slicing my flesh.

A scream rose in my throat, but I swallowed to choke it down. Screaming would put me off target and my father hadn't given up his stance, except for the slightest flinch when the windows of the lab burst into the parking lot. The two of us, both stubborn against defeat, willing to endure immeasurable pain to avoid backing down.

"Take me on, you coward," a voice shouted into the night, the sound so raw and distorted with anger that I couldn't even tell if it was Hawk or Christophe. The two guys I trusted above all else, twisting into something shattered and animal. Something darker. But which one? I cringed. Maybe both?

Flashes of limbs moved in my periphery. Thuds from bodies being slammed into the ground. The smack of skin on skin, then the clinking of metal as the gun skittered across the pavement. A slight relief bloomed in my gut—fists were far less deadly than bullets.

My father glanced at me, eyes wild, then charged right. One second. Two seconds. I stepped back and swiveled, dropping the bow three inches, then releasing the string. The lump in my throat ripped through my chest and landed in the pit of my stomach, heavy and hard, making it difficult to stand. The arrow grazed his leg. Drops of blood spattered through the air as the head tore through his pants. His low scream curdled through my blood, making my heart ache. He grabbed his calf and fell, red pooling around him on the concrete.

I surged forward, instinct kicking in and wanting to help, but instead of staying down he kept moving, crawling forward, designer suit slithering through oil stains and dirt. He couldn't get far bleeding out like this, but he didn't need to; what he wanted gleamed in the firelight only two feet away. The gun.

I ran as fast as I could. He reached out, fingers inches from the barrel. I jumped forward and kicked, sending the gun flying across the lot, his hand closing tight around my ankle.

"Let go." I yanked my foot from his grip and backed away as he collapsed on the ground, clutching his leg.

"You ungrateful brat," he yelled, pain staining the edges of his words.

"I told you I'd shoot." I crossed my arms and tried to sound tough, but watching him lying there, because of me, made it much harder than I would've thought.

"Everything I've ever done was to protect you. You and Mattias and your mother. Every hard decision I've ever had to make was so that you wouldn't have to make one."

"But it didn't work." I inched closer, trying to see the wound on his leg, but he had it completely covered by his arm. A familiar feeling built inside me. Doubt mixed with stomach acid. I swallowed to keep it all contained.

"No, it didn't." He let out a deep sigh. "And now you've gone and destroyed everything so many of us have worked so hard for and you don't even realize what you've done. Without this drug, the violence is going to escalate. The powers of the world will descend on us and there will be no way to defend ourselves. The entire country, and everyone in it, will be help-less." He paused, looking up at me without anger, only sadness. "You blew up our last hope."

It was a lie. It had to be. There had to be a better way to save the country than this. But what if I was wrong? I knew it wasn't right to sacrifice all those people, but what if I'd made every-thing worse?

"And I know I haven't been the best parent in the world, but I never meant to hurt you. Ever." My father inched closer to my feet. "All your pain is my fault and if you give me another chance, I know I can change. I can get help. I'm so, so sorry, Mercury."

I bit down on my lip as hard as I could, but it didn't help. Tears poured out of me and I couldn't stop them. I'd waited years to hear him tell me he was sorry, but he never had. I kneeled beside him.

"I wasn't trying to harm you. I was trying...." I gulped hard, choking on my own words. "I was trying to make things better. But there has to be something else we can do. There has to be another way."

Footsteps ran behind us and started to fade. I looked quickly to see the back of Christophe as he disappeared around the corner. He was okay. One small victory. But if Christophe was okay, where was Hawk?

I turned my head to look, but my father held my cheeks and stared at me. "I don't know what can be done, but maybe if you work with me, we can come up with a plan. Something you can be proud of me for." He paused. "And then I can work on everything else. Work on being a real family again."

"Really?"

His eyes watered and the lines in his face dug deep with conviction. He was finally listening. After everything I'd done. Every time I'd run. My chest tightened and made it hard to breathe, but it didn't matter because I had no words.

"But first...." He looked past me, probably worried about getting caught up in his emotions like me, or maybe the pain had become too much. He opened his arms wide. "Come here."

I hesitated, but he pulled me in. I closed my eyes and hugged him back, the smell of his musky cologne mixed with the scent of his skin brought me to a place where I was little again. Where he'd never hit me. Where he actually cared.

I wiped my face in his collar and let him go, but his arms stayed tight around my back. I pushed gently on his shoulders and he clamped on tighter.

"Okay," I said and tried to pull myself away again.

He gripped harder and twisted me around so my neck fell into the crook of his elbow.

"What are you doing?" I yelled, pushing at his arms.

But as the words flew out of my mouth, I looked up and got my answer—Hawk standing above me with the gun pointed at my father's head.

"Let her go," Hawk shouted.

The arm around my neck pulsed tighter. "Do you really think I'll be that stupid? You have no idea who you're screwing with, kid."

"I said let her go or I swear I'll kill you."

"Like I killed your father?"

His eyes widened and drifted off to a dark place, the ghosts that haunted him coming back for one hell of a show. "How do you know who I am?"

"The second you laid a hand on me in my office, I had your face out to every guard in the state. It didn't take long to put it all together. Besides, you look like Eldrin. That higher-ground air of conviction in your eyes. The look that gets people like you into trouble."

Hawk sidestepped for a better shot, but my father maneuvered himself beneath me as much as he could, refusing to give him a clear opening.

I pulled at the arm around my neck, digging in my fingernails, but the harder I tried, the tighter his hold, moments of the struggle disappearing into blackness when I lost oxygen. He was too strong.

My head ached, and the metal taste of my own blood dripped from my nose. Everything he'd said was a lie, and I fell for it. Part of me actually thought things could get better, but he wouldn't hesitate to kill me to save himself. He might be soon. Would Hawk risk taking the shot with me in the way?

I tried every hold breaker Tucker had taught me, but nothing worked. If only I could find a weakness. I pulled my head forward as much as I could while still breathing and positioned my foot. With all the energy I had left, I slammed my shoe into the arrow wound, grinding my heel hard against his leg.

"Argh."

My father's body convulsed under the pain and I threw my entire weight forward, breaking his hold and landing facedown on the pavement. I crawled away, his hands sliding over me, trying to grab on.

Hawk pushed the gun in my father's face. "You're never going to touch her again."

My father stared up the barrel at his executioner. A smirk curled across his lips. "The kid who can't mind his own business runs to her rescue again. She'll ruin you, you know that?"

Hawk's hand tightened around the gun.

"Who was foolish enough to trust the hands of justice to a boy?"

Hawk fired back, "Who decided to trust the lives of millions to a psychopath?"

"Such a naive, narrow-minded worldview." My father laughed and propped himself up on his elbow, staring at the gun as if it were plastic. "You know nothing of suffering. Of the true evils out there."

"You murdered my dad. You're why my mom died. I. Hate. You."

My father pushed himself up as high as he could and snarled. "I'll arrange to have you join them."

"Not if you're dead." Hawk's finger gripped tighter on the trigger. His arm held taut and steady. No nervous twitching. No hesitation.

"Don't," I yelled. The word tumbled out of my mouth, unfiltered and unexpected.

"What?" Hawk barked, but wouldn't look at me. "After what he's done to you. Your family. My family. Why not?"

I pulled myself to standing, every muscle in my body burning, and took a step closer. His jaw clenched hard enough to snap his teeth, and blood had dried and hardened down his cheek from the deep gouge across his forehead, but his stare frightened me the most. The cold emptiness of it. The detached void of having nothing left. I wondered if the old him looked like this. What his life had been before Ratchett found him. The darkness he had tried to run from.

"Shooting him won't change what he's done, but it will change you. It'll break you."

He took a deep breath, as if he was going to speak, but let it out with a faltering huff.

"Even if you get away with this, they will hunt you down as

a killer and never stop until you're dead. You're better than he is, and the world needs you. Don't let him win."

"What do I do?" Hawk screamed and rubbed his free hand over his face, smearing the blood into his hair. His body shook, but his arm stayed strong. "I don't know what to do."

"Whatever you need to. You shoot him and get revenge while you risk losing yourself. Or you give me the gun and run, still alive to fight another day."

"What do you want me to do?" He still wouldn't look at me.

I stretched out my hand. "Run."

He stood in silence, glaring down. In that moment, he was everything all at once—the hero, the terrorist, and the broken boy. He had every reason to shoot my father. To end this. And a part of me wanted him to.

Hawk grabbed my outstretched hand, his fingers twisting and squeezing around mine. I held my breath and waited for the gunshot, my body rigid with his indecision. A cry of police sirens cut through the night air. No time left.

"Okay," Hawk said as he lowered the gun to his side. "But only if you come with me."

FORTY-ONE

I slipped into the room and silently shut the door. Henrietta had only put Matty to bed an hour ago, but I hoped he would already be asleep. As I tiptoed closer to the bed, I could hear his deep breathing, his little chest rising and falling underneath the plush dark blue coverlet. He groaned as I sat, but within seconds he descended back to dreaming like I wasn't even there.

Looking at Matty lying there made everything harder. His long dark eyelashes curled against his soft pink skin. Unmarked and innocent. But I knew he couldn't stay that way forever. He would grow up in this world and they would try to make him one of them. Power and greed would corrupt him into something I wouldn't recognize. Like my father. Like Christophe. I couldn't let that happen.

I slid a small envelope into his tight fist. I needed to make sure he saw it before someone took it away. He wouldn't understand it right now, but that didn't matter. I just hoped he would keep it until he could.

He flinched as I brushed a stray curl over his ear. "Hey, buddy."

He didn't move.

"I really wish I didn't have to do things like this, but in some ways, maybe it's better that you're asleep."

Tears stung my eyes, the world turning hazy through the drops.

"I am going to have to go away for a while. I don't know where I'm going, or what's going to happen, but I promise I will never forget about you. When you get bigger, I'll come back for you, and it will be your choice for what you want to do. Not our parents'. Not anyone's. Make sure you don't stop being yourself. That big heart of yours will protect you until I can come back and do it myself. Just remember that I am doing this so that one day your world will be a better one. I love you. Don't ever forget that."

My lips quivered as I kissed his soft cheek. I tried to trap his smell in my nose so I could carry it with me forever. I always loved the Matty smell. A tear spilled onto his cheek, and I wiped it away. He rustled again but didn't wake.

I moved back toward the door, waiting until the last possible moment to take my eyes off him. No matter where I went, part of my heart would always remain here.

In the hallway, I leaned against the closed door. The tears came quick and hard now, streaming down my cheeks. I struggled to keep from gasping on my sobs, scared I might wake Matty.

I let my sadness take me until there were no more tears left to fall. I rubbed my face with the back of my sleeve and inhaled as deep as I could through my tight throat. I still had one more thing left to do before I could go.

I straightened up and headed toward the dining room.

Mom sat at the table holding a teacup in her hands. The TV was off, and only the small light over the buffet was on. It was quiet. Too quiet. Her eyes were puffy, and even from the hall I could see the depth of the lines in her face. I guess I wasn't the only one who had had a good cry tonight.

"It's rude to lurk," she said without looking at me.

I crept into the room and stood across the table from her. She didn't move.

I wrapped my hands over the top of a chair, gripping until my knuckles ached. "I came to tell you I'm leaving."

"Big surprise," she said, her face barely registering a reaction. "When things get tough, you just run away. It's what you always do."

I pulled out the chair and sat down. I didn't want things to end this way. She would never beg me to stay, but I hoped she would understand.

"No. I'm not running away this time. Running would be me slipping off into the night and never calling until you drag me back here. That's not what this is. This is me telling you that I'm leaving and no matter what you do, I'm not coming back."

She leaned back in her chair and raised her cup to her lips. The decadence of her sip put me on edge. I coped with this life by turning on charm; she did it by turning off her emotions. She wasn't my mother right now; she was the king's wife. Why couldn't she understand that all I really wanted was my mom?

"You can't. You're not an adult. You can't make that decision for yourself."

"Why not? Dad can make the decision to destroy people on a whim; that's not even human. He can decide to beat the crap out of me, out of you. Why does he get to make decisions like that and I can't decide what's best for me?"

"Fine." She stared past me. "But you're done. No money, no support, and no open door waiting for you to come back."

"I don't want your money."

"Well then, there is nothing left to say, is there? I suggest you get out before your father is released from the hospital. Pack your things and let security know when you leave."

She rested the cup back on the saucer. Slowly. Delicately. Her pointer finger still linked in the handle. I stared at her, waiting for something. Anything. She simply looked beyond me as though I'd already gone. But the coldness in her eyes had melted. She wasn't sad or angry that I was leaving. The look that remained seemed like it might be regret.

I stood and walked away. Pausing in the doorway, I turned back. "You can too, you know."

"I can what?" Her voice puzzled, her expression smooth as glass.

"Leave."

She chuckled. "I doubt you'll get very far with that naivety. You won't last a week."

"I guess we'll see."

I SLUNG my bow over my shoulder along with a small backpack of clothes. This was it. I was leaving.

At the door to the foyer, I turned and took one last look at what was once my home. My throat tightened, the weight of my decision starting to take hold. I would be okay. I was making the right decision. Wasn't I?

Behind me, the front door clicked closed. I swallowed and turned around.

Christophe stood across the room, his face twisted in a mix of shock and sorrow. He likely didn't expect me to be here, and he probably wished he wouldn't have to see me again.

He didn't move. Neither did I. We both just stared and tried to avoid staring.

"I'm leaving," I said finally, knowing that one of us would need to eventually break the silence.

He sighed, the thickness of his breath tangible from across the room. "Have you told your parents this time?"

I nodded.

"Well, best of luck." Flat. Cold. But I deserved it.

I dug into my backpack. "I was going to send this to you after I was gone. I'm sure you will find someone who deserves it more than I do." I handed him the little scrap of black satin with his ring wrapped inside. "I honestly hope you find someone that makes you happy. You deserve to be happy."

He walked toward me and snatched the ring from my hand. His lips quivered as though he might say something, but nothing came out. I gave him the best comforting smile I could. Touching him felt wrong, even if it was just a hug, so I kept to myself and headed toward the door.

"Did you ever really love me?" he called from behind me as I reached for the doorknob.

I stopped, thought for a moment, then turned around. "I will always care about you, Christophe."

"So no?"

"I didn't say that, I—"

"Then you just never loved me the way you love him."

I nodded and looked at the floor.

"How am I supposed to compete with everyone's ridiculous hero?"

Without looking up, I whispered under my breath, "You can't."

We stood in silence. Nothing I could say would make this better for him. I had crushed him. Betrayed him. At least he wouldn't have to see me every day anymore.

"Promise me one thing before you go," Christophe said, the edge falling off his voice.

I glanced up through my lashes, still unable to look him in the eyes. I wished I wouldn't have to remember him this way. "Sure. Anything."

"Let me know when he inevitably breaks your heart." The sadness drained from his expression, replaced by a glare of pure stone. "The pain is excruciating and you'll beg for it to kill you. I wouldn't want to miss that."

"That's not fair." Tears welled up in my eyes. I'd been beaten down and knocked around so many times over the past while, but his words cut sharper and deeper than anyone else's.

"Don't cry." He placed his hand gently under my chin and pulled my face up to meet his eyes. He gave me the faint hint of a smile, and I fought the urge to wrap my arms around his neck and bury my face in his chest. "You don't deserve to. All of this was your choice."

He snatched his hand away and stormed off without looking back.

Walking down the front stairs felt like falling. I stood on the sidewalk and braced myself on the stone railing so my legs wouldn't give out. My head fell back, and I stared up at the building that used to be my home. I couldn't see the top, just miles and miles of stone and glass towering into the sky. I'd never looked up before. I had spent my life looking down on something I didn't feel I was a part of. Now I stood on the outside looking up at something I could never be a part of again. It hurt. A sucker punch to the stomach knocking me down and leaving a big black hole. It would take time to breathe again, but in the end, I hoped it would all be okay. But what was stronger, the unsteadiness in my knees or the certainty in my heart that I'd made the right choice?

I refused to cry anymore. Crying would make this all too real and I needed to be as far away from here as I could before my actions completely sank in. My father said that all actions had consequences. Hopefully, the consequences of leaving home and shooting my father in the leg would be worth it. Besides, I wasn't sure I had any tears left.

The last few rays of sun before the pending twilight bounced off the buildings, making them look like sleek slate monoliths. A fortress closing around me full of secrets, lies, and corruption. I didn't know where I would end up, but I finally knew what I wanted.

"I've been looking for you," a voice breathed in my ear, as iron-like arms slipped around my waist.

This time I didn't fight. Instead, I let myself fall into them as they pulled me off the ground and around the corner into the alley. Hawk pressed me gently against the brick wall and I wrapped my arms around his neck, drowning in those blue eyes. A sense of calm washed over me. At least I had one person on my side.

"Where'd you go?" Hawk said as he placed his hands on my hips and sent a tingle from his fingertips up through my spine.

"A few last things I needed to take care of. Nothing to worry about."

His eyes narrowed as he scanned my face. His thumb rested under my chin. "It probably isn't safe for you to go back there."

"Doesn't matter. There's nothing left for me there anymore."

He brushed my hair back, his touch lingering over my ears and settling at the back of my neck. "It won't be easy, you know. Are you sure you still want to do this?"

My head nodded yes, but part of me wasn't sure. At least not yet. "I will be."

"I'll make sure of it." He held me in his stare, clear and crystal blue. There was honesty. He meant it.

I closed my eyes and inhaled. Part of the heaviness started to lift.

Resting my palms on the sides of his face, I leaned forward. "I know."

It was more than a kiss; it was a declaration. I was all-in. I had given up everything and now I was ready to start a new life. A life that didn't make me have to hide my feelings for Hawk. A life that wasn't dictated by my father or his position. A life where I could do something that had meaning. A life of my own.

My hands slid away from his face and clutched the muscles at his shoulder blades. He kissed me back, and we drifted away into the hidden world of the shadows. Just me and him.

"Does this mean we are going to have to watch you paw at each other like hungry dogs all the time? I definitely didn't sign on for that," a voice called from the end of the alleyway.

I peeled my face away from Hawk and sighed. "Hi, Tucker."

Hawk chuckled and looked toward Tucker, his fingers still tangled in my hair.

"In case you forgot, there's a lot of work to get done that doesn't involve whatever it is you're doing," Tucker said, pointing at both of us and wagging his finger.

"We're coming. Just had to grab a few things," I said.

Tucker shook his head. "Yeah, like Hawk's ass."

The heat in Hawk's cheeks radiated against my face as Red jabbed Tucker in the side with her elbow hard enough that he buckled over and grabbed his ribs.

"Right." Hawk backed away and shrugged, putting his hoodie back into place from where I had unconsciously pushed it off. "We need to let everyone know the truth about X9 and find a way to reverse the mind control on the cure victims. Ratchett has been working on compiling a list of those affected. Red, go to Iggy's and see Mrs. O'Connell to let her know what's going on. Tucker, we'll need your contacts again to find out how the poison is being spread and if the threat has been stopped after last night's explosion."

They both fell in line and nodded in agreement. Hawk was still in charge. Still focused on doing the right thing.

Red and Tucker turned on their heels and marched into the street. Hawk smiled and nodded for me to follow. *Here we go.*

His fingers linked in mine as we followed Red and Tucker back out into the setting sun.

"So what am I supposed to do?" I asked.

Hawk squeezed my hand and leaned toward my ear. "Maybe it's time to find you a code name."

Thank you so much for reading Mercury Rises.

If you are looking for more intrigue, mystery, and romance, try Keeper of Shadows also by Scarlett Kol.

When you find something worth fighting for

giving up is not an option.

Kellan Casey gave his heart to a girl, but instead she took his soul and traded it to a Shadow Keeper for her own survival. Now he has everyone fooled, hiding his curse behind a bad boy reputation as he transforms into a dimension-hopping wraith-like soul collector.

But when his neighbor, popular girl Abby Marino, accidentally uncovers his secret torment she insists on helping him—even if he doesn't want her to—descending them both deeper into the Shadow Keeper's dark and twisted world.

As the fatal end of the curse looms closer, any hope of finding a way out will mean working together. Except if they fail, Kellan won't just lose his life. He might lose the one girl he's willing to die for.

When night falls, all hell breaks loose...

Senior year was supposed to be the best year of Berkley's life—until it turned into a nightmare. Parental problems, boyfriend issues, scholarship competitions, and volleyball playoffs have her so stressed she can't sleep. But when an insomnia driven excursion leads her to cross paths with some amateur witches, she'll wish she stayed in bed.

Now she can finally sleep, but doesn't seem to get any rest. Each day blurs into the next as strange things start happening around her. Dark, sinister things that lead back to Berkley, except she can't remember any of them.

Desperate to regain control of her own life, she searches for an explanation to her nighttime amnesia. The answer will drag Berkley and her friends into a dangerous world of magic and mayhem—one where she may never wake up.

ALSO BY SCARLETT KOL

Paranormal

Keeper of Shadows

Sleepless

Wicked Descent

Faraway High Fairytales

Falling

Dreamer

Never miss a new release from Scarlett Kol by signing up for her
newsletter at scarlettkol.com.

ABOUT THE AUTHOR

Born and raised in Northern Manitoba, Scarlett Kol grew up reading books and writing stories about creatures that make you want to sleep with the lights on. She believed that the treasures in her mother's jewelry box were magic amulets that would give her immeasurable power and old books could transport her to secret worlds. As an adult, not much has changed. Connect with Scarlett on social media or on her website www.scarlet tkol.com.

facebook.com/scarlettkolauthor

instagram.com/scarlettkol

bookbub.com/profile/scarlett-kol

tiktok.com/@scarlettkol